LAST DITCH EFFORT

LAST DITCH EFFORT

MOONLIGHT DETECTIVE AGENCY™ BOOK ONE

ISOBELLA CROWLEY   ELL LEIGH CLARKE
MICHAEL ANDERLE

DISRUPTIVE IMAGINATION

Copyright © 2019 Isobella Crowley, Ell Leigh Clarke & Michael T.
Anderle
Cover by Fantasy Book Design
Cover copyright © LMBPN Publishing
This book is a Michael Anderle Production

LMBPN Publishing
PMB 196, 2540 South Maryland Pkwy
Las Vegas, NV 89109

First US edition, September 2019
Version 1.01, November 2019
eBook ISBN: 978-1-64202-455-5
Print ISBN: 978-1-64202-456-2

LAST DITCH EFFORT TEAM

Thanks to our Beta Readers:
Mary Morris, Chrisa Changala, John Ashmore, Larry
Omans, Kelly O'Donnell, Diane L. Smith, Suellen
Wiseman, Sara Keyes, Jackey Hankard-Brodie

Thanks to the JIT Readers

Dave Hicks
Deb Mader
John Ashmore
Jackey Hankard-Brodie
Jeff Eaton
Dorothy Lloyd
James Caplan
Peter Manis
Micky Cocker
Nicole Emens
Timothy Cox (the myth)
Misty Roa

If I've missed anyone, please let me know!

Editor
SkyHunter Editing Team

To Family, Friends and
Those Who Love
to Read.
May We All Enjoy Grace
to Live the Life We Are
Called.

PROLOGUE

In a dark and cavernous space, ancient stone ground heavily against stone and the scraping rasp echoed with mock finality. The lids of coffins, particularly those crafted in distant times, were not made to be opened and closed more than once.

Soon, the noise ceased and silence returned. The coffin was again still, its covering perfectly aligned with its body.

Those with sight that could penetrate the darkness would have seen a beautiful coffin, whose crisp, elaborate carvings had softened very little despite the long span of time since the ancient artists had shaped the stone.

It was an old, ornate house, which had been there almost as long as New York City had been independent of the Crown. The great metropolis was not far. But there, in the far and wooded outskirts, one could easily forget the city's proximity or even its existence. The venerable trees were both tall and dense. Dawn was delayed by their grasping arms that blocked out most of New York's light and noise and activity, just as they blocked the sun when first it began to peek over the horizon.

But each day, the sunlight crept in and filled the sky beyond with blazing light. And although the coffin's inhabitant would have no way of knowing, it promised to be a beautiful day.

CHAPTER ONE

Midtown Manhattan, New York City

Most people would have been horrified.

It would be a rare privilege to ascend to the top of the finest condominium in all of Manhattan and see the palatial penthouse, where most plebeians could never, ever afford to live. And then, if a visitor stepped through the door for the proverbial unveiling, they would find the place utterly trashed.

The expected opulence would be little more than polished turd—a gilded shithole and the obvious abode of a gold-plated shithead.

Of course, David Remington—the sole permanent resident and scion to the vast wealth of the New York Remingtons—had been called far worse things than that. Had someone flung such feeble insults directly into his face, he would not have cared.

In all honesty, he didn't really care about most things.

He had been unconscious—for one reason or another—and sprawled on the perfectly-shaped cushions of his loveseat in only his silk boxers. Now, however, he began to stir and wake up.

The inane prattle from his state-of-the-art television with its intricate sound system was what woke him. A news anchor with a standard-issue newsman's voice—a clear, self-important monotone and clipped, well-enunciated delivery—seemed to go on and on. His alcohol-dampened brain began to recognize the words.

"Two weeks ago," the uninspiring anchor said, "we reported on an incident in which the police were called to restore order at the bacchanalian bash hosted by a wealthy Manhattan playboy."

David allowed one eye to drift open. He wondered who they could possibly be talking about.

"A number of lawsuits were issued in the wake of the chaos. Due to confidentiality issues—as well as the fact that this is a family-friendly program—we cannot divulge all the details. However, information is still coming in, even now, and we do have one important update. The lawsuits are still being pursued. There are, at present, no fewer than three of them."

He rubbed the one eye that seemed to have returned to life. "No, they're not still being pursued, you imbecile. Not all of them." He scowled with moody displeasure while he fumbled beside the loveseat for the familiar and comforting neck of a large glass bottle. "We're down to two. I paid that slut in Twelve-A off with a spare Rolex last week. Get your research right—there might be more after last night, after all."

If there was anything he truly hated, it was journalists.

They prided themselves on informing the public but half the time, they couldn't even inform themselves.

His fingers finally brushed glass and with tremendous relief, he wrapped his hand around it and hoisted it up with a semblance of a grin. It felt awfully light. He held it in front of his eye and his grin turned to a frown when he saw it was empty.

"Fuck." He tossed it halfheartedly to the floor, the thud muffled by his excellent plush carpets. They absorbed sound almost as well as they absorbed fluids of various kinds.

With a heavy sigh, David decided he ought to open the other eye. It took a fair amount of effort but he managed. The lids and lashes parted, and depth perception returned to his otherwise fuzzy and blurred vision.

And now, he realized, came the hard part—getting up.

"Uhhh..." He rocked forward to test the proverbial waters. Moving his head did feel like being on a boat in a storm, so the metaphor was apt. He took a couple of deep breaths before he made another attempt.

This time, he summoned enough momentum to roll clumsily forward, far enough that his feet had no choice but to spasm off the couch and find the floor to support him.

David wobbled but did not fall. He also heaved but did not vomit. That reassured him that he was doing fairly well thus far.

He was still a young man—relatively—but not as young as he used to be. It showed in a weakened resilience to the ravages of partying. There ought to be, he thought, some kind of boot camp to prepare people for this kind of shit.

And he'd not even done any of the drugs which had been passed around last night—joints and lines and colorful pills. Wasn't sticking to booze supposed to be healthier?

The dizziness and nausea eventually subsided after a couple of long, deep breaths. A little more sure of himself, he rubbed his eyes and looked around.

Someone would definitely have to do some cleaning. Sadly, the last few cleaning services he had engaged had all terminated their services with him, stating unreasonable working conditions. This was an issue he might have to contemplate resolving right away.

"My friends," he observed, "are all mysteriously gone." They must have wanted to give him time to himself since they were such good friends and all. He'd wager that they'd even continue to respect his space and privacy if he were to call them and ask them to come over to help tidy up the present fiasco.

He picked at a crust that had formed in the corner of his eye and tried to ignore the inner sinking feeling as he surveyed the devastation. Ridiculously, he felt like a politician making a show of touring a natural-disaster area.

"Ugh. I might actually have to do this myself." Something brushed against his toes. He glanced down at it and noted with approval that his vision was returning to normal, which meant he hadn't permanently damaged his eyesight. That old saying about "drinking yourself blind" was full of shit. However, everything about headaches was all true.

The object at his feet was a disposable takeout container that had probably contained Chinese or Thai food at some point but now held a mixture of ashes, seeds, and torn condom wrappers. It gaped like someone who had passed out, open-mouthed, with their head sprawled back on the floor.

David knelt and closed the carton. He picked it up, along with a few other random scraps of party detritus, and went in search of a trash can.

Bizarrely enough, it almost felt good to do this. For a moment, it occurred to him that he might even be accomplishing something.

The problem was that he couldn't find any of the fucking trash cans. The penthouse was large enough that they could be anywhere. Wasn't there generally a big one next to the kitchen sink?

"Where are you?" he asked and grimaced when he heard how wheezy his voice sounded. "Bastard. Trying to evade your duties." He was now tired of holding the carton and all the other garbage.

A hasty exploration under the sink unearthed a plastic trash bag. Relieved, he stuffed the flotsam and jetsam elbow-deep into it and left the bag on the floor for now. It was a start.

"Maybe," he suggested, "I should drink some water. Eat some food. Something like that..."

He had drunk an entire glass of water last night and he was very proud of himself. But perhaps he needed more than one? And he'd forgotten the aspirin.

Unfortunately, he made the mistake of opening his refrigerator.

"What?" he exclaimed and his jaw dropped. "How the hell did the trash can get in here?"

Someone had removed one of the empty shelves and placed it lengthwise against the inner wall of the fridge before they shoved the trash receptacle into the wide bottom space that was left. David was almost angry but mostly merely flabbergasted.

He shook his head and seized the can by its edge. It was slick with cold condensation and it took a fair amount of effort to pull it out. He had to jerk it a little from side to side to gradually free it from its tight and chafing confinement.

This made it impossible not to imagine the difficulties that must have been involved in putting it there, to begin with. The person responsible would have had considerable time to think about what they were doing—although whether they had been capable of thinking at that point was open to debate.

When David finally managed to yank the can out, he found it was stuffed with food. He selected a bag of shredded cheese and sniffed it.

"Oh, God." He gasped and immediately recognized his mistake. "Why didn't I throw this out sooner?" He dropped it back into the garbage can. It occurred to him that whoever had put the thing in the goddamn fridge might have been trying to control the stench by preventing all this crap from ever reaching room temperature. There was a certain logic to that.

Other, similar smells were everywhere, though. He looked around, sniffed again, and once more felt his gorge rising. It took a fair amount of effort to force it down.

"And this is why I stay drunk," he remarked to the room at large.

By this he meant events of the kind that had taken place last night, not to mention two weeks before. It also included mornings like the present one. These were the types of things that had happened far too often for the last decade or more.

When he thought about it, this really meant his entire life.

He removed the mostly full bag from the can, tied it off, and set it aside. He replaced it with the mostly empty one into which he'd shoved the carton a moment before. So armed, he made his rounds through his living space to impose order upon the chaos. As he picked things up, he noted their existence and hastily disposed of them.

"One more or less clean pair of panties with a bow on the front. Bow untied." He flung them into the receptacle and moved on.

"One syringe, residual contents unidentified and possibly unidentifiable. Which is probably as well for the good of mankind." Into the trash it went.

"One opened can of expensive caviar mixed with vomit." He unfortunately had to pause his process to clean the vomit that surrounded said can. This unpleasant experience made him truly long for a restorative drink.

And so it went, seemingly without end. After half an hour, though, he had made considerable progress—an entire quarter of his living room now looked perilously close to being fit for human habitation.

Once the bag was full, he decided he needed a break—the type best taken leaned over the toilet while he supported himself against the wall with one hand.

David walked to the bathroom, opened the door, and stepped in.

"*Jesus fucking Christ on a cracker!*" he screamed and he stumbled out, his face ashen and sweat running down his temples and jawline.

That was it. He had, beyond any possible doubt, reached the limits of his ability to resolve this predicament on his own.

"Why?" he gasped. "Dear God, why?" He shuddered, closed his eyes, and wiped a hand over his face.

Finally, he straightened with grim resolve and made a solemn vow.

"I don't care how much it costs—I *will* find cleaners in this damn city. That is a job only professionals could manage."

A series of sharp knocks interrupted his nascent plan. Someone was at the door.

Soundview Waterfront, The Bronx, New York City

The small man was dressed far too nicely for this neighborhood. Especially at this hour of the night.

He rarely ventured this far into the Outer Boroughs and when he did, it was generally during the day and with a specific destination in mind. Usually, it would be somewhere reasonable and respectable—a legitimate business, a cultural event, or a landmark he'd always wanted to see.

A location where no one would question the presence of a diminutive, pudgy, middle-aged accountant.

This current location, however, was the complete

opposite. Anyone who saw him now would know he had no good reason to be here.

Very ill at ease, he looked around. "Which alley?" There were two that looked probable. He opted to stand where he was for a moment and consider both of them before he reached his own conclusion as to which one James had meant.

The neighborhood was well-suited to the night's business—an almost abandoned slum that sprawled next to a desolate waterfront. He looked inland for a moment, through and past the shadowed alleys, decaying houses, shuttered stores, and old, creaky apartment buildings that brooded in the dim city night.

Behind him, water lapped faintly against the rotting wood and weathered concrete of a pier. There was something vaguely sinister and downright unwholesome about its irregular sloshes and gurgles.

The accountant took a couple of steps forward into the stark, cold-white glow of the streetlamp. His hands looked ghoulish in the light when they emerged from the cuffs of his crisp, charcoal-hued suit so he could read the note again, instructing him where to meet his contact.

Making his presence so obvious was risky but the individual he'd come to meet needed to know that he had, indeed, shown up for the appointment. Truancy was a far greater risk than visibility.

Thick, hot sweat formed on the accountant's chest and under his armpits to roll down his body beneath the suit in fat, acrid beads. More perspiration appeared on his palms. He wiped his hands on his pants and stepped forward, out of the light and back into darkness.

"Well," he muttered breathily. "I guess we'll start to the left, and—"

Something scuffled behind him and he spun while his muscles tensed and his heart froze in a convulsive halt. Almost as soon as he'd turned, he saw what it was. A dark shape about eighteen inches long and seven inches tall yowled and screeched in fear that probably equaled his own.

"Fucking cats." He grunted in relieved annoyance and resumed his path into the alley. "Don't they have anything better to do than sneak up on people who are already..."

His words trailed off. He'd been about to say nervous, but terrified might have been a better word.

Merely being there was dangerous. Someone might easily mug him, with no witnesses and no one to help. He could stumble onto a homeless junkie, crazed and irritable, who might do God knew what in a chemical-induced mania. Or the police might appear and assume he'd come to buy drugs himself. The idea that they might harass him with leading questions before they hauled him off on some bullshit charge almost equaled the junkie scenario.

But the man whom the accountant had come to meet was the most frightening thing of all.

He breathed deeply, steeled himself, and stepped toward the nearer alley.

As he drew closer, a looming silhouette detached itself from the inky pool of shadow between the buildings and moved toward him. The footfalls were heavy, yet somehow soft.

Near the mouth of the narrow walkway, they stopped

at the same moment—the accountant about six feet outside, the other six feet within.

The shadow spoke first in a tone that was low, deep, raspy, and almost bestial. "You came. Smart man."

This, the small man thought, was what it would sound like if a guard dog tried to form human words around its angry growls.

"Of course." He tried to sound confident. It wasn't easy to gather the nervousness in a tight ball and hide it deep within himself but he made a valiant effort. "Your instructions were perfectly clear. Shall we begin negotiations?"

A barking, snorting sound transformed into a harsh, hacking laugh.

"Negotiations? No. I am here to tell you how things will be. You have no say in the matter."

The speaker took three long, striding steps forward, emerged from the jaws of the alley, and entered the dim light of the empty street.

A lump formed in the accountant's throat and he swallowed instinctively. Previously, he had not had a good look at the larger man. Now, however, he saw that his appearance unfortunately matched the voice.

His companion was even taller than he'd seemed at first and stood in a hunched posture as if readying himself to pounce. His hair was fairly short yet unkempt, and it spiked wildly. A full beard covered most of his face. His skin was dark and leathery and his eyes narrow and gleaming. At a glance, he seemed something other than human.

The accountant desperately wanted to back away from the advancing figure. But he had not attacked yet and backing away would be interpreted as weakness—perhaps even a lack of resolve.

"If," the smaller man began, "you can indeed offer me 'protection,' let's say what I pay you per month can be based off—"

"No," the other retorted. "You pay whatever I tell you to pay." His eyes seemed almost to glow with a yellowish hue like the reflected light of a full moon. "I am the alpha of the pack. You are the least. You now exist at my mercy."

He took another step and leaned forward, and the long fingers of his powerful hands clenched and unclenched.

The accountant was on the verge of fleeing, but he knew he would not be able to run fast enough to escape.

The bestial man continued and his voice rose in volume. "Displease me in any way and I'll rip your throat out and feast on your flesh and blood. You have no—"

He stopped abruptly. His gleaming eyes flicked to the side and his hair rose like that of a threatened animal.

Both men turned to face the woman at the same time. Her chuckle was soft and precise, completely out of place, it seemed, beside the hulking werewolf she'd startled.

"Hello, James," she said.

The accountant realized that James, his would-be extortionist, was afraid of this petite stranger. That was all the encouragement he needed. He turned and ran toward the waterfront, faster than he would have thought himself capable of, and vanished into the night.

James turned his head slightly to yell after him, "I'll find you. This is not over yet." His gaze, however, remained locked on the approaching figure who had emerged, almost catlike, from a slanting shadow beside the building to the east of the alley.

He growled low in his throat. "I thought you didn't mess with humans, Taylor."

Small, light footsteps sounded on the concrete as the new arrival drew closer and stepped out into the harsh light.

She was dressed entirely in black and in clothing halfway between formal and exercise gear. Her shoulder-length hair was so dark that its gleam was almost blue. Her skin was almost unnaturally white.

"I still don't mess with humans, James, unless they can help me." She smiled. "For example"—she nodded in the direction in which the accountant had fled—"I might use them as bait."

"Bait? For what?" the werewolf demanded. His teeth extended to grow longer and sharper and the familiar painful itch heralded the fur that sprouted from his skin as his whole body was suffused with anger.

Taylor took another step toward him. She cracked the knuckles of her slim hands. "Discovering who is responsible for the recent spate of wanton killing of humans. It would appear that I have succeeded."

"Hah!" James spat. He repositioned himself slowly while he spoke and slid slightly back toward the alley's mouth, where the woman would have less room to maneuver—if she tried anything. "Since when does your kind have any scruples about the sanctity of human life?"

His adversary followed his subtle movements with her gaze, which had taken on a pale reddish glint. "I am not above killing when there's actual cause for it," she explained, "but your childish and irresponsible acts of slaughter draw far too much attention. The humans will find you and when they do, that will become a problem for me."

He allowed his lips to curl away from his mouthful of fangs. "You don't give a shit about the rest of us, Taylor." He snarled to emphasize his point. "You simply want to protect the domesticated ones so no one comes looking for vampires and finds you."

The woman took another quick, light step. She now faced the werewolf and effectively backed him into the alley toward which he'd begun to retreat.

"Yes," she remarked, "I am among those who will be inconvenienced by your recklessness. I have no time for that, James." Her eyes narrowed in anticipation of his attack before he moved. He thrust into a broad, powerful leap with both arms outstretched and the claws already unsheathed from the tips of his paw-like hands.

Taylor ducked and rolled under his hand. His brain was too engulfed with red fury for conscious strategy, but his instincts and reflexes had reached the peak of their lupine efficiency. Grunting and drooling, he pivoted and struck with a fist. His movements made up in strength and unconscious ease what they lacked in sophistication.

Something crunched and gave way against his knuckles and the woman catapulted into the wall of the west building. He paused for an instant to assess how much damage he'd done. If he pounced too soon, he might fall into a trap she'd laid for him.

The vampire stood. A trickle of blood came from her mouth and her jaw seemed to have cracked inwards, but the bone was already resetting itself beneath her ivory skin. She wiped the blood away with the back of her hand and licked it with a long, dark-red tongue.

"I wondered," she began, "if you would be all bark and no bite, James. It's a pity you'll shortly no longer be around to spar with."

They both lunged.

CHAPTER TWO

Taylor was not incapable of fear and felt a trace of it now. The lycanthrope was a more formidable opponent than she'd assumed.

He swung a furred fist at her face, most likely intended to cave the rest of her skull in, perhaps. She moved faster to duck under it, seized his arm, and prepared to rip his throat out before he could attempt another blow. He shifted his position instead and simply half-shoved, half-threw her toward the deserted courtyard behind the alley.

She landed, rolled, and vaulted up at once to elevate twenty feet before she glided with arms outspread to land in the low branches of the area's single tree.

James glared at her and spittle trailed from the lips around his fangs. "Coward!" He barked a scornful laugh.

Taylor ignored the insult. She had no intention to retreat. After all, she had defeated monsters worse than him.

"Don't worry, James," she explained. "I'm not going

anywhere. I shall stand triumphant over your ravaged corpse."

She leapt with the unnatural grace of her kind directly toward the werewolf, who prowled and clawed at the dirt in his almost frenzied need to kill her. The bloodlust of the beast was dominant over the man now. Any conscious thoughts his mind might try to find, at this point, would quickly be forgotten in the mental chaos of enraged predatory reflex.

Crazed with rage, James pounced and his jaws snapped toward her head. She made her move at the same time, threw herself down and aside, and landed in time to swipe her own claws through the lycanthrope's stomach as she rolled away from him.

He grunted and gurgled, then howled as he spun toward her while blood poured from his slashed abdomen. His recovery was faster than she would have liked.

She tried to pull out of his reach, but his hairy, powerful hands closed on her right wrist and yanked hard. Her upper arm snapped near the elbow. Pain surged through her and she fell back and wrenched away from his grasp. He staggered in place as the delayed reaction to his own injury suddenly affected him.

His yellow gaze fixed on her, his pupils wide with adrenalin. "You—" He snarled in place of words. Her nails had ripped half his gut but already, the flow of blood had lessened in force and volume and the torn flesh worked to repair itself.

He was a powerful creature indeed, she thought, to be able to regenerate so quickly. No wonder the Southern Tip Pack had elected him their alpha.

But he was not the only one with that ability. She backed away and slapped her humerus into place, and the familiar tingling prickled as the bone mended and the flesh around it eased itself together.

She allowed her mouth to hang open so her enemy could see her fangs. "You're no pushover, James. I half-expected to be disappointed. But I've gone easy on you. I didn't want this over too soon. Let's have some real fun, now."

The blue-black hue of the night in her eyes began to shift as they took on a reddish sheen. Her own instincts—every bit as predatory as his but less chained to the conventions of animal nature—kicked in and rapidly attained their highest level of power and sensitivity.

Her adversary took a step toward her and drool flowed freely as he growled. "Stop talking and fight!"

"Very well."

With a lunging motion almost too fast for even a were-wolf's eyes to see, she swept her left arm to the side, yanked a brick from the rear corner of the building behind her, and hurled it at him in the same movement.

He raised a paw and deflected it with ease, but the momentary distraction was all Taylor needed. She had already surged toward him and pivoted in midair to kick him hard in the stomach with both feet—one landed firmly on what remained of the gash—and drove him back in a snarling flurry of limbs.

She landed beside a trash can and threw that as a follow-up. He braced himself with his feet and launched toward her and shouldered the can aside. She seized him around the neck, hauled him off-course, and delivered an uppercut to his face that careened him into a heap of garbage along one side of the courtyard.

Parts of his jaw and skull had shattered in a very satisfying fashion under her small, hard fist.

She walked over to a metal pole cemented into the ground. "There are reasons why you never provoke a vampire, James," she lectured him.

The werewolf spasmed in anger, flung the trash away, and struggled to his feet, his movements pained and awkward. Her flying kick had reopened his gut wound and probably cracked a couple of ribs, and his skull was still in bad shape. The injuries also weren't regenerating fast enough.

Taylor wrapped her hands around the pole as her opponent, now in a blind animal rage, roared and charged.

Sharp cracks echoed through the courtyard when concrete gave in and fissured violently. Taylor heaved the pole free of the earth, with a large chunk of dirty cement still attached to the end like the head of a giant mace. She swung it easily as if it weighed less than a small baton.

That cement mace connected with the same side of James' face she'd recently punched. The force of the impact pounded his head to the side before the weapon drove into his upper chest to shatter his collarbone, shoulder, and a couple more ribs. He crumpled and made a painful wet noise when he tried to breathe.

The vampire tossed her makeshift weapon aside. It thumped onto a broad slab of pavement and left a spiderweb of cracks where it struck.

"You," she began, "have broken the rules. You've killed

innocent people even after you've extorted 'protection' money from them—like the poor bastard you met tonight. If you do shit like that, you'd best understand that some of us are willing to stop it. At any cost."

The werewolf was still alive, twitching and bleeding, and while he attempted to get himself back into fighting shape, he'd taken too much damage in too short a time. For the next few minutes, he was at his adversary's mercy.

Not that she intended to show any.

Her beautiful face, by now, had finished its transformation to reveal her true nature as something even more terrifying than he was. Her eyes were fully red and her jaw had fallen open like a python's.

"There's always a way to kill a lycanthrope," she observed. Her voice had become a sharp, hollow rasp. "Silver isn't the only one. There is also what the medical profession refers to as massive trauma."

Her clawed left hand stabbed viciously through James' ruined chest. He tried to howl but couldn't drag in enough air through his injured face and neck. Her hand found its target and she withdrew her blood-soaked arm slowly. His heart beat once in her grasp before it fell still. She raised the organ to her mouth and bit half off. After a moment, she spat out a sliver of ribcage that had broken off in the tough muscle.

"Tasty," she commented. His blood ran down her chin. "You are good for something, after all."

He was almost dead, but not quite there yet. His body, stupid as it was, continued its attempt to regenerate from damage that would have killed a human twice over.

Taylor opened her mouth still wider, her gaze on the werewolf's neck. She leaned over him for her last drink.

Above and around them, the noise of their battle had risen to the rafters of the abandoned buildings. There was, however, no rustling, no flapping of wings, nor high squeaking cries. It was night and the bats were all out hunting.

Midtown Manhattan, New York City

Approximately twenty-four hours had passed since David had made his solemn vow to pay someone else to finish making his condo fit for human habitation. Now, at last, he was able to complete that vow.

He stood near the door and scrawled in his checkbook, as a line—a long line—of people prepared to file out. It looked like the new cleaning company had sent their entire staff.

He licked a finger. "Let's see...one thousand, nine hundred and eighty-seven dollars, and sixty-nine cents. That was the figure you quoted me, right?" He folded the check away from the stub and began to tear along the perforation.

"Yes," replied a pinch-faced older man near the front of the column, who frowned with disapproval. His overalls were covered with stains and his hands looked red and painful, despite having worked in gloves. He smelled awful.

David ignored the implied moral criticism. "Excellent." He smiled and handed the check to the crusty old bastard.

The geezer took it and they exchanged their last formal pleasantries. Most of the other cleaners simply looked relieved that it was over. A few looked...broken, somehow, as though their souls had been damaged by sights—and aromas— not meant for mortal senses.

After the door closed behind them, he sighed wearily. Once upon a time, a mere two grand to save himself some unpleasant hassle would have been nothing.

An assortment of envelopes, however, rested on the nearby table to remind him that things had changed. Most of them were things like credit card advertisements, charities begging for money, personal letters from people he used to know who wanted money, bills, and various other inconsequential things.

There was one, however, that was far more interesting. The knock on his door yesterday had been for the envelope in question, sent via certified mail. If he had to sign for it, the implication was that it was actually important.

Not only that, it looked important—or, at least, unique. The envelope was a deep yellowish-brown color as though handmade to resemble old-fashioned parchment. The sender had listed neither their own personal name nor the name of an organization, and the return address was not one he recognized.

David slit the envelope with a knife and sat at the table to read the contents. Within, the letter was handwritten in a beautiful, fancy, almost archaic script—the kind of fancy, archaic script it was a real bitch to read.

Once he deciphered it, he had to read the letter twice to fully grasp its significance.

"The Moonlight Detective Agency. I wondered what the hell had happened to it."

Of the various businesses he'd owned, the Moonlight

Detective Agency was perhaps the one he knew the least about. He did not even know what they did—what kind of agency they were, exactly, or where they operated—or how many personnel they employed. He usually paid little attention to such matters.

But lately, anything in his possession that might bring him revenue had rekindled his interest. His proverbial stream had been drying up.

Now, he had this letter. Its author was rather cryptic but they had alluded to specific things he'd mentioned when, a week or so ago, he'd dispatched his attorney to inquire about the firm's status. At the very least, he could be certain they'd received his message.

The letter's author wanted to know why he was looking for the company and promised to deliver what information he required if he'd agree to meet for dinner and a discussion. That sounded quite reasonable to him. The letter even included an email address for easier communication.

"Well, then..." He breathed deeply. "I'll have to take care of that directly. This might even be entertaining."

He leaned back in his chair and stretched his arms over his head. To be honest, he didn't feel very well. His head spun and swam a bit, his skin itched, and he felt strange— as though he were hungry or thirsty, even though he'd eaten only an hour ago and washed it down with a full glass of water while the cleaners did their thing.

Obviously, his body was still under the impression that it needed a fix. He longed for a joint to soften the hard edges of the world. Or a drink, and not of water. But he knew he needed to stay clear-minded, at least for the moment.

David stood and went to the desk in his study, where he opened his laptop and turned it on. The password screen flashed before him, and his brain suddenly turned to wet cotton.

"Uhhh…" he stammered while he simply stared and blinked at the screen. "I, ah…what the hell is my password? Fucking withdrawal symptoms…the human body is ridiculous and stupid. It doesn't even know what's actually good for it." He scratched his face, chest, and armpits.

He honestly wished he'd tried to quit drugs a few weeks earlier. If he had, he might already be past this crap.

After a moment—and once his brain stopped the active attempt to remember— the password flickered into clarity within his mind. He hunched over the keys at once, faintly afraid he'd forget it again unless he punched it in immediately. The task complete, he struck the Enter key.

The computer came to life and all was well. He sighed.

His first task was to draft a brief message to the email address mentioned in the letter. He wanted to have this taken care of soon. If he was lucky, they might even respond quickly enough to have this dinner meeting that night. He pressed Send and leaned back to rub his eyes.

"Now," he said, "let's see how my…things…are doing."

His first instinct—powerful, insistent, and totally evil— was to send a coded Facebook message to his dealer. It seemed the normal, logical, healthy thing to do.

"No." He grunted with irritation. "We will not waste our time like that again. Or our money."

Plus, he'd promised the cleaners that they would never again have to clean up…that. The abomination in his bathroom. Even he wouldn't have permitted that if he'd been sober.

He honestly even felt sorry for the team for having to deal with it.

It occurred to him that the mere fact of his having to make such a promise indicated that the time had come to make some permanent changes. In that light, getting high again would only keep him where he was.

No matter what, he refused to stay where he was. That left him with only one option since it was unlikely he could sink any lower—move up.

David logged into his bank account. While he wasn't exactly destitute yet, it would only be a matter of time.

"It could be worse, I suppose." He sighed and rubbed a hand over his face. "I'd rather have two hundred thousand in the bank and at least be able to afford lunch when I go looking for a job than nothing but a goddamn hat in my hand and a cardboard sign under my arm."

This was, in fact, the lowest he could ever remember his balance being. Regrettably, the cardboard sign scenario might become a real possibility.

He needed income and he needed his business to keep generating revenue like it was supposed to. And finally, he needed some kind of miracle that would persuade his family to speak to him again.

But first, he'd have to arrange this meeting with whoever the hell was responsible for the Moonlight Detective Agency. Which meant ensuring there was enough money on his credit card to pay for appropriate transportation. He rubbed his temples and focused on his bank's site again, prepared to transfer the necessary funds to—

"*Shit!*" He bolted from his chair when he suddenly realized there was no semi-flat lump in the back seat of his pants. He had no idea where his wallet was. Had he simply left it lying around when the cleaners had come through? Had one of them seized it with their grubby little paws and slipped it under their shirt?

David raced to his bedroom, which seemed like the best place to start his search. He glanced around frantically, seeking a dark leather object which, hopefully, ought to be somewhere in plain sight.

There—on the dresser and very obviously placed atop a white doily. One of the cleaners must have stumbled onto it and left it there for him. How courteous of them, he thought, and his relief was such that he'd already forgotten his unfair suspicions.

He rushed over to it and flipped it open. All his cards were still there. He exhaled and relaxed.

Another pang of craving clawed at him as he trudged back to his laptop but he ignored it. Once settled in his chair, he transferred an amount from the investment account to his personal checking. He didn't want to deal with possible overdrafts if he could help it.

A new message appeared in his inbox. Someone at the agency had already replied with a time and place for their little dinner date.

"It's so nice when my employees don't make me wait for things," he commented.

Now, David merely needed to arrange for transportation. Traveling in style was no longer really affordable. He'd have to settle for a ride-share instead of a chauffeured limo. It was cheaper and would still get him from Point A to Point B.

He did, of course, have three cars of his own, but like any sane person, he hated driving in New York City. It was much easier to pay someone else to do it.

CHAPTER THREE

Sotto Suolo, Chelsea, New York City

David had a tendency to swallow continuously on the rare occasions that he felt anxious. Saliva seemed to pool under his tongue and his Adam's apple would roll up and down, over and over again, as he tried to ingest it all.

It irritated the hell out of him. Somehow, it didn't seem right for a Remington—a goddam Remington—to have a nervous tic, especially one so common.

"So," he began and pretended to adjust his tie to disguise the weird undulations of his throat, "this...uh, is the right place?" He shifted his position in the back seat, suddenly conscious of how uncomfortable the seatbelt was.

The driver glanced into the rearview mirror. "Yes, Mr Remington," he responded in a polite monotone. "I triple-checked the address and I've taken people here before. Don't you worry, sir."

That was exactly what David was afraid of.

"Oh, uh...good. Thanks." He removed his hands from

his silk tie and wiped his sweating palms on the car seat. Sweat did not belong on his Armani suit.

When his mysterious contact had first told him where they'd meet, his mind—still somewhat addled by the ravages of sobriety—had only dimly registered that it was an Italian restaurant.

It wasn't until later—after he'd already climbed into the car and placed himself at the driver's mercy—that he'd recalled that the place had a reputation. Which was a polite way of saying that everyone knew it was owned by the Mob.

Whatever, he'd thought. The person who'd written the letter probably merely liked the cannolis and was ignorant of any of their behind-the-scenes activities. A naïve foreigner or nerdy suburban kid, someone who didn't understand the subtleties of New York. That was all.

The car came to a stop. Before it, the restaurant loomed like a square island of bright red light amidst the glare of the lamps and night-blackened concrete of the city.

David drew in a deep breath as the driver got out and opened the door for him. He pulled his phone out, went into the app, and left a tip—the bare minimum amount that could be considered appropriate.

He reminded himself he was the Remington scion and turned with fully assured haughtiness toward his destination. Assuming he wasn't murdered or threatened with murder, this slightly off-putting endeavor would still be worth it—he'd find out, at last, what was going on with his agency.

Almost as soon as he pushed his way through the front doors, the host appeared before him. "Mr Remington!

We've been expecting you. Please, come with me." The man wore an almost theatrically fancy tuxedo with a blood-red rose in the lapel.

"Oh?" he remarked as he adjusted his tie again and tried to sound calm. "I didn't realize I had made a reservation."

The host did not reply to this but only led him into the far wing of the establishment. In the main dining area, a group of five men ranging from muscular-going-to-fat through the-full-Pavarotti conversed in low voices over heaped plates of penne and meatballs.

Infuriatingly, his palms were sweating again. Being expected when he had not even contacted the place struck him as very definitely odd. The individual he was meeting must have made the reservation and given his name. That was not acceptable. He'd have to talk to him about that.

The tuxedoed man ushered him all the way into the farthest corner of the restaurant, he noticed.

Exactly what kind of company do I own?

He wasn't particularly scrupulous about where his money came from, but he sure as shit did not want to be associated with anything blatantly illegal. For some reason, he'd assumed that the Moonlight Detective Agency was a talent firm for wannabe super-sleuths with daytime jobs that wanted to kick.

But now, as the host guided him toward a table in the darkest corner of the establishment, the word agency conjured up far more sinister images.

David flicked his gaze around to take in the details without moving his head. There was no one in this section. If he were meeting with a Mafia underboss, he would have expected to at least see a couple of goons hanging around as protection. The only person he could see was a rather small woman seated at the table in the rear corner with her back to him.

He released the breath he'd been holding and relaxed a little. Women were strange and wily creatures and could be fucking dangerous in their own way, yes. But a lone female did not portend an immediate life-or-death threat.

The maître 'd nodded and walked away. David ignored the man and circled to the far side of the table. The lighting was terrible and he could not see the small woman's face. He decided to greet her in a show of confidence.

"Hello. Is this seat taken? I'd be shocked if it was but, you know, politeness and such."

She extended an arm toward him and a slim white hand gestured toward the chair, indicating he had her permission to sit.

He complied and cleared his throat. "Well, then. How are the cannolis here? I—"

Suddenly, a waitress appeared. "Are you ready to order, sir? I can get you some cannolis as an appetizer if that's what you'd prefer?"

"Ehhh, no," he told the server, "let's start me off with a cup of coffee, like a normal, sober person. One creamer, no sugar." Until he knew exactly what this meeting was about —and how safe he was there—he intended to stall on ordering food.

The waitress jotted the order down. "Certainly. I'll be right back with your coffee." She glanced at the dark figure in the corner. "Uh, anything for you...madame?"

The shadowed woman shook her head and held up a flat palm.

David turned away from the waitress and tried to study his still silent companion across the table.

It was odd because it didn't seem like the far side of the normal-sized restaurant table should be almost totally covered by shadows. Still, he could make out no more than a vague silhouette, a darker shape amidst the darkness. Only the lady's tiny, red-nailed hand was visible in the dim light.

A voice emerged from the blackness. "You are Mr David Remington?"

He tried to give her a jaunty, playboy smile. "Yes, I am he." He re-adjusted his tie.

The woman spoke in a soft, musical, almost girlish tone. Part of him immediately found it appealing and yet the whole situation still felt subtly wrong. The setup was like something out of an old noir film. And her voice, while suggestive of all manner of tantalizing promises, also carried a cold undercurrent of threat.

"Why," she began, "do you want to know so much about the company all of a sudden?"

David, wondering what he'd gotten himself into, almost wiped his hands on the legs of his pants but stopped himself at the last instant and shook open the cloth napkin in front of him.

"Oh, you know," he drawled. "I wanted to do an audit to make sure things are being run profitably."

The waitress materialized and set a steaming mug of coffee before him, along with a tiny jug of half-and-half. He dumped the creamer into the black liquid, stirred it with the spoon, and sipped immediately.

It burned his tongue, of course, but he did not visibly

react. Instead, his toes curled into fists of sorts within his polished shoes.

The woman drummed her fingertips on the tablecloth, but only once. "I see. Well, I can assure you that everything is being managed properly. All the i's are dotted and every t is crossed. From what your attorney told me, it sounds like you somehow managed to lose your own paperwork, which is why you had difficulty finding us."

He took another sip, more carefully this time. At least the coffee tasted good and fresh.

"Something like that," he remarked. "Although I don't seem to have records of even receiving any such paperwork to begin with. It's all very mysterious. Not that I really care about the specifics, but I invest in businesses to make money and I don't want any...problems to develop. Problems are expensive."

The woman readjusted her chair. "There are no problems. And I can deliver the most up-to-date reports. The agency is profitable. Every quarter, you will find, we are in the black. I will have my assistant send you the accounts post-haste so that you may look them over at your leisure. Then, you can rest assured that all is well."

She paused and drummed her fingers again. It occurred to him that she might be trying to get rid of him. Perhaps she was busy and didn't want to waste time having to summarize her activities for his benefit. His curiosity sharpened and he leaned forward, almost spilling coffee onto the fine red tablecloth.

The woman seemed to sense that he would not be fobbed off so easily. She continued. "In fact, I wondered if you might be interested in simply selling the company. I can make you a good offer and then, of course, you would have the money and no further worries about it."

David had not expected this. He blinked and gave it a moment's thought.

"Errmm, no," he replied before he returned to his coffee. "What I really need is not a lump sum but reliable, long-term income. I need companies that can be trusted to pay dividends every quarter."

The woman did not speak. After a moment, the waitress returned to top up his cup.

As she traipsed away, he guzzled another half of the beverage and set it down before him to look across the table again. "I didn't catch your name."

"You may call me Taylor, for now," said the shadow.

"Taylor...lovely, yes." He kind of had to pee but he decided it would be best to stay where he was until he'd prised more information out of the mysterious lady. Taylor was a modern name, yet something about her seemed... old. Her hand showed little sign of visible aging, though.

Somehow, knowing her name was Taylor made him less nervous.

"So, what kind of agency is this?" he asked. "I'm curious."

He felt, rather than saw, her smile faintly at him from behind her curtain of darkness. "Private investigation. By and large, we acquire useful information that interrupts trouble before it happens. I'm proud of the work we do."

David nodded. "Fascinating. Vague, but fascinating. It sounds like the kind of thing that would definitely be profitable—with the right kinds of clients."

"Of course," she returned. "If you insist on knowing

more, I can arrange that, but it would involve a considerable amount of boring, tedious paperwork."

The obvious ploy made him chuckle. "You won't get rid of me that easily. I hate paperwork, yeah, but I do technically own you."

Putting it that way might be risky but sometimes, a hard turn of phrase was exactly what was needed. It would allow him to test her reaction and better determine what he was dealing with.

The slightest tension seemed to ripple through the woman. "Technically."

She's toying with me, he realized. *In a sadistic, cat-and-mouse kind of way.*

"Well," he said, "I can tell that you want me to go away and leave you alone. So, let's make a deal. Provide me with enough information to know that my revenue stream is secure—and legal and kosher and all that—and I'll go away and leave things in your obviously capable hands."

Taylor nodded. "It's true that I've become very comfortable with being able to run things on my own without interference. Imagine how much fun you'd have if your parents—or the board of directors of one of your parents' companies—constantly poked into your apartment during one of your half-a-million-dollar parties, wanting to make sure that the money was spent well. Picture it that way and I'm sure you can appreciate my position."

"Indeed." He honestly didn't even want to think about that. "If you know about my parties, you must be a hell of a good private investigator since I never mentioned them to you."

"Hah!" she retorted. "Everyone knows what the

Remington kids get up to in their spare time. Which is to say almost all their time. This is the first time you have ever inquired about the agency's status so obviously, you must be having financial problems."

He wasn't about to challenge that statement. In fact, he was unexpectedly impressed by her.

"Yes," he admitted. "I...uh, have had a few unforeseen expenses, you know, important things that later turned out to be not as important as I'd thought. And my family seems to feel that it's time I learned my lesson and took control of my own finances. I hate the fact that they're probably right. So, I want a more active role in this firm. I'd like to know what I can do for it—you—and what it can do for me."

He sipped his coffee again. The cup was almost empty by now. He hadn't lied to her, but neither had he revealed too many details of the kind that were none of her business.

"Interesting," Taylor quipped. "Most people have to 'learn their lesson' several years earlier in life. But we'll allow that late is better than never. What I want to ask, though, is why you are specifically inquiring about this company. Why not any of the others?"

David frowned. "I already sold the other three in my portfolio," he confessed. "Yours is the last one I have. If I try to start over with something completely new, I might well run out of cash first."

"That's understandable. Wanton substance abuse is quite pricey, isn't it?" She did not make this blunt statement sound as cold and bitter as she could have and for that, he was thankful. Mostly, she simply sounded slightly amused. But even that stung. It was true, after all.

"I've managed to stay off the drugs for a few weeks now," he explained, "and with the aid and advice of my doctor, am working my way through the withdrawal symptoms. So much fun. I've also...uh, partially scaled back on my alcohol consumption, although I should have stopped altogether, I suppose. It's at least within normal-person bounds."

He didn't see any point in lying to her as she clearly already knew a few things about him. She probably wanted to make sure he wasn't the type who would demand a position on the company's management simply so he could raid her petty cash and hand it to his dealer. Admitting to his worst excesses—while pointing out that he was leaving them in his past—must allay the worst of her suspicions.

The silhouette nodded its head. "I see. Your family has cut you off from their proverbial teat until you clean up and grow up. And you claim to have been off drugs. But what about that party two weeks ago?"

"Oh...that." He grunted and adjusted his tie. "I guess you heard about it on the news?"

Taylor laughed, a light bell-tinkling sound. "David, everyone with the ability to hear heard it. The news only confirmed what half of Manhattan already knew."

He nodded. "I was about to ask if you lived in my condo, but 'half of Manhattan' broadens the possibilities."

She laughed again. He hoped it was because she enjoyed his wit but there was an edge to it. There was still danger there, even if it had taken a back seat as their conversation had progressed.

"I have told you what our company does. I would not

even need to live in Manhattan to know you were partying again last night."

Footsteps approached and he turned toward the waitress. "Are you ready to order food, sir?" she asked.

He noted that she'd given him and Taylor considerable time to talk before she intruded. "Yes, I'll simply have the special of the day, or whatever the house recommends."

"Certainly." She jotted the order down. "Would you like any more coffee?"

"No, thanks," he said. "I'd rather sleep tonight, actually."

The waitress left and he turned to his host.

"So, tell me," she continued and picked up where they'd left off. She sounded legitimately curious. "Why have you been so irresponsible and self-destructive? I don't mean that as an insult, exactly. I'm simply keen to know why you've chosen to live your short life the way you have, thus far."

By now, David had finished his coffee. He set the cup down with a firm motion.

"Because I can," he stated. "I'm a fucking Remington. Even my parents never really punished me for anything, now that I think about it. I was born to do whatever I wanted and still get my ass kissed for it." He shrugged. "Until now. Maybe."

"Hmm." Taylor's fingers curled into a small white fist and her knuckles cracked slightly before the hand uncurled. "Why now? What happened to make you want to change?"

He leaned back in his chair and considered the question. "I'm not sure, to be honest. I'm merely...tired, I guess. Tired of seeing people passed out, half-dead, on my furniture and wondering if they were actually happy. What would happen to them after they went home from the party. Whether or not any of it might even be my fault. Well, that and being cut off from my family's proverbial teat, as you called it."

She seemed about to say something else but he decided to push ahead and test her response to a different kind of question. "So, you're with the Mob, right?"

The silhouette showed no sign of being fazed by this inquiry.

"No," she replied mildly. "I simply have an understanding with the Family. I'm able to request small favors which are always granted."

David peered into the shadows again and tried to discern her face with as little success as before. "Who are you?"

"Someone," she said, "whom even the Mob respects. If I ask for privacy and security, they oblige." She gestured with her visible hand toward the restaurant.

He glanced aside and saw that it was now empty. The table out front had cleared and they were the only two who remained. And the waitress, of course, who now approached with his food.

Given how little time it took her to return, he was not surprised to see that she held a plate heaped high with penne pasta and meatballs bathed in marinara—the same thing the men had been eating.

"Thanks," he told her as she set it before him. "Now, check back in another, say, ten minutes and we'll discuss this matter of the cannolis."

She nodded and left.

David forked and sawed at a meatball, then added it to his mouth along with a couple of the cylindrical noodles. He finished most of his chewing before he resumed the conversation.

"So," he began and allowed a smile to creep onto his face, "this is my last meal, I suppose. I wish I'd known so I could have ordered something more specific. I prefer alfredo over marinara."

The woman seemed taken aback. "Why? Are you committing suicide tonight?"

She almost sounded genuinely baffled. He allowed himself to relax a little. Snark had long since been his usual way of dealing with any situation, even the veiled threat of murder, but it was always nice to know that someone didn't specifically plan to kill him.

"Oh, you know," he retorted, "I basically assumed that someone who has the Mafia under their thumb might conceivably be plotting my demise themselves. As for my own intentions...I actually want to clean my life up."

As he said this, it struck him that Taylor hadn't had anything to eat or drink since he'd arrived. And she'd declined to order anything when given the chance.

Her fingers drummed the table. This time, he found it faintly irritating. "And that fracas two weeks ago? The party last night?"

"Tests," he said.

"Of what?"

He chewed another mouthful before he answered her. "Of my ability to resist temptation."

"Did you resist?"

"Last night I did." He smiled. "I only had enough alcohol

to make myself moderately hungover the next morning and that was all. And this while there was enough snow to make my condo look like Mount Fuji during winter and enough pills to set up as a pharmacy. Oh, and enough weed to intimidate a Rastafarian."

There was a long pause from the darkened side of the table. "Well, if you are truly dedicated to cleaning yourself up, I guess you will do."

David blinked. "I'll do for what?"

"For helping me with a project."

He half-gagged on a mouthful of food. "Now, hold on. I'm not looking to get involved in the day-to-day operations of the business. I merely wanted a better understanding of—"

"You will," Taylor interrupted him, "understand after you've aided me. Only with one or two things, we'll say. This interview is concluded. I'll send you information on when and where to show up for work. If you want a stream of revenue, you should try earning it. It will help you to 'grow up.'"

In the moment it took his brain to process the ramifications of this statement, she had somehow stood without him seeing it and already snaked between chairs and tables with easy grace.

As he started to rise himself, she looked over her shoulder and he could almost see her pale face. "Don't be tardy, David. I always go to sleep on time and I won't have you making me late for bed."

With that rather cryptic statement, she was gone.

He glanced at the table and saw a handwritten note

with an address and an hour. The first was meaningless to him, but the second seemed odd.

"Who the hell goes to bed at five am?" he marveled. "I mean, who among people who actually work for a living? Unless they work the night shift, I suppose."

David sat again, shook his head, and decided he might as well finish his food. The waitress managed to reappear at almost the same instant as he set his fork down.

"I'll skip the cannolis, after all," he told her, "so you might as well get straight to the bill."

She held the palm of one hand up as she slid his plate onto a tray with the other. "Oh, no. The lady has already paid. It would...insult her to accept anything more."

He shrugged. "Well, hopefully, she also tipped you while she was at it since it's not like I carry cash. If not, there's always the leftover cannolis."

Taylor's strange words and even stranger manner still gnawed at him as he stepped out the door and into the New York night which seemed, to his somewhat bemused senses, simultaneously so dark and so vivid.

CHAPTER FOUR

Midtown Manhattan, New York City

Another night, another rideshare. It was a step down from what he was used to but he'd have to manage.

He greeted the concierge as he stepped out the front doors of his building. "Hi, Enrique. Have you seen any attractive prostitutes so far tonight?"

The man frowned slightly and responded in the appropriate and professional manner. "None, sir. Of course, I can't vouch for the professions of all the ladies I see coming through, but certainly none who were obviously in that line of work. We...ah, strive to keep that kind of thing out of this neighborhood."

"Well," he countered, "the night is still young." He glanced at his Rolex. It was 3:29 am.

Going to work at this hour seemed beyond bizarre to him, but he tried not to think about it, let alone complain. He didn't want to upset the Scary Mafia Lady. Who, furthermore, was probably as hot as all hell—he hadn't managed a decent look at her, but something about her had given him a special tingly feeling in his nether regions.

He sighed and muttered, "Just my luck. Meeting her under these kinds of circumstances."

His car pulled up, carefully avoiding the puddle that had formed beside the curb after the rain earlier that evening. He was dressed nicely, once again, and he nodded with approval. It was remarkably pleasant when people overcame their natural urges as New Yorkers to simply splash anyone who happened to be in their way.

"Hi," he said and leaned toward the vehicle as the driver rolled down the window. "I'm your customer, obviously. You have the address in your system, right? We need to be there before 5:00 am. And the more before, the better."

The man at the wheel was about the same age as him—thirtyish, a little overweight but noticeably clean-cut and eager-looking and probably reliable.

"Yes, sir," he replied, checked something on his phone, and gestured with a wave of his hand. "Hop in."

David tried not to grimace too obviously. He was accustomed to having car doors opened for him. Fortunately, Enrique had already rushed up to do the deed himself.

He nodded his thanks to the man, climbed into the back seat, closed the door, and belted himself in.

The driver chuckled in a good-natured way. "You can ride shotgun if you want, you know."

"Oh, I'm fine," he responded. "The back seat looks more comfortable."

"Whatever you say, my man." He pulled the car out into the street and accelerated. Enrique and the condo vanished behind another, slightly less opulent building and a row of streetlamps.

"So," David began, "are you familiar with that address? Does it ring any bells? Do you know where the hell you're going, in other words?"

The shaggy head nodded vigorously in the rearview mirror. "Oh, yeah. I know where this is. The neighborhood, at least. And it shouldn't take more than a few minutes, probably, to find the individual house."

"Good," he murmured. "I honestly have only the vaguest idea where the hell that is. Somewhere outside the actual city, it seems. So either someplace unimportant or so important that even I would have no reason to be familiar with it."

The drive proceeded and things went relatively smoothly. Even the City That Never Sleeps saw some downturn in its traffic during the wee hours of the morning. And, to his satisfaction, his new coachman seemed highly competent.

The man's name was Stan—short for Stanislaw, apparently. David, without specifically wanting to, learned this as well as a fair-sized chunk of the guy's life story. His family came from Poland when he was six years old. He went to school mostly with a ton of Asians and he was heavy into role-playing games, both video and tabletop… blah blah blah.

"Fascinating," he remarked and rested his cheek on a fist, which in turn was propped up by his elbow on the armrest. "It's astonishing how much you've managed to talk over the course of the last…uh, almost an hour. Are we there yet? I'm hoping we're close by now."

"Oh, yeah, definitely." Stan laughed. "You can basically tell by the types of houses they have here."

He looked out the window. The driver had spoken the truth. He almost felt as though they'd driven into nine-teenth-century England, barring a few telltale modern contrivances. The houses were not so much "houses" as "estates" and the landscaping more than matched their quality.

Shaking his head, he could not help feeling slightly... intimidated? That wasn't exactly the right word, but it was the best one he could think of.

This was an area purchased by old, old money that would have looked down its nose upon the mere decades that the Remington fortune had existed. Compared to these peoples' wealth, his looked like last night's casino winnings. The families that lived there were among the ones who'd put New York on the map.

Stan coughed. "Uh...well, I've been to this neighbor-hood before, but I'm not sure where the hell this particular road is."

There were multiple small, private drives that wound their way along the forested grounds that surrounded the mansions. He probably would have gotten lost himself, had he been driving, but he was paying this guy.

"Don't you have GPS?" he inquired. "Turn-by-turn directions and all that? I thought you all had to have that?"

"Yeah," the driver replied, "but it doesn't seem to recog-nize half of these little private streets and stuff. I can't tell which of them are driveways. Don't worry, though, we should stumble onto it nice and quick."

David adjusted his tie. "Should, yeah." He brushed off

the longing to ask if the man had a joint. While it would most definitely take the edge off, perhaps an edge was exactly what he needed tonight.

Fortunately, after a couple of moments, they took a turn around a tall hedge and Stan cried, "Ah, here we go!" He swerved onto a narrow, winding drive that led slightly uphill.

They arrived at a half-circle turnaround before a tall, wrought-iron gate set within a long stone wall draped with curling ivy.

"Right," said David. "Let's see, it's…uh, 4:43 a.m." He exited the vehicle. "Five or ten minutes earlier would have been better, but I'll still leave you a halfway decent tip of some kind." He didn't have time to dick around on his phone at the moment but made a mental note to keep his word on the matter.

Stan waved. "Good luck," he quipped and rolled the window up before he drove off.

He turned to the gate. A buzzer was set into the column to the right of the ironwork, and he pressed it with his finger and leaned close to the intercom.

No one spoke on the other end but the gate clicked and swung open, creaking a little as it moved.

"How theatrical," he remarked. He stepped through, pushed it shut, and heard it latch behind him.

The path ahead looked like a walk through some kind of park. In the darkness of pre-dawn, all that nature was almost sinister. Again, he found himself reflecting on the woman's slightly ominous words and disturbing choice of meeting place. This, he thought, would be an excellent place to murder someone.

Fortunately, nothing assailed him as he strode along the path. It took almost five minutes, though, before the actual house came into sight.

The gnarled and towering trees fell away to either side and he stood in a broad clearing. In the center, directly before him, was a paved area where at least six cars could park with ample space to maneuver.

And beyond that stood the house.

It was two stories high and not merely "nice," but downright ornate. It was built partially into the base of a small rocky hill—the peak of the incline he'd been slowly climbing since he'd entered the gate. He estimated the size of the entire home at a good seven to eight thousand square feet.

Trees, each looking at least a century old, had been planted all around the perimeter, which made it very private.

"Exactly how much is this company worth?" Something did not seem right. His family, who owned the company, might have had some difficulty procuring a property like this. He pushed the thought from his mind—five am was not far off.

Heavy, wooden double doors loomed portentously above him. He was a few paces away and about to climb the three stairs leading to the landing when the door on the right opened. In the dark space beyond stood a wizened, elderly butler in an old-fashioned black tux.

The droopy-faced man looked at him with eyes that were at once watery and bright. "You are punctual," he observed in a soft drawl with a slight, residual British accent. "That is good. Welcome, Mr Remington."

David smiled and stepped over the threshold. "Thanks, Jeeves. And yes, I'm always punctual for the right people."

"My name, sir," the butler retorted, "is Presley."

"Presley, then. But we all know that every butler answers to 'Jeeves.' It's tradition. Feel free to close the door behind me, old chap." He unwound the scarf around his neck and heard the man do as he'd suggested. The latch clicked into place with surprising volume.

Within, the house was elegant, but something about it was ever so slightly oppressive. Its age, its formality and outdated quality, and the difficulties of keeping such a venerable estate in good condition after what had to have been a very long time indeed all added up to money…and mystery.

On a small table a few paces before him lay a book. The lighting was dim, but he thought he could make out the words *Music Theory* on the spine.

Someone cleared their throat. David's gaze snapped toward the sound and settled on Taylor, who stood in an archway.

"Right on time," she said in her soft, musical voice. "I'm glad you weren't late. It would have been unfortunate to have to rush to bury the body, although it wouldn't be the first time."

David laughed as he assumed he was supposed to.

"Oh," she went on and took a step forward. "You can laugh even in the face of legitimate danger. That's a good trait to have."

His gut roiled somewhat at that, and fine hairs on the back of his neck stood at attention. He kept smiling, though, and decided to hear what else she had to say. Later, he could make up his mind as to whether she'd been joking or not.

Taylor walked into the room, her stride brisk and self-assured. She did not speak. He took another moment to appraise the foyer around him and the sitting room beyond.

The house, he decided, was more beautiful than it had seemed at first—and daylight would likely improve his opinion of it even further. It also appeared to be even more expensive than he imagined. In the sitting room was what looked like a staggeringly old piano, maybe even a harpsichord. And the furniture he could see was of absolutely top-notch craftsmanship—the kind of stuff his parents would fawn over and make sure to put where guests would see it.

"So," he began, "I'm a little confused. You're my employee?"

Taylor stopped a few paces from him. He could almost see her face now. It was still somehow indistinct in the poor lighting, but he could make out fine, almost aristocratic features to go with the ivory skin and dark, gleaming eyes.

She smirked. "In a manner of speaking, I am, yes. The Moonlight Detective Agency was sold to you, with you being the primary investor, during a party when you were twenty-one."

David blinked. "I don't remember."

"How many details from your drug-suffused revelries do you normally remember?" It was difficult to tell whether she was chastising him or faintly amused.

He adjusted his tie. "Not many, I'll admit. But I would

have thought I'd recall you, at least. I usually remember women who are exceptionally beautiful."

She stood, impassive and entirely unmoved by his compliment.

A little disappointed at the lack of response, he pressed on. "The only things I do remember, really, are some of the more interesting people I've met—sadly, not you—and some of the god-awful bets I took and the ridiculous things I ended up doing. They seemed funny at the time but now, I think I'd rather forget them."

Taylor nodded. "Perhaps you're finally beginning to grow up. Now, I will give you a very brief and efficient explanation of the reality you are about to enter and which you must comprehend. You have..." She glanced at an ancient grandfather clock. "Twenty-seven minutes to understand and make your decision."

David looked at the clock himself. He tried to think of what might be happening at about 5:20, but nothing sprang to mind. "Why twenty-seven minutes, exactly?"

She looked directly at him. Her eyes were like black pools and he almost felt as though he were being drawn forward—as though her eyes had somehow grown in size while the rest of the world shrank.

"Let's say," she began, her voice lower now but harder, "that for me, life can be very painful. There are things in this world that most people know nothing about and are better off in their ignorance. I am one of those things."

Part of his mind felt he ought to be frightened by a statement like that, but he'd become utterly fascinated. None of his usual fear responses were active. His throat was calm and his palms were dry.

The woman continued. "Our world is full of those supposedly mythical Things That Go Bump in the Night, David. The lycanthropes...the fae...the unquiet spirits of the dead...all those things humankind has decided not to believe in anymore, relegating us to no more than the fever dreams of classic horror novels and fantasy films."

David had almost no idea how to reply to that, but the hour of 5:20 am suddenly made a small amount of sense. "What about vampires?" he asked and smiled.

Taylor spread her hands wide. "You have now seen one with your own eyes."

"Well," he replied and tried to play for time. Obviously, he didn't believe her in the slightest but decided he ought at least to play along, "I guess that would explain why the Mob respects and even fears you. Are you the current Godfather? Or Godmother, I suppose." He tried to chuckle. It didn't work.

"No." She shook her head. "They leave me alone and provide small services when I ask for them. In return, I don't slaughter a score of them on the occasions when they aggravate me."

"Huh. Well, that is very handy. I love the idea of a vampire being a secret force behind the Mafia."

She placed her hands on her hips, stared at him, and declined to speak for almost a full minute. Finally, she asked, "Do you believe me, David?"

He chuckled. It worked this time. He was getting on top of the situation. "Well, compared to some of the shit I've seen and heard at parties for the beautiful and noble elite, this isn't even the weirdest thing I've been told. So, yeah, sure, I totally believe you."

He peered at her face, then—at her mouth. So far, he could not see any fangs.

His examination was not lost on her. "No. Do not ask to see my teeth," she advised him. "You would not like what would happen after that."

David swallowed and hastily thought of something else to say instead. "So, I was twenty-one, you say? Ten years ago—"

"And my plan has worked well for those ten years," the woman went on. "Unfortunately, you have proven to be a horse's ass whose family has all but tossed you to the curb for your extraordinary ability to party like a teenager even well past puberty, and then some."

He shrugged. "Go hard or go home," he quipped with a grin. She did not return his smile. "Yeah, that joke gets old quickly, I'll concede that. So…you're apparently a vampire and I own the company, but even though you work for me, I can't sell it? Or can I?"

Taylor glanced at the clock again, then back at him. "There are a few things you have wrong," she explained and extended her red-nailed fingers to tick them off as she listed them. "First, your ownership is in non-voting stock. Effectively, therefore, you cannot tell me to do anything, so don't even try. Second, you need money and maturity before anyone will take you seriously enough to let you run any further companies. I'm sure this is starting to become clear to you by now."

He grimaced but did not respond as she moved on to the next finger.

"And third, I—perhaps the only one of all fools in this world—am willing to give you a chance to redeem yourself, David Remington. You should not refuse my offer." She curled her third finger back into her hand.

"I can't refuse," he responded, "on pain of?"

"Death, most likely," she stated.

David had fidgeted in place, almost ready to stroll around the perimeter of the foyer, but stopped abruptly. He stared hard at her. "You're really serious, aren't you?"

She smiled in a subtle, disturbing way. "There is only one way to find out, David." She pointed toward the front door. The butler, Presley, was gone. "Walk out and pass up the chance I've given you."

He snorted a breath from his nose. She'd made him a dare, and one of such magnitude that it was almost impossible for him not to test it.

With a small smirk, he turned and walked to the door.

CHAPTER FIVE

Harrison, Westchester County, New York

"I'm David Fucking Remington," he told himself, placed his hand on the knob, turned it, and opened the right-side door. He paused and looked over his shoulder.

Taylor stared at him, calm and focused like a poised animal waiting for its cue to strike.

He chewed on the flesh inside his cheek. After a moment, he pushed the door shut, pivoted, and strode back to his place near the grandfather clock.

"Well," he said, "if you can't accept a vampire as your first boss, what's the point of going on living, anyway?"

A hint of a smile flickered across her face. "That wasn't quite the answer I anticipated, but it will do."

She glanced beyond his shoulder again toward the clock. "You have the advantage of being able to walk around in the sun. I obviously work the night shift so you get the day shift. The agency will now be open for business twenty-four hours a day. And you will run the mitigation projects."

"The what?" he asked. He knew what the word meant but the context was meaningless to him.

"Mitigation," she repeated. "We have three types of projects—the Three M's. Mitigation, Mindwipe, and Murder." She cracked her knuckles absently.

He nodded. "We solve murder cases?"

"No," Taylor explained. "We murder the guilty."

Now, David felt drawn back into the land beyond snark where things grew too serious for him to simply joke his way out of. "Uh...how often is the murder option employed?"

"Not too often," she reassured him.

He relaxed slightly. It was probably merely a contingency measure they kept on hand for particularly desperate circumstances. "Well, that's good to know. When was the last time, though, that you had to kill someone?"

The petite lady frowned, her white face cold and solemn. "Two nights ago. A werewolf had decided to pretend the rules didn't apply to him. He'd extorted money from humans and often killed them for sport, even when they did pay. We cannot allow that kind of behavior. His punishment was death."

Something about the matter of fact way she made this statement brought a chill to his spine. He wasn't used to encountering people who meant exactly what they said.

"'We?' Who is 'we?' Who decided to kill him?"

Taylor waved a hand dismissively. "It was approved by the Council."

"Fantastic! Who the hell are the Council?"

The woman smirked again. "Me, primarily." Perhaps it was simply his imagination but this time, he almost thought he could see the sharp point of a tooth protruding over her lower lip.

David fiddled nervously with the knot of his tie. "Of course, yes. It makes perfect sense." He forced his hands down. "May I sit?"

"Yes," she agreed, "but you won't be here much longer, anyway. I was about to brief you on your first assignment."

"I see." He planted himself in the nearest chair. Taylor did not sit, which made him feel awkward, but she likely had to depart soon. Dawn was coming, after all.

Then he thought of something and his eyes narrowed. "Wait—first assignment—do you mean I'll be starting today?"

"Correct," the woman confirmed. "Your task is the mitigation of a dispute between two nests of fae—or fairies if you prefer—who seem to be based in Fort Washington Park. Probably under the George Washington Bridge, but I can't say that for certain. Look around. They like cover and seclusion but also like being within easy access of New York pizza."

"Who wouldn't?" he mused, certain the words she'd said would eventually make some kind of sense.

Taylor ignored him. "An argument has broken out between the nests. The only explanation I received was badly garbled, so I can't say exactly what they're fighting over, but the fae are capricious and fickle little creatures so it almost doesn't matter." Her gaze flicked toward the grandfather clock. "Now then, I go to sleep in eight minutes. You'd best get along to the park."

David stood quickly and tried not to squirm. He felt almost as if he'd been caught with his pants down. "What?

How the hell am I supposed to resolve a goddamn fairy dispute? How do I mitigate something I know nothing about?"

The vampire walked slowly toward him. "How you effect the mitigation is your own problem, but I can give you two pieces of advice."

She stood less than an arm's length away now. Although a head shorter than he was, she seemed to somehow loom over him.

"First, I suggest you find something they all can agree upon. Fairies love to bicker, but when faced with a serious issue that affects all their kind, they will tend to band together and forget their differences."

He nodded warily. "Okay...that's slightly better than nothing."

"And second," Taylor went on, now holding his gaze once more with the ebony pools of her eyes, "remember that it's real. It's all real." She tapped his forehead lightly with the tip of her finger.

David went utterly still. The woman's touch was ice-cold —shockingly so—and yet it was not unpleasant. Something about it almost reminded him of the refreshing quality of stepping into proper air-conditioning after being forced to actually walk somewhere in New York on an August day.

"This is a test, David. Your opportunity to prove to me that you are worth keeping around. I am testing your initiative, your intelligence, and your ability to succeed under pressure. Remember that. I doubt you will succeed, but it would be nice if you do."

Taylor smiled. "Good morning, David. And good luck."

She spun on her heel and sauntered into a compound layer of shadows under a staircase. An interior door opened and shut and she was gone.

"Great," he muttered and glanced at his phone. There were no bars. "Now I can't call for a rideshare. How the fuck am I supposed to get back to civilization?"

He trudged toward the front entrance. The butler reappeared again, apparently from some half-hidden alcove near one of the large bay windows, and opened the door for him. In greeting the man, he almost called him Presley, but he was in too bad a mood.

"Thanks ever so much, Jeeves." The snarled tone suggested the opposite of gratitude.

"You're welcome, sir," came the reply in precisely clipped words. "However, I would appreciate it if you called me Presley."

David waved disdainfully at the old geezer and descended the short staircase to the front parking lot.

He tried not to think too hard about how in God's name he would get out of this medieval neighborhood and all the way to Fort Washington Park. He supposed he could walk until he reached a major street and then hail a pleb-taxi, distasteful as that would be.

By the time he'd descended the estate's gently sloping forest walk and passed through the gate, the sun was already creeping over the horizon. He pictured Taylor climbing into a coffin in some deep crypt below the mansion. The mental image should have been funny but somehow wasn't.

"Which way," he sighed as he glanced left and right, "did

we come from? Ugh, I hate rich people's neighborhoods. This is why I refuse to live in a house."

Finally, he chose right and started off at a slow trot.

To his surprise, the car that had brought him was parked only a short way down the street around the hedge they'd navigated before Stanislaw had found the correct road. He approached the vehicle hesitantly. Something seemed wrong there.

The driver was quite literally asleep at the wheel—slumped forward uncomfortably with his cheek pressed into the curve of the wheel. Snores droned faintly through the closed window. At least he wasn't dead.

David walked up and knocked on the window. "Good morning!" he announced. "Your services are once again required, Garrulous Polish Guy. Hello?"

Stan jerked up, blinked, and rolled his head around. "Whuh?" he stammered, his face momentarily zombie-like. "Oh. I...uh, yes, I'm working. Do you need a ride, sir?"

He frowned and regarded the other man a little nervously. "Yeah, not back home, though. Somewhere else—for business and such."

The driver seemed confused. He stared at Remington and almost appeared to wrack his sleep-addled brain. David assumed it was merely the usual stupefaction of morning until he realized something.

Chatty Stan stared at him like he was a stranger. The man had no memory of him whatsoever.

"Oh," he said quickly to avoid the honest explanation. "Uh...yeah, sorry. My mistake. I thought you were...the other guy. You are a driver though, right? Well, I do need a ride."

"Sure," said Stan. "Hop in. What's your name, sir?"

He opened the back door and climbed in. "Remington. I need you to take me to Fort Washington Park. Is that doable?"

"Certainly. I'm Stanislaw, by the way. You can call me Stan, though."

A sinking feeling of despair worked its way through him upon hearing this—he'd undoubtedly end up having to listen to the man's entire life story all over again.

But, he wondered, how the hell had he lost his memory like this?

Mindwipe, Taylor had said. "The second M." He wondered if she had slipped out while he approached the door, moving at the speed of darkness to render Stan oblivious to anything a normal human being should not know.

"Well," Stanislaw began, "we have a fair drive ahead of us, so let me tell you a little about myself. It makes the trip less awkward, you know? See, I was originally born in Poland…."

He ignored the man's ramblings. Instead, he reflected on something else.

The cold, bright, weirdly pleasant sensation when Taylor had touched him on the forehead hadn't gone away yet.

Fort Washington Park, New York City

Stan brought the car to a stop. "Fort Washington Park, as requested. How far do you want me to—"

"Try to get close to the bridge," David interrupted and craned his neck to look around the area.

"Okay."

Whistling and muttering inane commentary to himself, Stanislaw wheeled the car around and sought a place to pull over that would put the George Washington Bridge within reasonable walking distance.

His passenger slowly registered the unexpectedly beautiful morning, all rose-pink and gold. The park wasn't exactly deserted—it was rare for anything in NYC to be free from people—but it was far from bustling. A couple of joggers and one person nearby walking their dog were the only signs of life.

The whole scene was too banally every-day to seriously accommodate the possibility of actual, honest-to-fuck supernatural beings floating around.

David shook his head. In the light of day and far from Taylor's spooky mansion, the rational and conscious part of his brain tried to tell him this was all a shitload of nonsense. Vampires? Lycanthropes? Fairies?

But something within him felt different. It had ever since that icy tap on the head.

He saw things he wasn't sure he'd ever seen before. Colors in the sky seemed brighter and more vivid. Shapes that scurried along the ground or flitted through the air, furtive and sinister. Things that appeared to glow in ways not intended by either nature's original dictum nor the technology of mankind.

It was as if a bright, cold light had begun to shine out of his head to add a hazy extra dimension to things that, in the past, had looked like they were all that was there. Now, he could see there was so much more.

"Okay," Stan announced and intruded on his brief reverie. "I think this is as close as we'll be able to get to the bridge. Is it acceptable?"

"Yeah," David said, "here is fine." He still had only the vaguest idea of what he was supposed to do there once he located this lair of the supposed Fae.

The driver put the car in park and shut the engine off. He twisted to look back and draped an arm over the seat. "Do you want me to wait for you, Mr Remington? If it'll only be an hour or two, that won't be a problem. But if it'll be all day...well, it's in my best interest to—"

"Yes." He cut him off again. "Wait. It will probably only be an hour, I think. If it's longer, you can leave."

Stan faced forward again and settled himself comfortably. "That sounds good. Enjoy your walk in the park. See you later, sir."

David unbuckled himself. "Thanks, Stan. Yeah, a walk in the park." He opened the door, stepped out far more confidently than he felt, and took a deep breath as he scouted for the path of least resistance.

The grass seemed fairly well-maintained, so he decided to simply walk over it and directly toward the bridge. "Hopefully, the fairies aren't accompanied by junkies or gang members," he grumbled under his breath. "I always wondered how they got some of the graffiti so high up. They must have the little flying bastards carrying the spray cans while the taggers direct from the ground."

An athletic middle-aged woman in skimpy jogging gear, sunglasses, and a white baseball cap ran past and gave him an odd glance. She must have overheard part of his conversation with himself.

He waved a hand sharply in front of his face to clear his mind to focus it on the business he had to attend to. It wouldn't help to be distracted by people who wondered why a well-dressed upper-class gentleman strolled through a park and mumbled to himself.

The bridge's huge posts were made of industrial pale-gray metal resembling construction scaffolding that had never been finished. They clashed with the nature elements—trees and grass and flowers and all that—of the rest of the park. The whole scene did not look supernatural in the slightest, even with his seemingly altered perception.

David scowled and tried to focus.

What, he wondered, did a fairy's nest even look like? He glanced all around him as he walked and paused here and there to examine anything that looked out of place in more detail.

His exploration found an old, dead beehive and a rather boring hole in the ground, but no fairies.

"The bridge," he told himself. "Keep heading under the bridge— Wait, what about trolls? I know trolls live under bridges but I'm not so sure about fae."

He passed into the shade of the great structure, which spanned the Hudson river and allowed easy access to New Jersey for anyone who actually wanted to go there for some strange reason. A few cars cruised above in both directions.

"This is bullshit," he murmured. "They're setting me up to get robbed or something, aren't they? Some thugs will pounce and take my wallet and say they know where I live, and Taylor will materialize and offer to 'protect' me from them in exchange for a small ongoing donation to her ultra-legitimate Italian restaurant. I should have known. They're all in it together, trying to—"

He stopped abruptly when both his brain and mouth ceased to function.

Two small bi-pedal forms with wings floated—definitely airborne—about twelve feet in front of his face. Both had hands with thumbs—that somehow seemed important —and hair on their tiny heads.

"Uhhhh…" he said as the breath leaked out of his lungs.

"It's not a lie!" the fairy on the left shrieked, although given its size, the shriek was not particularly loud. "You merely have a narrow and uptight definition of truth. You've spent too much time around humans."

For a moment, David was afraid the creature had spoken to him. It pointed at the other one on the right, however. Neither of them seemed to have even noticed his presence.

"How dare you," the other retorted waspishly. "Your nest is the one that keeps getting fat on deep-dish. You would rescind any word you'd said simply for human table scraps!"

He stared and could almost hear the gears of his brain clanking as it tried to process this information.

Both creatures looked similar—roughly humanoid but definitely alien, with flapping translucent wings like those of a dragonfly and delicate antennae protruding from beneath their moss-like hair. Their skin was a bizarre color that he could only describe as greenish-pink. However, the left one's extremities were tinged with pale blue, whereas the right one tended toward peach or amber. Both were about the size of a grapefruit.

"Now you're the one who's lying. Oh, the stench of hypocrisy."

David adjusted his tie. The argument seemed on the verge of violence, which meant it was no doubt time to do some of that mitigation.

"Um...excuse me," he said, in a clear voice but well below shouting volume. "It...uh, seems you two are having some...problems." He wondered what they were fighting over and recalled Taylor's advice that it was unlikely to matter much.

Both fairies turned in midair to look at him. Their eyes were almost human but with an iridescent sheen like a fly's.

"What the shit?" the orange-tinged one burst out. "You can see us?" The other one looked equally as shocked.

He smiled at them. "I certainly can," he confirmed. "I'm from Moonlight Detective Agency, actually. I've been sent to help...uh, mediate this discussion. What seems to be the nature of the disagreement here?"

The two fae fluttered to face toward him and drew a little closer together, and he had the odd sense that a kind of silent communication had passed between them.

"What is your name, mortal?" the bluish one asked.

David, to his own surprise, blushed. Two emotions struck him at once. The first was a vague sense of caution —something he recalled from old legends about a person's "true name" having power or some crap like that.

The second was shame. He thought back to the news

report on his now-infamous bacchanal and decided that he simply didn't want to be known as David Remington.

"My name," he began, "is Remington Davis. What about yours? If they're unpronounceable, round them off to the nearest syllable, I guess."

"What?" a thin voice screamed off to the right somewhere. "What? Who dares?"

He glanced toward the new sound. From an ordinary-looking mound of dirt near one of the bridge-posts, three other small, winged forms had emerged. They now glided directly toward him.

The orangish fairy looked at them. "This human can see us," it squeaked, "and he said our names were unpronounceable."

Blinking in confusion, David glanced to the other side when another cluster of fairies—more blue-tinged ones this time—wafted up from another nest.

Seeing its brethren approaching, the first of the blue ones turned toward its amber-hued rivals. "You probably were the ones who hired him," it accused. "Sure, that was a clever plan. You hired the mitigation agency to send this idiot to insult us so we lose control and you win the argument. Well, it absolutely won't work."

"Horseshit!" two of the orange fairies shouted in unison.

The two tribes immediately returned to their heated argument.

"Hey," David interjected. "*Hey!* Shut the hell up, you little—fairies! For fuck's sake. Neither of you hired me. I came here to knock some sense into you tiny-ass pricks."

All the fae turned to look at him.

"You shut up," they howled, almost perfectly unanimous.

One of them then added, "Yeah, *Remy*. What a stupid name. It probably isn't even your real one."

Now, he was pissed. He opened his mouth to let them know exactly how much.

CHAPTER SIX

Harrison, Westchester County, New York

In a dark, cavernous space, stone ground against stone. A slim white hand pushed away the heavy lid of the enclosing sarcophagus to reveal the more conventional but beautifully carved wooden casket within.

Taylor drifted upward through the cold, stale air and her eyes opened slowly as the last of the sunlight died away. The night was newborn, and she was awake.

Once she'd cleared the edge of her coffin, she allowed her feet to fall gently to the earth and stood in the natural fashion. Behind her, the stone lid scraped into place of its own accord.

She listened intently but the house was silent. That disappointed her, but she'd had many, many years in which to learn to cope with disappointment.

Only a moment later, her sharp ears discerned a slight commotion aboveground. Presley sauntered over the floor above her head, opened the front entrance, and admitted someone, who entered with heavy, shuffling steps and grumbled his way into the foyer.

"So," she whispered to herself, "he's not dead."

"Taylor?" David's voice called. "Where the hell is she? It's, like, two minutes past sunset already. *Taylor?*"

She wondered with amused curiosity how her inept human problem-child had managed to resolve the task she'd set him. Without thought, she floated to the door and took a moment to remember to put her feet on the ground before she opened it. She stood in silence and studied the mess of a human in front of her.

"What," she asked coolly, "happened to you? Did you complete the assignment?"

He was covered in bruises and cheap, pharmacy-bought bandages and walked with a slight limp. His hair was untidy and tousled, and one of his eyes had swollen half-shut. In keeping with that, his clothing was ripped in various places, his jacket was gone, and his tie was askew.

"Oh, yeah, sure," he replied with bitter sarcasm. "Your goddamn fairies are now all one big happy family of murderous, height-challenged pricks with purty wings."

The vampire smiled inwardly but kept her face impassive. "Come with me into the kitchen," she instructed and waved for him to follow her.

He did, and she stood in the corner while he shuffled into the center of the room. She pointed toward the sink.

"There's running water and some paper towels. Wipe your face. It looks like it's been oozing on your trip over here."

"Thanks." He grunted with moody resignation.

While he washed his face and hands, she inquired, "What did you get them to agree upon, David?"

The flow of the faucet stopped. "They all agreed that they needed to kick my ass." He sniffed. "*Ow.*"

"Why?"

He sighed and explained.

"It seems my attempt at 'straight talk' with them wasn't appreciated. They were arguing over...I don't know, who is more of a slut for human pizza or some crap, and I tried to get them to all shut up and listen to me. Each nest also thought the other had hired me to cause problems. Which I did, obviously. They didn't like my tone and thought I was being condescending. They went from yelling at each other to yelling at me.

"So," he went on, "they all started buzzing around, all pissed-off, and I got angry as well and accidentally swatted one of them out of the sky because I had flashbacks to stepping on a fucking hornet's nest when I was a kid. I hit one of the blue ones, and one of the orange ones caught it before it crashed, which I guess was enough to unite all of them against the invading human. So they all ganged up on me and I ended up like"—he swept a hand down the length of his body—"*this.*"

Taylor nodded. "You should have simply caught one of them and eaten it."

His eyes fluttered and normal functionality returned. "First of all, eww. Come on, eat a fairy? That's messed up. Is that some kind of vampire thing?"

She laughed softly. "You are already making my nights more amusing. Don't believe everything you hear about vampires, David. Most tales are false. You'll learn what's true soon enough."

"Oh, I can't wait." He groaned "By the way, they asked me my name and I told them to call me Remington Davis. We might as well run with that. On, the job, I don't think I want to be David Remington."

"Very well, Remington Davis. You found a novel solution to resolving that issue. Let's find you a more challenging assignment, shall we?"

David slumped against the door of the car. They were almost home. That was good, but he simply wanted to collapse into bed right now.

"Damn," Stanislaw remarked as the condo came into clear sight, "you live here?"

The man's memory had mysteriously vanished again after he had left Taylor's mansion for the second time. This failed to surprise David anymore.

"Yeppers," he said wearily.

"Isn't this the place where that party happened a couple of weeks ago and there were all those lawsuits? I heard about that on the news." Stan shook his head and uttered a low whistle.

"I heard about that, too." He sighed.

Earlier, the bleeding and battered man had told the driver that, while searching the park, he'd been jumped by a pair of homeless individuals suffering from an excessive dependency on controlled substances. He didn't want to bother contacting the police, though—too much trouble.

Stan had chewed his lip in concern but accepted his explanation without comment.

And now, they were strangers again. David begrudgingly concluded that he'd have to start finding alternative transportation arrangements.

He leaned forward. "Drop me off here. I can cross the street on my own. And…uh, thanks for waiting for me all day."

The driver was obviously confused by this remark. He seemed to have no idea that he'd now worked as his chauffeur continuously for almost eighteen hours.

It was probably for the best, though, given all the odd trips they'd taken. He dragged himself out of his seat and gave Stan a somewhat more generous tip this time. The man thanked him and took off, whistling cheerfully to himself.

"Doesn't he ever get tired?" he wondered. Then again, the guy kept passing out whenever he got mindwiped.

The concierge noticed his condition as soon as he came into sight and immediately made a fuss over him.

"Yes," he mumbled, "I'm fine, Enrique, thanks."

The man escorted him into the lobby. A couple of snooty bitches in fur and Louboutins were there and gasped in disgust as he trudged by.

"What happened, sir?" Enrique followed him and continued to fuss. "Did you get robbed?"

"No," he replied, speaking louder and not really thinking as the words flowed from his mouth. He was tired and sore, and he had a headache. "I had my ass kicked trying to break up a fight between some fairies."

The Paris Hilton wannabes looked shocked. Some of their best friends were totally gay people.

David realized in irritation how that had sounded, and he slapped a hand over his face to drag it gradually downwards. "Oh, for fuck's sake. No, I meant, real, actual—"

He stopped and literally bit his tongue. There was absolutely no way he should blurt out his sincere conviction that he had, earlier this very day, had a violent altercation with the gossamer-winged denizens of the enchanted Realm of Faerie.

There was no point in trying to explain any of that to either Enrique or the socialites. He limped into the elevator and smacked the button for the penthouse.

By the time the light reached "P" and the elevator pinged, he was slumped against the doors. They opened and he stumbled out. Around him, the penthouse was clean and orderly, one hundred percent sane and normal.

"Ugh." He breathed deeply. "At least being gone all day meant there was zero chance of me turning this place into a satanic ritual aftermath scene again."

He stopped abruptly where he stood when a disconcerting thought intruded. In the course of his job to come, he surmised, there might come a time when he could no longer consider that a joke.

"What the hell have I gotten myself into?" he wondered. "How is this even real? A vampire sent me to have the crap beaten out of me by the fae. Christ on a cracker...this is even more absurd than the time me and that Rothschild shithead had a puking contest while trying to sing death metal lyrics."

Furthermore, he and Taylor had not even discussed the

subject of his pay. That would be the first thing on his agenda tomorrow.

But for now, he needed to sleep. He took off his shirt, his tie, and his slacks and slouched his way to the bathroom, brushed his teeth in a painful daze, and tried not to think too hard.

Part of him desperately wanted a drink. And by a drink, he meant half a bottle or so of Swedish vodka. But that was about how much he had left in total. He settled for two shots. After all, he needed to wean himself off.

"How," he asked aloud, "will I stay off drugs if I barely even drink? Whatever. I'm a Remington. I can do anything."

He dragged himself to bed, reset his alarm, and collapsed onto the soft mattress, already dozing off as he pulled the warm covers over his sprawled body. Consciousness faded so quickly that he might as well have passed out on the floor.

The alarm went off at 3:00 am.

"Huhh?" David protested, both against the noise and the drool on his pillow. His arm flopped out and his fingers groped in the general direction of the alarm clock.

"No," he mumbled. "Please, Mom. I'll be good. Just not the little asshole flying people again. Anything but… Come on, I mean it."

CHAPTER SEVEN

Harrison, Westchester County, New York

Taylor walked into her garage and stood before her five cars.

Three gleamed in the low light and two others were protected beneath tarps. But one, in particular, was her usual chosen mode of transportation.

It was a Tesla Model S, P100D and only about two years old. Already a beautiful, efficient, and well-functioning vehicle on its own, its appeal was even stronger since she had made a few alterations. Of course, she had requested it with Ludicrous Mode. Acceleration was a beautiful thing. And *Spaceballs*, along with Mel Brooks' entire oeuvre, was a guilty pleasure of hers. The Tesla could take it and she was not a chicken.

In addition to these standard features, she'd had the interior upgraded in several key ways. The seats and floors were all recovered with real, premium leather, not the synthetic, vegan stuff. Nothing beat the feel—and smell—

of genuine leather, she felt. And as a true predator, she felt she had the right.

There were also a few nifty gadgets on or near the console and various minor hacks had tweaked the car's main system. Not all of these were what you'd call street-legal, but legality was more of a guideline than a rule—a white-and-orange roadblock that could be driven around or plowed under.

Shortly after purchasing the car, she had tracked down and mesmerized a Tesla engineer. The man was the type who didn't believe at all in the paranormal, which made him easy prey for manipulation. In minutes, he happily did whatever she'd asked.

Which, in this case, meant removing every last barrier on her vehicle's speed. She could drive as fast as she wanted to. However, the car's computer would give her an alert when she exceeded the manufacturer's stated lockdowns so that at least she'd know to be cautious.

The car was black, of course. All five vehicles were.

Taylor climbed into the vehicle, pressed the button to open the garage, and piloted the sleek ebony vehicle out into the night. She quickly navigated the labyrinth of private roads surrounding the estate and soon found herself on a major street, heading into the heart of the city.

Something beeped on her dashboard and Presley's voice came through. "Madam," he began, "it appears that Mr Remington put a handprint on your harpsichord. He barged in there looking for you before I could stop him, I'm afraid. Shall I call for professional cleaning and restoration, or will my own ministrations be sufficient?"

She bit her lip and realized she would have to inform

David that he was not to touch anything unless given permission to do so first. "I trust your abilities, Presley. If they prove insufficient, you may call the pros."

"Yes, madam." He ended the call.

The rest of the drive passed uneventfully. She enjoyed driving, even in the thick of Manhattan's traffic. It was almost like fighting—the interplay of speed and force along with the technique and exhilaration—only less physically intimate. Usually.

Her destination was a club of sorts—arguably more of a bar-and-grille and one frequented almost exclusively by preternaturals.

The term "supernatural" was already close to played out by around 1880, many individuals felt, and she was one of them. Now, a good one hundred and forty years later, the term had acquired all manner of cheesy, banal, and ridiculous connotations, which only served to remind her that they'd been right.

Besides, those few humans who knew the truth didn't like it when the world's other sentient beings went around referring to themselves as "super." It made them edgy and hostile and was simply bad PR.

"Preternatural" was a more neutral and less clichéd term. It conveyed the same essential meaning—beyond the normal standards of what is considered natural.

As Taylor eased her Model S into the establishment's parking lot, she saw that her usual space was occupied by an obnoxious red pickup truck. It looked like it burned a ton of fossil fuels and she grimaced.

She didn't feel like starting shit. Not yet, at least, so she let it go and parked in the next space over and swung her legs out of the vehicle to stand on the pavement.

New York City glimmered all around her. The artificial lights made by humanity never failed to impress her. It was a welcome sight for someone who hadn't glimpsed the original source of Earth's illumination for so, so long.

The building was unassuming from the outside—a fairly standard, blocky, yuppie-restaurant type establishment, clean and modern-looking. There were no flashy advertisements to draw undue scrutiny. Along similar lines, it was located slightly off the beaten path and surrounded by vacant but well-maintained lots, yet they'd managed to select the location to avoid it seeming too private, either.

Taylor strode in through the front door. Beyond the entrance lay a small lobby, with doors leading to the right and left. The left opened onto an exclusive dining parlor, where the guests were expected to dress nicely and be on their best behavior. The right led to the bar, where things were rather less formal.

She went left and nodded at the hostess. The maître d' noticed her presence once she'd taken a step or two into the restaurant area.

"Ms Steele!" he greeted her, beaming politely beneath his well-groomed mustache. "Welcome. It's so nice to see you again."

The vampire nodded to him as well. "Thank you, Chagnon." It was unnecessary to say anything more as he was already leading her to her usual place, a booth in the extreme rear. This was also the darkest part of the restaurant where only those with excellent night vision would even be able to see she was there.

She, on the other hand, had her back to the wall when she sat and could see the entire dining wing. And she could hear, quite clearly, anything the humans were saying.

As Chagnon moved toward the front, he dispatched another waiter to her booth. It was a youngish man she recognized, although she'd only seen him two or three times.

He seemed a little tense. "What will you have, madame?" he asked.

"Historical Bloody Mary," she responded with a smile.

The waiter wrote it on his pad. "At once." He turned and left.

The Historical differed from a standard Bloody Mary in that it was made with something other than tomato juice. There were ways to acquire such ingredients for a place like this. Some of them were even relatively ethical.

While she waited, she looked around. The current clientele was a motley group but everyone seemed to be minding their manners so far.

A moment later, a man strode down the aisle toward her booth. He was short—Taylor was taller than him—but broad-shouldered and barrel-chested and looked extremely strong. He wore a fine tuxedo and had a long, full beard that hung almost to his waist.

When the bearded man reached the booth, he nodded respectfully and eased himself into the seat opposite her. "Good evening," he said in a voice somehow both gruff and elegantly formal. Many people thought he had a vestigial accent, although opinions varied as to whether it sounded more Scottish, Yiddish, or Scandinavian.

"Good evening," she greeted him. "It seems that all is well with the warring fae."

The man nodded again. The fae of Fort Washington Park lay within his sphere of influence and were his responsibility. He'd long since learned that it was best to resolve their disputes before more powerful preternaturals were drawn in and all hell broke loose. While the diminutive folk largely kept to themselves, they did have friends with more violent tendencies.

Slowly, he withdrew a handwoven sack from his tux. As he loosened the drawstring, she saw a flash of gold within. His kind always paid in antique coins of precious metals. Human paper money was regarded as worthless. Like the species who created it, it was neither stable nor enduring.

He counted out a few coins. All were large and heavy and inscribed with obscure writing and symbols. "So," he began, "is the rumor true, then?"

Before Taylor could answer, her waiter reappeared with her drink.

"Thank you." She sipped almost immediately but kept her eyes mostly lidded as she drank. While she'd been hungry and knew not to wait any longer to assuage it, she did not want to advertise the slight red glow that emanated from her pupils.

Even before the waiter could ask, her guest raised a hand and requested a stout. "The darker and stouter the better, please."

The server gave a curt bow. "Of course, sir." He moved quickly toward the bar.

Refreshed, she now turned her attention to the man's query. "Which rumor? There's never exactly a shortage of them."

"The rumor," he replied, "that a human—during the day —went to the fairies' nest in the middle of one of their arguments and picked a fight with all of them at once. Which of course forced them to come together against the invading giant in their mutual defense and thereby resolved the feud." He ran a hand through his beard.

"It was a unique way to solve the problem," she agreed, "but let's not tell the human that. The important thing, though, is that everything turned out well…assuming the fairies didn't track him home and poison him and he hasn't died in his sleep overnight."

Seeing her faint smirk, the dwarf rolled his eyes toward some distant upwards point. "A new partner for you?" he asked.

She took another sip. "Let us say…an old partner who may decide to take the daytime shift. I'll give him the mitigation tasks, if so."

The waiter returned with a bottle of beer. It was sufficiently dark and stout to be almost black, by the looks of it.

The man spoke first. "It's a good enough beer," he pronounced. "While it's not quite as strong as I'd like, the humans are getting better at this kind of thing."

Taylor smiled. "The craft beer revolution, my friend. As for mixed drinks, though, at first, I had to show them exactly how to make a good Historical myself. Don't worry. No one was harmed."

He snorted. "Of course not. I understand the 'tomato juice' comes from a…bank, these days."

The dwarf finished his beer and set the bottle firmly in the table's center. "There is another rumor, you know—one alleging that the alpha of the Southern Tip Pack seems to have lost his head. And his heart."

She acknowledged this with a small movement of her head. "I have also heard that. I should assume it is accurate."

"The rumors also say," he went on, "that James tried to run shakedowns on humans, the way the Mob does, and that he may have bitten off more than he could chew."

"Hmm," she said calmly, "that would have been a bad decision if so. Everyone knows that the rules state to leave humans to humans."

The dwarf grunted. "Those are your rules, Taylor. Many feel that they never had the opportunity to agree to them. Or disagree. Some even say this part of the country would be ripe for the plucking if it wasn't for your personal authority over New York."

Their eyes locked. The dwarf was stolid and poker-faced, but even he was not impervious to her abilities. She could read, almost immediately, that he himself was not amongst those who agitated against her. No, someone else had said such things. He was merely trying to warn her.

Taylor broke the silence. "I know of quite a few who seem discontented yet have nevertheless behaved themselves. Such as…"

She rattled off a list of names, speaking fast enough that the dwarf could not get a word in edgewise but with enough of a pause between each one that his brain had time to register them individually.

While she spoke, she watched his subtle reaction to

each name, noted every nuance, and filed the information away.

There were three agitators, it seemed. Two werewolves —that didn't surprise her—and a relatively young male vampire, only about two hundred years old. She was not well-acquainted with any of them but had heard their names and seen their faces on the odd occasion. They'd all struck her as potential troublemakers, even though none had done anything egregious.

Yet.

Something in the dwarf's demeanor suggested that the hints they'd dropped were not merely the desire to call a forum and debate the issues. More likely, the three suspects actually imagined a world in which she was dead.

Taylor betrayed no sign that she had gleaned so much information from nothing more than subtle cues. "I see," she acknowledged. "Yes, the young and ignorant never seem to think that the things they dream up could possibly be flawed. They look around and see no one else implementing their plans and assume it's because they are the first geniuses ever born in this world and everyone else is too stupid to understand them."

The dwarf fingered his beard in silence and she continued. "I imagine that the aforementioned pack alpha was a member of the malcontents. What has happened to James will send a message to the remaining ones."

"Well," her guest responded with a firm air of finality, "I have been around long enough to know when we have a good thing going. Fools and troublemakers are not wanted. I hope the message is received."

She nodded. The dwarf had told her what she needed to

know—that he had voted for measures to be taken to preserve the peace, if necessary, and that she had his support if things started to get ugly.

Her drink finished, she stood and prepared to leave. Before she could say her goodbyes, however, her attention snapped toward a table near the front where a trio of idiots —almost certainly lycanthropes—had been gradually raising their voices. Now, one of them shouted and cursed violently, disturbing the entire room.

With no more sound than a shadow would make as it flitted across a wall, she strode toward their table. They did not even notice her presence until she was beside them.

"Excuse me," she remarked to the noisiest of the three, slapped her hand on the back of his head, and drove his face flat into the table in the same motion.

Not only did that quiet the other two but the rest of the room, as well. With piercing black eyes, she stared at the other two. "This side is for quiet dinner, not outbursts and rowdiness. Please do not make me complain to the management about the inconvenience of your blood on my clothing."

The two nodded slowly. To emphasize her point, she seized the arm of the one she'd accosted and gave his wrist a sharp twist. That ought to give him something to think about.

"Now," she went on, "eat in peace or go to the bar side."

Their jaws clenched, the two unscathed young were-wolves gathered their drinks—and their disoriented friend —and shuffled away from the table toward the lobby.

Taylor followed them but remained a few paces behind. They did as instructed, passed the host and entered the bar, and gave no indication that they intended to cause further trouble. Satisfied, she turned aside and pushed out the front door.

Her Tesla waited for her. No valet was ever needed as it drove itself. She smiled.

CHAPTER EIGHT

Harrison, Westchester County, New York

Remy—the nickname the fairies had given David had kind of stuck in his own mind—sighed and shifted the vehicle into park. Or, rather, he thought he shifted into park but apparently, it was into neutral since the car began to slowly lurch backward and down the slight incline immediately before Taylor's house.

"Shit, shit, *shit!*" he cursed, fumbled for the gearshift, and stamped on the brakes. "Park is all the way forward. Remember that." He pressed the button on the side of the lever and shoved it where it needed to be. The car came to a stop.

He exhaled. "Well, I'm getting better. I'm a tad rusty, is all." He probably wasn't supposed to park there, though. He wondered if he could get away with it or if Taylor would try to chew his ass on the matter. At least he was inside the gate, Presley having buzzed him in.

Not that she was likely to be up and about. Remy had overslept by almost half an hour, not to mention that driving himself all the way to Harrison in Westchester had taken another half-hour longer than he'd expected. The sun had been up for a good forty-five minutes by now.

He was about to remove the keys and exit the car when the garage door opened.

"Damn." He shifted into drive again and inched gently toward what seemed to be his reserved space.

There were already several cars within but the structure was large enough to accommodate at least six, maybe more. he selected an empty space and eased into it.

A strange sense of claustrophobia set in as the garage walls seemed to hem him in and the other vehicles loomed close by. He had no physical fear of collision, but in his current financial straits, he did not like the idea of damaging his new boss's property and having to pay to repair it.

"Okay," he said to himself as he ventured forward an inch or two, "I think we're all the way in now. Right?" It was hard to judge.

To be safe, he shifted into park—and checked to be sure —then left the engine running as he climbed out to examine his surroundings. He was fine on both sides but, annoyingly, his rear bumper was still almost directly below the edge of the garage door.

He climbed into the driver's seat once more and nudged the car an eensie bit forward.

"That should do it." He nodded and got out again. Thankfully, he'd managed not to run the front end into any of Taylor's belongings, and he'd keep his rear bumper intact, also. He then remembered that he should probably shut the engine off and remove the key. With this accomplished, he examined his surroundings.

Doubt assailed him and he froze in place. He wasn't sure if he was allowed to enter the house via the door within the garage or if they expected him to circle to the front entrance. After a few minutes' deliberation, he decided to try the easier option first.

He grasped the knob on the heavy wooden door leading from the garage to the interior and tried it cautiously. It failed to turn.

"That figures," he muttered, walked to the front, and ascended the steps as he had on his first morning there. He'd no sooner reached the landing when the butler opened the right side.

Remy spoke first. "Good morning, Jeeves. Sorry I'm a little late, but you know how New York traffic is."

The old man frowned. "Morning, sir. And do please call me Presley, thank you. Come in." He motioned for him to follow him and turned to disappear into the shadowy foyer.

Presley turned to face him, now, and his hands were folded behind his back. His droopy face frowned even more deeply than before.

"Uh-oh," he said, reading the disapproval.

The old man cleared his throat. "Ms Steele wished for me to express her intense displeasure at your tardiness," he stated, his voice low and cold with disapproval.

"Intense displeasure?" he inquired. "That sounds as kinky as all hell, Jeeves. I thought your relationship was purely professional."

"I am uncertain what you are implying by that," Presley

retorted and his frown became almost a scowl, "and don't think that being a smart-arse is some kind of compensation for having failed to arrive on time. You're only making things more difficult for yourself."

Remy sighed. "The sympathy is appreciated, old chap. It's good to know that you feel sorry enough for my predicament to have forgiven me already."

The elderly man sighed and turned his eyes heavenward. "I can see it's utterly useless to try and lecture you, Mr Remington. Let's get straight to your assignment, then, shall we?"

"Good idea," he quipped. "We shall. That way, you get to pay me for doing actual work instead of standing here talking."

The butler motioned for him to follow as he led the way into the kitchen. He stopped after a few paces and gestured with his hand toward the table, where a large stack of envelopes lay.

He looked at them. "All those are for me? I didn't realize I was already so popular."

The butler remained stony-faced. "They are for you to deliver, sir. Ms Steele wishes for you to act as her private courier in taking these important messages to various clients and contacts of hers throughout the city and its surrounding environs. You will have all day to do so, although sadly, you have wasted your first hour."

Remy frowned at the prospect of more driving. He knew he would simply have to get used to it, but the notion still almost curdled his bowels.

"So," he began, "if she expects me to be her delivery boy,

taking her letters to her contacts, does that mean I can use one of her cars? It looks like she can spare one."

Presley sniffed, although that might merely have been to disguise the sudden flaring of his nostrils. "Absolutely not," he stated.

There were only four locations to which Remy had to deliver the letters as some of the stops had several envelopes each. It was now approaching late morning as he drove toward his first destination, which was all the way down in Brooklyn and near Prospect Park.

It made sense to him to start with the stop farthest south and work his way back north toward Westchester. In fact, the third stop would be in some bumfuck village upstate, northwest of Taylor's mansion. For some reason, however, Taylor and Presley had explicitly instructed him to leave one stop in Lower Manhattan for last. That made no sense to him, but whatever.

According to his map app and GPS, it should have taken only about an hour to get from the estate to the middle of Brooklyn. He had thought that sounded rather optimistic. But, of course, even after he'd added half an hour to be safe, he had still come up short.

"For fuck's sake," he grumbled and tried to navigate the narrow and winding residential streets at a consistent twenty-six miles-per-hour. "This never would have happened if there were some standardization of what constitutes right versus straight at those diagonal-ass intersections."

A little farther ahead, a family of Hasidic Jews seemed to be having a friendly neighborhood argument with a pair of Puerto Rican teenagers in the middle of the road. He waved half-heartedly to them as he passed in the faint hope that one party or the other might spontaneously A, ask him if he was lost or B, get out of the road. They all ignored him and he was forced to drive around them.

With a suddenness that actually startled him, he was back in a business district of sorts. But at least his GPS finally seemed to have caught up and he was heading south again.

When he'd first departed the village of Harrison, where Taylor's ancient neighborhood lay, he'd gotten onto 95 South, intending to take it to where it became the 678 when it crossed the East River. That was what the app recommended and it certainly made sense.

The plan had gone well at first, and he'd begun to congratulate himself on his brilliance and success. In fact, he grew so confident that he changed lanes at high speed to avoid getting funneled into an exit and almost clipped some lady with a "May I speak to the manager?" haircut in a pearl-colored SUV. She reacted in usual New Yorker fashion.

Directly after that, something had gone wrong. At the interchange, he'd misinterpreted exactly what the hell the robotic voice from his phone meant by "bear to the right" and somehow ended up on Cross Island Parkway, which had borne him to the east and into Queens.

Cursing and pounding his fist against random sections of the car's interior, he had gone along with it, ignored his GPS's garbled attempts to get him back on course, and taken Grand Central Parkway southwest into Brooklyn… until it suddenly ended in a labyrinth of diagonal streets.

"I'm sure I'm somewhere fairly close, by now," he muttered, nodded, and stared straight ahead. "I'll stumble onto the place any minute now…any minute now…."

He did not stumble onto the place that minute or even the next. After driving around randomly and getting stuck in congestion at every red light, he pulled into a metered parking space and thumped a single quarter into the machine. He only needed long enough to sit for a moment and check his phone to determine exactly where he was.

"Okayyy." He breathed deeply and zoomed out on the map as the app pinpointed his location. "This is beginning to make some sense…"

Thankfully, it appeared that he was only about a mile away. He backed out into the street—spinning the wheel as rapidly as he could to correct his position once he realized he'd left the front corner of his car in the oncoming lane—and hurried toward his destination.

The place turned out to be an unusually small block of rowhouses—four individual residences. There was only one address for the entire complex, which suggested that whoever lived there owned or rented all four adjacent houses.

Remy turned to the items on the passenger's seat. This location had four envelopes assigned to it.

Taylor had also written a few notes on a piece of paper to go with the pile of mail. Her handwriting was beautiful and elegant. He recognized it as the same script he'd seen on the missive he'd received before the meeting at the

Italian restaurant. The notes themselves, however, were terse.

Her comment for this address simply said, *Elves—beware temptation.*

"Interesting." He turned the paper face-down on the seat. "I wonder what kind of temptation we're talking about here?"

He narrowed it down to two things on the short walk from his car to the front entrance.

The door with the address plate in front of it seemed like the sensible place to start. Remy tapped the knocker three times. While waiting for a reply, he heard jangling and unstructured music wafting from somewhere within the building.

Light footsteps approached and the door clicked and opened.

He wanted to get this over quickly, so he began to speak even before the door had swung all the way inward. "Hi, I'm from Moonlight Detective Agency and have a few letters for...you..." He trailed off and his mouth went slack.

The person—elf?—who'd answered the door was a young woman wearing little more than a loose skirt and multiple necklaces of brightly colored beads, which mostly hid her breasts. Mostly. She had huge golden eyes and long, messy, silver-white hair which barely concealed the points of her elongated ears.

"Uhhhh..." he slurred and tried not to stare.

"Hello," she greeted him. Her voice was soft and musical and her facial expression somehow wise but also strangely innocent. "You may come in if you want."

He swallowed. "Well, I only need to drop these letters

of, from…you know, Moonlight Detective Agency. You…
uh, know us, right?"

In the middle of his reply, another elf—a male—came
up behind the woman. He was an inch or two taller and
noticeably flatter-chested but otherwise looked little
different than she did.

"Hey, brother," the elf said. "We were a little bored and
we've actually been looking for someone who might want
to expand their mind a little, you know? It's on us. No
charge."

Even despite their obviously non-human eyes, there
was something distinctly familiar about them, which he
noticed immediately. They possessed a kind of sheen and
displayed an overstimulation and dilation of the pupils.
Quite obviously, both were as high as kites. Behind them,
the music revealed itself to be Pink Floyd, although
someone in another room strummed a sitar in a way that
toyed with and reshaped the music.

His palms itched and sweated and he worried he might
be drooling.

"No," he said after a moment's hesitation, "thank you. I
merely need to drop these off."

"Aww." The woman pouted. "You're not into free love?
It seems like not many people are anymore. We thought it
was a good idea so we've tried to keep it alive." She smiled
pleasantly.

As if to agree with her and emphasize her words, the
male elf fondled her breasts, which caused the pert nipples
to protrude through the layers of beads. He smirked in a
way that reminded Remy of some Euro-trash prick he used

to know who had a thing for watching his girlfriend with other men.

"Sorry," he apologized quickly. "Interspecies relations is one of the few kinks that even I feel should remain off-limits. Now, if you'll please take these—"

Another elf suddenly wandered past the doorway, swaying as he moved. "Whoa," he exclaimed, noticed the visitor, and snatched the letters from his hand. "They finally showed up, man. Ha." Smiling goofily, he staggered and started to close the door.

Remy waved to the couple who had first greeted him. They looked disappointed.

"Maybe some other time," he said, using the classic blow-off line.

The elves merely stared at him. He exhaled sharply and made himself turn and walk back to his car.

He fell into the driver's seat and fumbled for the air conditioning as soon as he turned the key in the ignition. The temperature had been set at seventy but suddenly that seemed too hot, so he reduced it to sixty-five. He was sweating excessively.

"God," he drawled and fought to clear his head. "Come on. I assume elves live longer than humans, but I still would have thought they'd be over the Sixties by now."

His next stop was in Hell's Kitchen. Once across the river and onto Manhattan Island, he was at least back in relatively familiar territory and he made good time as he drove north on 9A.

This time, the problem was finding a goddamn parking spot.

The public housing structure he sought wasn't difficult

to find, but there were almost no actual lots nearby and the curbside parking situation was not encouraging. He circled the building four times. Each time he saw an open space, some other asshole appeared out of nowhere, cut him off, and slid home before he could react in time.

"This," he grated as his jaw muscles tensed, "is why operating a motor vehicle in the City of New York should be left to the professionals."

Eventually, he cruised down a nearby side street and found another metered space. He was grateful that he kept each of his cars stocked with a handful of quarters in the case of exactly such a contingency as this.

Remy gathered the two envelopes and checked Taylor's notes again. *Gremlins—knock loudly*, she'd written.

"Gremlins," he muttered and eased out of the vehicle. "I can't even imagine what we're in for now."

He wandered around until he found Building C, ignored the sidelong glances of a few dudes who loitered about, and was surprised to discover that there was no concierge or receptionist or anything. Instead, he simply entered the building and ascended to the second floor.

As soon as he found the correct hallway, Taylor's note started to make some sense. Seemingly, this half of the floor boomed with gunfire, explosions, and colorful swearing.

"I wonder," he said under his breath, "which *Call of Duty* that is. The thirty-ninth one, perhaps."

He took a few steps toward the door marked with the correct apartment number. Halfway there, he was stopped in his tracks by a stream of curses from a high-pitched, thin, ragged voice unlike any he'd heard before.

"Oh, that's fucking bullshit!" the voice shrieked. "You're simply taking your incel rage out on people who are better than you because your fucking dog's pussy isn't tight enough ever since you lost your Fleshlight. Just admit you're going to lose and tell your mom to bring you more pizza rolls down to the basement."

Remy blinked. That horrible voice made him feel nauseated—as did the particular word-picture it painted—but at least he could take comfort in knowing that the world of competitive online gaming hadn't changed much over the years.

"Hello?" he called and pounded on the door. "I have some—"

"Fuck, yeah!" another voice squealed, perfectly timed with another blast of gunfire. This one was similar but sounded like it belonged to a different gremlin. "You just transitioned to female because you're a pussy and you got fucked. Go tell everyone to learn your new pronouns, bitch!"

Remy raised his voice. "*Letters.* I have letters for you... people." He pounded on the door again. When no one answered after several more moments of noise, he squatted to see if there was a mail slot or even if the crack under the door was wide enough to admit a couple of envelopes.

He had no luck in either case, kicked the door, and pounded on it again.

Suddenly, someone lowered the game's volume to merely loud, rather than deafening.

"What?" a voice demanded.

He gritted his teeth. "Important letters."

The door unlatched and opened. Almost before Remy

could see what happened, a small, dark, mottled claw appeared and snatched the envelopes from his hand. His eyes locked onto a knee-high figure that scuttled back into the apartment, and the door slammed in his face. A moment later, the sounds of simulated combat again echoed through the whole floor once again.

"So sorry to disturb you," he mumbled.

Somewhat relieved that nothing more had been required of him, he descended the staircase, departed the housing complex, and returned to his car. His ears were still ringing from the racket.

He sighed. "Well, I'm about half done. And it's only around lunchtime." He was already getting tired—not so much physically as mentally. It was the stress of having to focus on driving and finding the right location and dealing with whatever weirdness both humanity and inhumanity threw at him along the way.

His next destination was all the way in Tuxedo, which he was reasonably sure was where they held the Renaissance Faire. He'd gone to that with some friends when he was sixteen or seventeen although he'd been too fucked-up to remember most of it.

"Ugh," he grumbled and checked the directions on his phone, "the shortest route cuts through New Jersey. At least it's only a small part of the northeastern corner." He contemplated going farther north within New York and then taking the Tappan Zee Bridge across the Hudson River, but that would take longer. He sighed mournfully.

A short drive to the west brought him to 9A, which he took north. From there, he headed west across the George Washington Bridge into Jersey and bore northwest, first on

4 and then on 17. To his pleasant surprise, he arrived in the vicinity of Tuxedo after only about fifty-five or sixty minutes, which was what his app estimated. He seemed to be well ahead of rush hour.

The area grew sleepier and more rustic. Without having to actually focus as much on the act of driving, he was able to glance at his notes. His destination seemed to be some kind of farmer's market outside the town, where his task was to seek out whoever was in charge of the whole mess.

He took his foot off the gas and let the car slow to a crawl while his head moved from side to side to scan the countryside for the correct streets. Some of them barely even appeared to be marked, but at least he didn't have half a city's worth of traffic behind him now if he needed to go ten miles per hour.

Fortunately, once he found the road, he was quickly assured of his success by a bevy of pickup trucks, some of them with trailers attached, parked all over a broad field filled with stands and wandering pedestrians.

"Well..." Remy stopped the car and studied the scene. "Isn't this all picturesque and peaceful and shit." He chewed the inside of his cheek a moment. "Now, how do I..." A tickle in his sinuses stopped him. With his eyes open wide, he searched desperately inside his car. Before he could locate a paper napkin—one of many that seemed to accumulate in all his vehicles—and bring it to his nose, he sneezed loudly and wetly all over his dashboard.

"Well...shit." Finally finding the napkin, he wiped his nose followed by his dashboard and gathered the three letters while he double-checked the notes. He tossed the napkin on the floor, snatched a fresh one, and shoved it in his pocket.

Taylor did not indicate what kind of fantastical creatures he'd be dealing with this time. He looked through his car windows at the assembled crowd of marketgoers. They all looked perfectly normal.

Perhaps this delivery is for mere humans, for once?

He stepped out and shut his door, and the little beep-beep of his alarm cut through the air.

Hey. The sun feels good.

He squeezed through a couple of rows of parked trucks and cars and walked into the market itself. A good seventy or eighty people had to be milling around and there were perhaps thirty stands and tables set up in no obvious order.

An old couple in overalls passed to his left.

"Hey!" He waved and hurried over to them. "Who runs this place?" He barely managed the last word before he felt a desperate tickle, yanked the napkin out of his pocket, and shoved to his face. He sneezed loudly enough to wake someone back in the city.

The couple stopped and stared and their eyes narrowed.

Damn.

They'd pegged him as a typical rude SOB from the city and were very obviously and not necessarily politely waiting for him to recover from his attack of unexpected clean air.

The man started to speak but another sneezing fit struck him. He doubled over, spewed phlegm loudly onto the grass, and finally straightened.

He sniffed and rolled his hands in a circle, his eyes watering. "Sorry. Sorry. Please, go on."

The old guy pursed his lips and scratched his beard. "The organizer here is a man about your age with tawny hair and a beard." He pointed ahead. "He's probably off at the north end of the market. His name's Felix. He's a nice enough fellow and very polite."

Remy nodded and pinched the bridge of his nose to try to cut off another sinus eruption as he waved goodbye to the couple. "Awesome. Thanks. Hope you guys find some nice...uh, vegetables." He turned and marched toward the northern extremity of the hubbub.

As he wove through the crowd and ignored the heaped piles of fresh fruits and vegetables—many of which did look as appetizing as all hell, he admitted—he sneezed twice more and wondered what the hell was going on.

The only thing he was allergic to was cats, as far as he knew, and he didn't see any of those around. Maybe some had nested there—or whatever cats did—before they'd set the market up? Or, since he rarely ventured this far out into the boonies, perhaps it was merely an exotic flower whose pollen had never found its way into Manhattan?

Toward the north of the space was a covered pavilion where a large throng had gathered to talk. Many of them held plastic cups that seemed to contain beer.

"Hey," he called, "I'm looking for Felix. Does anyone know where he is?"

Four or five of the people closest to him turned toward the sound of his voice. For a moment, he thought he noticed something odd about their eyes but it was gone before he could pinpoint it. They exchanged glances and one of them disappeared into the crowd. Everyone turned away and ignored him.

He continued to sniffle and tried to choke off the sneezes before they happened while he waited. This time, he succeeded.

A moment later, the guy who'd left returned beside a relatively short and thin man whose head and face were mostly engulfed in a mass of dull orangish-brown hair. His eyes were sharp and narrow but he looked kind and relaxed, nonetheless.

"I'm Felix," he said. "How can I help you?"

Remy held up the three envelopes. "I'm from Moonlight Detective Agency. Taylor, whom I assume you know, wanted me to—" He broke off and sneezed. "Uh...to give you these."

Felix's eyes widened in curiosity. "Oh, Taylor has a new assistant? Well, I'm not sure how long you've worked for her, but I want to assure you that you're safe here. Compared to some of the folks you've probably had to deal with, we pose no threat to you." He took the letters.

"Oh...uh, good," he responded, somewhat confused as to what the man was talking about.

The man took him a few paces aside. He wanted to simply leave but somehow, he felt that the friendly bearded guy was about to reveal something important.

"It's true," he went on, "that many other shifters have developed a taste for human flesh. But not us. No, we are a commune of werecats who have taken a vow of vegetarianism, the better to live in peace with—"

He stumbled back but caught himself. "Werecats— wow," he commented. His nose was already tingling again.

"I've never encountered any of you...uh, guys before. I never had cats as a kid, either. Unfortunately, it took me a while longer to find this place than I thought, ha-ha, so I really need to be going—"

Felix frowned slightly. He noticed for the first time that the man had oblong, vertical pupils and what looked like a tail twitched around in one of his pant legs. "Oh, sure. Some other time, when you're not in a hurry, let me know how Taylor is doing."

Remy sneezed and said desperately, "I will. She's doing great. And vegetarianism. That's impressive for a carnivorous species, I must say. Gotta go, sorry! Have a nice day."

He turned and despite his desire to run, restrained himself to a fast power-walk.

In the midst of his flight, another brutal attack on his sinuses stopped him in his tracks and before he could turn away, his nose exploded again to scatter droplets all over someone's lovely display of tomatoes.

"Hey! What the hell?" the farmer cursed, bolted to his feet, and glared.

"Oh God, sorry about that," he muttered and inched away. "It must be the...uh, ragweed pollen out here in the country—"

Someone nearby said in a slightly jeering tone, "Maybe you ought to get yourself back to the city, then."

"That's the plan," he responded and took another couple of steps toward his car. "You can send us a bill for the produce if the phlegm makes it unsaleable. My apologies."

A few of the agriculturists began to talk in low voices and to his mind, the sounds they made were almost like the yowling of felines. He waved toward them as he opened the door of his car and climbed in.

"God," he gasped and locked himself in. "Regular-sized cats are bad enough. These are the size of people. I don't even want to think about the amount of dander they produce."

He sneezed again.

Por's Bar, Lower Manhattan, New York City

The day's light was all but spent when Remy arrived at his last delivery of the day—someplace called Por's Bar, all the way back in Lower Manhattan. He had no idea why Taylor had insisted on this being the final stop.

As he parked his car off to the side of the establishment in an alley that didn't look too suspicious, he debated whether to simply go straight home from there and call her to inform her that the work was done, or whether he actually ought to go back to Westchester to punch out his time-card or whatever.

His allergies had continued to bother him for the first half of the drive back to NYC, although they seemed to have eased by now. He'd already made a mental note never again to deal with werecats if it could possibly be helped.

He dragged himself out of the vehicle, holding the final envelope as well as Taylor's note-sheet, which he stuffed into his pocket after reading it. *Porrillage the Gnome*, it said. *Ignore his attitude (typical New Yorker).*

"That," he observed, "sounds nice, in comparison."

The bar seemed to be located in the basement of a rowhouse that hosted a New Age paraphernalia shop on the ground floor and apartments or condos higher up. He walked into the alley beside the building, where a discreet sign pointed down a narrow staircase protected by a black iron railing.

After a deep, calming breath, he descended, opened the door, and stepped in.

"Hello," he said, to no one in particular. "Special delivery, I guess." He glanced around.

The place wasn't exactly large but it seemed to fill most, if not all, of the basement, and could probably accommodate eighty people or so on a good night. He idly imagined the werecats from the farmer's market crowding in there, downing screwdrivers and talking about the difficulty they'd had lately in keeping the rabbits out of their turnips.

At present, there were only three patrons—one loner at the bar itself and another two men seated at a table, discussing something in soft, gravelly tones.

Wood clacked as someone emerged from the bar area. Remy glanced toward the sound and blinked in confusion at first, wondering if he was about to have a conversation with an invisible entity. Then, he looked down.

"Oh," he said, "there you are. Are you Porrillage?"

The little man—all three and a half feet of him— looked up sulkily. "The sign says Por's Bar and I stepped out from behind the bar. Whaddya think?"

He nodded. "So yeah. Nice to meet you, too. I'm from Moonlight Detective Agency with a letter that apparently couldn't wait to go through the postal service." He waved the envelope in the air.

The diminutive man put one hand on his hip and

snatched the missive with the other. "Hmph. Taylor and her 'urgent' messages."

Remy raised a finger. "Speaking of urgent, before you open that, I'd like to order a beer. It doesn't really matter what. One of those with alcohol in it."

With a heavy sigh, Por motioned him over and retreated behind the bar. He took a seat on one of the stools as the gnome climbed a small pyramid of stools and wooden blocks to fill a glass with golden, foaming brew from one of the taps.

He watched him idly. Porrillage almost looked like a "little person" of the mundane, mortal variety, and most of the patrons probably assumed that was what he was. He wondered if the slight abnormalities were visible to them, though—the pointed ears, the greenish tint to parts of the skin, and the odd, sparkly eyes.

Probably not. No one else had seen the nests of fairies in the park, after all.

Por set the glass in front of him and the gnome tore the envelope open.

Remy drank. It had been a while since he'd imbibed anything with such a low alcohol content, but it was much appreciated and refreshing after his long, tedious, arduous, bizarre workday.

Low grumbling noises came from the gnome as he read the letter. "Hah!" he scoffed after a moment. "So Taylor thinks that some kind of plot is being hatched against her and now, she's reaching out to everyone she knows with promises and threats in case any of us know something useful. Isn't that typical? The people on top always think someone is eroding the foundation they stand on."

The human raised an eyebrow. This wasn't what he'd expected to hear at all.

Porrillage shook his head and muttered again. "No, ignore me, I'm merely in a bad mood. You never know what kind of idle chatter will work its way back to her. Well, let me assure you since you're her errand-boy"—he wagged a finger for emphasis—"that I mind my own business here, and that's it. I don't plot against anyone or participate in any plots, but I'm not much interested in any counter-espionage, either."

So I'm not the only one annoyed with how overbearing that woman is.

"Yeah," he began as the warmth of the booze seeped through him, "let me tell you about the crap she's pulled with me. I basically own the company but suddenly, she seems to think I'm her employee because I got in a little financial trouble and had my lawyer ask for the accounts. Seriously, what kind of horseshit is that?"

Por shook his head. "Hmph. It sounds to me like you're a rich kid who screwed the pooch one too many times and now you're complaining about merely having to work a normal job like the rest of us. It's simply your luck you ended up with someone like Taylor as your taskmaster."

Remy waved a hand dismissively but turned the gnome's words over in his mind.

So what he's saying is that someone of my status needs to be more assertive or else she'll walk all over me. He nodded and felt confident that he'd come to the right conclusion. He set his empty beer glass down on the bar.

"Por," he proclaimed, "you're right. There's no reason I should have to put up with this kind of treatment simply because this is my first actual job. I'll go straight to Westch-ester to explain to her how things will be from here on."

Porrillage cleared his throat and raised his eyebrows. "Good luck with that."

"Thanks," he said and was glad he had the gnome's moral support.

CHAPTER NINE

Harrison, Westchester County, New York

This time, when he steered his car up the drive toward Taylor's garage, Remy at least felt confident that he knew how to park again. The sun had set not long before so despite his late start, he felt he was perfectly on time. That would show her.

Presley had already buzzed him through the front gate. Now, once more, the garage door opened for him as he approached. He drove in slowly and carefully and slid out to examine his handiwork.

"Ha!" He laughed in triumph. "I always was a fast learner. Perfectly aligned."

The large automatic door made a grinding sound and lowered itself to the earth as he stepped out the side of the garage and strode down the walkway toward the front entrance.

This time, oddly enough, the butler did not open the door until after he'd reached the stone landing and actually knocked. The old boy must be slowing down.

The latches clacked and the heavy wooden rectangle swung inwards. "Good evening, sir," Presley said.

"Hiya, Jeeves. I'm glad you came and all. I started to get worried and think I waited almost half a minute for you to open the door this time. Have you been hitting the brandy stashed behind the fridge?"

He stepped past the butler, noted the lack of expression on the man's drooping face, and stretched. It occurred to him that he'd spent far too much of the day crammed into a car seat.

"Sir," Presley intoned, "I do not answer to 'Jeeves,' I'm afraid, and I cannot possibly see how the joke is still funny to you. Do please call me Presley. And refrain from jokes about intoxication on the job. You may relax for the moment. Ms Steele is occupied but will see you shortly."

Looking around as the butler wandered off, Remy saw that the light was on in a sitting room down the hall. He wondered, vaguely, if vampires truly needed light to see what they were doing or if turning the lights on was a kind of formality to help them blend in with humans.

He sat on one of the foyer's big, old, roomy chairs and contemplated taking his shoes off but decided against it. Taylor might see that as too informal. The old-fashioned high-society types were obsessed with manners and decorum and bullshit faux-pas.

Besides, he didn't want to look ridiculous or "compromised" in any way when he confronted her over her absurd and unfair treatment of him. He intended to win this argument.

After all, he'd driven all the way to fucking Harrison from Por's Bar rather than skipped home from there instead of reporting back to the proverbial office. He wanted to make sure his efforts paid off.

Three or four minutes passed and Presley returned, saying, "Ms Steele will receive you now. And do be honest in describing to her everything that transpired. She always finds out when someone lies. Always." He stepped aside and extended his hand graciously toward the lighted sitting room.

Remy stood and walked past the man. As he crossed the threshold, he noted that the sitting room was furnished in a highly tasteful but somewhat outdated fashion, which was about what he would have expected. It reminded him of his grandparents' old home—which they had modeled on magazine photos from even earlier in time.

Taylor was seated in a leather chair before a low oak coffee table. "Hello, David. Or Remington, rather. You did say that you'd changed your professional name to Remington Davis, didn't you?"

He smiled a diplomatic smile. It would be best to open with friendly small talk. "I'm flattered that you remembered. And Remington as a first name does have a certain ring to it, although those fairies thought it was funny to call me Remy."

Taylor set down the book she'd been reading. His gaze focused on the word *Maths* on the cover, although he didn't catch the full title.

"Hmm," he observed and pointed at it, "they misspelled 'math.' I'm not sure I'd trust a textbook that can't even spell a four-letter word."

"No." She sighed and her voice took on a patronizing edge. "That's the English spelling."

Remy blinked. "Oh, really? I never knew that. All this time, I'd been learning about math in Hungarian."

Taylor pinched the bridge of her nose. "English, meaning England. The United Kingdom of Great Britain and Northern Ireland. The country that named the language. A sub-dialect of it is spoken here in America."

"Ohhh," he said and spread his hands in an over-dramatic motion, "that place. Yes. Well, at least we got rid of all those pointless extra U's in words like 'colour' and so forth."

Taylor did not visibly react. "They weren't strictly necessary, but I thought they added character. Nevertheless, I can adapt when I must."

So she's originally from Britain. There's no accent but some of her quirks make more sense now.

He gestured toward the book again. "Are you studying to get your GED?"

"Not quite.".

"Well, I can't quite understand why you would be interested in 'maths' otherwise. I knew a guy once who enjoyed math problems but then again, he freaked out after a total of three hits on a joint—three—and he used to keep all his old grocery receipts for five years and arrange them carefully in a pile on the corner of his desk with the edges perfectly aligned."

Her mouth quirked into a smile. "He was probably a brilliant man. I keep up with my studies because they are useful and remind me of more dignified times. The idle rich used to spend their days differently. We lazed around but used our leisure to learn new languages, pursue scientific discoveries, and try to push the boundaries of the human mind."

Remy nodded and puckered out his lips. "That's a unique approach. Back in my day, we spent our time doing coke and licking jello-shots out of a woman's belly button. Those were fun times."

"Oh, I don't doubt it," Taylor said in a monotone. She no longer looked at him and began to shuffle some papers under her book.

He gestured toward them. "And what is that, if I may ask?"

Taylor flicked her dark gaze toward him for a moment before she returned her attention to her materials. "I'm reevaluating a paper I wrote on Quantum Loop Gravity a few years ago. There has been some interesting work done on topology in mathematics, and it might alter my original conclusions. We may be looking at a breakthrough in our fundamental understanding of science in the coming months if I'm not mistaken."

Blinking, he almost took a step back. He'd never even heard of whatever a Quantum Loop Gravity was and had to admit he was rather impressed. "Damn, I wish I still did drugs, too," he remarked. "Although I guess it's good you've kept busy. Personally, I always thought immortality might get boring."

She looked evenly at him. "It does."

Remy matched her stare. "Tell me all about it some time. Quantum Loop Gravity, I mean."

"So," she went on and ignored the comment, "tell me how things went. Presley already made it clear, I would hope, that you are not to be late again. And that you are not to touch my cars or other possessions. We'll add a fuel stipend to your wages. You kept track of your mileage, right?"

"Uhh…" he stammered, "I seem to vaguely recall about how many miles I had before I drove the car today for the first time in two years, so yes, that should work."

"In the future, please keep all your gas receipts and turn them over to Presley once a week. With the edges perfectly aligned." Finished with her book and papers, she folded her hands in her lap and turned her full attention to him and motioned for him to sit in a chair across the table.

He seated himself and adjusted his tie. "Well, I delivered all the messages, so mission accomplished. And I even resisted temptation with the elves. So don't worry about that."

"Indeed," she said, unimpressed.

Since she didn't say anything else, he kept talking. "I'm allergic to cats, though. That farmer's market…ugh, I sneezed all over someone's tomatoes. Don't send me back there. I don't think they'd want to see me, anyway."

Taylor pursed her lips. "I will make a note of that, but necessity is necessity and I can't make you any promises at this point."

He went on to briefly describe his experiences at each stop and the reactions—or lack thereof—which he had from each of her contacts. He ended with a rough summary of Porrillage's grumpy indifference to the whole affair but omitted the part about having a beer while he was there.

The woman nodded through his anecdotes, politely attentive but never surprised. "That is satisfactory. We'll want you to speed up in the future," she stated, "but with this being only your second day of work—ever—I'd say you did acceptably."

"Acceptably. Gee, thanks." He inhaled through his nose. Now was the time to assert himself as he'd vowed to do.

She started to speak again. "In a moment, you may—"

"Listen." Remy cut her off. "I'm not necessarily opposed to helping with some of the operations, but I'm the owner of this company. Officially, the entire company exists under my authority and for my benefit. As such, I'm entitled to be treated as an equal partner in all this—not merely some errand boy whom you can boss around and assign all the menial labor to."

Taylor leaned back in her chair and extended a hand to drum her fingernails on the surface of the table—only once, as she'd done in the restaurant.

"No," she said quietly. "On the contrary, this is your apprenticeship. If you want to have an equal hand in running the place, you must first learn all the ins and outs. And the only place to start from is the bottom. That's how it is for almost everyone on Earth in almost every situation, even those of us born to wealthy parents."

He scoffed. "This isn't some philosophical work-ethic situation. It's the cold hard facts. My name is on the documents that ultimately control the flow of money. The company can cease to exist if I want it to. I, as primary shareholder, can have you fired and replaced."

When he saw the hard, black coldness of her eyes on him, he almost quailed but took a deep breath and pressed on. "So I insist on being treated with more respect. I will not do any more bullshit chores."

Taylor opened the bathroom door. "How is it coming along?" she asked, her voice gentle but firm.

Remy was on his hands and knees in front of the toilet and scrubbed at the inside of the bowl. A can of cleaning chemicals designed to neutralize mineral buildup in water stood on the floor next to him.

"Uh..." He gasped. "Fine...yeah, great. I'm almost half-done with this one." His hair was disheveled and he'd removed his overshirt and tie, exposing the sweat stains on the undershirt.

She nodded. "Good. Once you're finished with this one, you may take a five-minute break to have a glass of water. Then, scrub the one upstairs in the guest bedroom and I'll allow you to call it a day."

He cleared his throat and said earnestly, "You're so kind. Thank you, mistress."

The vampire turned to leave but stopped on her way out. "Oh, before you depart, though, speak to Presley. We have paperwork to do to ensure everything is kosher as far as having you officially on the payroll is concerned. We'll need your Social Security number and all that kind of thing. You will be paid at the end of the week. Keep up the good work."

Before he could annoy her with inquiries as to how much he'd actually earn, she stepped over the threshold, shut the door behind her, and strolled to her sitting room.

She was almost done reviewing the paper. It looked as though it would indeed be necessary to make a few adjustments and revisions. The march of science moved on, swifter and swifter all the time, to make more and more of yesterday's knowledge obsolete by morning. Or dusk.

Of course, she would have already completed the paper if she hadn't had to waste time playing surrogate mother to the problem-child she'd taken under her wing. There were other, more important things she still needed to do tonight and only a few hours before dawn.

Footsteps approached, not from the bathroom but from the kitchen, and they were both lighter and yet more studied and deliberate than Remington's, anyway. By now, she could recognize Presley's even gait against every other pair of human feet in the world. Each person had their own subtle rhythm and frequency.

"Madame," the butler said, "I've brought your tea."

Taylor looked up. The aged man held a saucer in both hands. Atop it was a generations-old, ornate cup, and a delicate spoon lay next to it. The spoon was made of stainless steel, not silver.

She motioned him to bring it in and set it on the table. "Thank you, Presley."

He walked up and set it before her. Within the cup was a dark crimson liquid—Red Salt Tea was the beverage's traditional, formal name. It had long ago stained the cup's interior a deep, rusty brown.

"How is our supply doing?" She stirred it with the spoon and inhaled the bouquet.

Presley, standing beside her, folded his hands behind his back. "Quite well, quite well. We shouldn't need another delivery for three and a half, perhaps four weeks, I'd estimate. I will contact the bank tomorrow, though, just to be safe."

"Good." She took a sip. For the sake of her family dignity, she suppressed the almost electrical tingle of pleasure that went through her. Even after all these years, it still happened whenever she fed.

Some vampires got addicted to that feeling. It was far too easy to succumb to helpless bloodlust. She'd seen it happen even to individuals whose self-discipline she had once respected.

The butler waited a few moments as she drank the first half of her tea. After a respectful pause, he asked, "Is there anything else I can do for you at present, madame? Far be it from me to pry, but it seems something is troubling you."

Her jaw tightened a little, and the sharp points of her teeth dragged against the porcelain of the teacup.

"I am troubled," she admitted, "by the fact that several individuals who ought to know better may be planning my demise. That kind of thing tends to be troublesome, yes."

The old man gave an apologetic frown and immediately, she regretted snapping at him.

"I'm sorry, Presley. I know you're only concerned. But we have several situations going on that are…still developing. I haven't sifted my own thoughts on all of them yet."

He nodded. "I see, yes." He did not leave.

"Ohhh." She sighed and gestured toward the bathroom down the hall. "I'm already growing tired of this. For so long now, it's been only the two of us and that arrangement really has worked well, hasn't it?"

The butler's eyes grew distant as he seemed to ponder her words. He always thought through his responses before he gave them. She liked that about the man.

"In most regards, yes," he agreed. "We've kept things

running smoothly. But sometimes, a state of affairs can stagnate when it never seems to change."

Taylor ran a fingertip over her chin. "I suppose that's true in a fashion. But Remington is such a colossal handful...even by the standards of a short human lifespan, he's more of an overgrown child than anything. His arms can reach where mine cannot but suddenly, it's as though I'm responsible for a wriggling mass of inexperienced arms."

She shook her head and half-reclined in her massive chair. "It's only been a few nights and I'm already growing nostalgic for the good old days when I had only myself to worry about. I knew exactly what had and hadn't been done, and how, and when, because I did it all myself. Well, aside from the things I trust you with, of course."

"Mm, yes, ma'am."

"And," the woman went on, "every moment I have to waste trying to lecture him or correct his behavior is a moment I don't spend on my own work. And since I know what I'm doing to a far greater extent than he does, it's really quite inefficient. I have to spend ten minutes instructing him for every five minutes' worth of work he does, which I myself could accomplish in merely one or two."

The butler nodded but replied calmly, "Yes, madame, but there's always this period of investment early on, the idea being that the extra time you spend now will pay for itself in the future. And there are many minutes in the day. Not to mention that your future extends somewhat further ahead in time than mine does...and much further than Remington's."

She considered the ramifications of this. "That's true

enough. But we're entering a potentially difficult and even deadly time. I'm on the verge of another power struggle. Dealing with that as well, I'm not sure how much longer I care to keep up with babysitting duty. At what point, exactly, is the hassle of playing nanny no longer worth the extra anonymity he brings to the table?"

"Well," Presley began, "I will agree that he needs to shape up, and quickly. But let us not be too hasty to dismiss him. For all his immaturity and obnoxiousness, he does bring numerous potential advantages."

Taylor raised an eyebrow.

He continued. "Furthermore, well…it's rare for you to express interest in any mortal. The mere fact that you selected him yourself for this job suggests that you might end up getting along with him quite well."

While the surface content of the man's words made sense, Taylor saw the subtext equally as clearly—Presley was worried about her, given her long years of self-imposed isolation. He wouldn't be so bold as to try to push her in a direction in which she did not want to go but he cared deeply about her welfare.

"Thank you, Presley," she said. "You know that I tend to…bear down on myself and focus too much on…work. Or distractions, such as a paper I wrote twenty years ago that has no bearing on the current situation." She sighed again. "It does help to talk about things. I will come to my own conclusions, in the end, but I do value your advice and will weigh it against my own instincts."

He smiled. "Thank you, madame. A second opinion never hurts, and I am honored to provide it."

In the bathroom, Remy seemed to be finishing up.

Taylor could hear him flush the toilet to rinse it, knock the excess droplets from the brush, gather the can of cleaning chemicals along with his clothes, and scrape his pants and shoes against the floor. She could hear everything.

He didn't make a great deal of noise, all things considered. But she was used to her house being quiet. It was a peaceful, orderly place and she'd adjusted to the sounds of Presley, the birds and insects outside, and the occasional settling of the wood and stone.

And that was all.

"That racket, however," she muttered, "hurts my ears."

CHAPTER TEN

Gold Reveal Hotel, Park Avenue, Midtown Manhattan, New York City

Three men had gathered in the Presidential Suite where they would be guaranteed both comfort and privacy.

Midnight was the hour of their meeting, but the suite itself was well illuminated. All the lights were at their brightest and glinted on the gold-leaf which covered the fixtures and appliances. An oval table stood in the center of the broad sitting area, where three huge leather-bound chairs were arranged.

There was also a bottle of wine on the table but only two glasses next to it.

"Gentlemen," said Gabriel, who did not have a glass resting before him, "I will assume that all of us have heard the news by now."

The other two nodded.

Both of them could be talkative but they tended to restrain themselves when he had things to say. And even when, as now, he kept his mouth shut for the moment and only leaned back in his chair, flexed his hands around each other, and cracked his knuckles.

The light glinted on his eyes but did not penetrate them. They were wide black voids, deep-set beneath his heavy brow—the only coarse feature of his otherwise elegant and symmetrical face. Given his ivory pallor, he could stand still and almost be mistaken for a statue.

His light brown hair, although neat and short, had a curious tendency to waver in even the slightest of breezes. It never seemed to shed, though, onto the snug black turtlenecks he always wore.

"This," Gabriel continued after a long moment, "is not the result we were hoping for and yet, we still succeeded in learning what we most needed to know."

In front of him and to his right, one of the other men responded.

"Yessir," chortled Tucker, "we learned that James was exactly what we all thought he was, after all—a mangy dog that changes into a dumbass human when the moon ain't out." He spoke with a thick Southern accent which many decades living outside the South had not softened in the slightest.

Opposite Tucker, the third man added his own two cents' worth.

"Yeah," Albert began, "he was a stupid, low-level enforcer type who got to thinking he was a self-made man." He adjusted the cuffs of his dark gray suit.

Gabriel almost smiled considering that the phrase "made man" had a certain pedigree in the background Albert came from.

Their leader cracked another knuckle. "Had he survived, James might have been useful as a low-level enforcer and nothing more. But with him dead, at least we know he won't fuck anything up for us, either. And we know that the precious, all-important rules are still being enforced."

"Yep," Tucker agreed.

Albert frowned. "Some rules are worth enforcing," he suggested. "Codes of honor, basic standards to keep mad dogs from stirring up too much shit, yeah. But Taylor's little moratorium on doing anything…it's a load of crap is what it is."

Gold light flashed from Gabriel's black eyes. "That's putting it very mildly, Albert," he stated. "What she's doing is unnatural. It is the equivalent of putting every bat and spider in a glass cage and allowing the flies to proliferate. She runs this town like a cattle farm and yet no one ever seems to get any steak." He separated his hands and clenched both into fists.

Tucker smirked. "Steak ain't the only good part of a cow, Gabe," he remarked. "It's all good, far as I'm concerned."

Albert looked across the table at the Southerner. "It doesn't mean you have to put it on a skewer over an open barbecue pit where everyone can see the carcass, ya uncivi-lized reprobate."

The other man gestured toward the mobster. "This from a body-disposal guy."

"Disposal's a private matter," he retorted. "The whole point is that no one ever sees the body."

"'Cause you ate it." Tucker laughed. "There ain't no

proper difference between having a pig roast and ordering prosciutto at a restaurant."

Gabriel was already tired of this nonsense. "Shut up," he snapped, "both of you. All your kind can talk about…meat, as much as you want once our task is accomplished. But for now, we need to focus on the common objective."

"Agreed," Albert replied.

"Yessir," Tucker added.

He nodded. As lycanthropes went, he could have done far worse than these two, even if he did have to keep them away from each other's throats. A dyed-in-the-wool Confederate who remembered the actual Confederacy and a relic of Prohibition's glory days in Chicago…both brought the kind of cut-throat attitude he needed if his plans were to come to fruition.

As far as he—and every other vampire—was concerned, all werewolves ranked lower on Nature's totem pole than vampires. That still put them above humans, however.

"Now," he went on, "despite the danger to my person, I will continue to perform reconnaissance during the day. No one has caught on yet. They simply don't look for me when the sun is up. I do believe I brushed past a couple of acquaintances and they did not even recognize me."

Part of that, granted, was because he'd worn a hood, jacket, gloves, and sunglasses in addition to a thick layer of sunscreen. He made certain to be very careful with the application of the sunblock and the draping of the hood—the burns from before had healed but the searing memory of their pain remained fresh.

"And," he continued, "Taylor's own sleeping habits seem to be entirely predictable. The chances that she herself will appear during the day are slim to none. She's content to sleep in safety with her own pet werewolf to watch over her. The fact that I am willing to brave the sun and she is not is all the evidence we need that we will win. She is old and lazy and complacent. We are the future."

He folded his hands over one another—first the left over the right and then vice versa.

Tucker produced a flat green cylindrical can and popped a wad of chewing tobacco into his mouth. Gabriel and Albert both watched him with quiet disgust but relaxed when they saw him pull a golden ashtray toward himself.

"In a manner of speaking," the man said as he chewed, "that's true, but it sounds strange when you consider what we all agreed on—that we're bringing the old days back."

Gabriel nodded impatiently. "Yes, but we can save the philosophizing and semantics for later. For now, I want to know how things are coming along with each of your individual assignments. Albert, you first."

Albert unfolded himself from his position in his chair and drained his wine glass of its remaining contents. His beady gaze darted around the room. The man never seemed able to entirely relax.

"My guys have been all over town," he explained. "We visited every establishment Taylor does business with—all those run by preternaturals or have dealings with them. A couple are too powerful to threaten directly, yeah, but we got the message out to anyone who has ears to hear."

"Yes," Gabriel said, "that's what you were supposed to do. And?"

The mobster grimaced. "And we haven't made much

progress. We sent a couple of tough guys to each of the main places—that occult bookshop, the blood bank, Por's Bar, the restaurant, and the trucking company that moves coffins in refrigerator packaging—and they all gave us the cold shoulder, basically. They acted all respectful, but my guys said that the sons of bitches are still more afraid of Taylor than they are of us and they didn't get any straight answers from them. We rustled 'em, yeah. But it doesn't look like we'll be able to cut her off from her usual suppliers anytime soon. Maybe after she's dealt with."

The vampire looked somewhere off into the distance before he returned his gaze to his co-conspirators. "That is disappointing but it's almost to be expected. She runs this town with an iron fist and has convinced almost everyone of what will happen to them if they cross her. For these last few decades, people simply aren't as terrified of your type of organization as they used to be."

Albert tensed. He clearly did not like hearing the truth.

Gabriel recalled that Albert had grown up when the American Mafia families had been at the peak of their power, thanks largely in part to the government's ridiculous ban on alcohol. The man had idolized the celebrity mobsters of his day and adapted to that lifestyle, rising in respect and authority as he used his preternatural abilities to make people completely disappear.

But after what had happened first to Al Capone and then to John Gotti, he had grown increasingly paranoid and sullen. Now, he had Taylor to deal with as well, and watching the Family kowtow to her was a nightly thorn in his side.

The vampire's black eyes turned to his other werewolf

cohort. "Tucker. How are things coming with our weapons shipments?"

Tucker picked up the golden ashtray carefully and spat some of his chewing tobacco juice into it discreetly. "Things are coming fine, Gabe. Just fine."

"Would you care to enlighten us with details?"

The heavyset Southerner readjusted his position so that rather than sitting at attention, he slouched to appear more relaxed. "Everyone came through. The first shipment has already been received and distributed to all my people, with some of the guns on their way to your place as we speak. And I've received confirmation that the second shipment is on its way and ought to be here in another day or two. There's a group of good old South Carolina boys handling it. They trust me, and I trust them." He chuckled. "It's gonna be like Fort Sumter all over again."

Albert scoffed. "Weren't you all of five years old when that war started? You didn't actually fight in it."

He turned his head slowly toward the mobster. "My pa did. I remember him not being home—ever again. That's close enough, friend. And for all your talk about being more civilized and sophisticated, you seem to be the one having trouble on your end of the mission."

Gabriel saw Albert lean forward in his seat with his jaw jutted out menacingly, and he held a hand up. "Stop. There will be no infighting. We don't have time for that. Tucker, good job but don't get cocky. Albert, your men have still done good work in providing us a better picture of the overall situation."

Both men relaxed and returned their attention to the vampire.

"And," he continued when satisfied that he had their full focus once again, "we know that at least some of the other preternaturals in this area sympathize with us. Not all of them have the courage to do so openly but I strongly suspect that Taylor's reign is widely resented. In addition, our own subordinates have all been cleared for loyalty."

"Yessir," Tucker agreed.

He allowed himself a smirk. When he was younger, he'd been overly brash and even arrogant. Elder vampires told him even today that he was still young and foolishly hotheaded.

But over the course of three human lifetimes, he'd learned a few things. One of those was how to project an image of charismatic leadership that people would naturally want to follow.

He'd been carefully vague about exactly what the endgame was. This let his potential allies project their own goals and desires onto the proverbial blank sheet. So far, with these two—his top lieutenants—it seemed to be working.

Albert saw his alliance with Gabriel chiefly as a business opportunity. He and his associates in the world of organized crime stood to profit from a New York freed of restrictions on who was and wasn't fair game. In his mind, Taylor was little different from an aggressive and meddling prosecutor who could not be bribed and therefore had to be silenced.

Tucker's motivations were more romantic. The vampire was, after all, the leader of a rebel cause, and the South Carolinian werewolf had never gotten over his obsession with that particular conflict. Through him, he would be able to re-fight the war.

It occurred to him then that Tucker was smarter than he seemed. He'd proven himself competent thus far and his affected image as a stereotypical redneck shit-kicker from the Deep South was in all likelihood a way to make people underestimate him. In fact, Tucker might not even have been his real name. He made a mental note to investigate the matter in more detail.

Later, anyway. For now, they had work to do.

"The time is approaching," Gabriel pronounced, "in which, at last, we are able to act. Soon, our natural prey will no longer have artificial protection and the creatures of the night again can flourish with freedom and self-determination. The pieces are almost all in place."

He paused and cracked the base knuckle of his left hand. "There is one other order of business to discuss before we go our separate ways."

Albert raised an eyebrow and scanned the room, apparently concerned that he might suddenly betray him.

Tucker spat more black juice into his ashtray. "Oh?"

"There are rumors," he continued, "that Taylor has a new human assistant—someone running errands around the city for her and even working his way upstate. This is likely nothing of major concern. He may be no more than an errand boy. And, of course, he is merely human. Still, it represents another potential loose end that ought to be tied off."

Albert nodded. "Yeah, yeah. I'll have some of my men tail the guy—see what he gets up to and where he pokes his nose. Anything he sees or hears will probably make its way back to the lady, after all. And let me tell you—Capone was taken down by a group of fucking IRS accountants. Never assume that someone isn't a threat if there's even the slightest chance they can do you ugly. If we have to rub this guy out, we will."

"Good." Gabriel sat back in his chair. A tremor of excitement went through him—the thrill of the hunt. It reminded him of the incredible sensations he'd experienced the first time he'd run down a hapless mortal and fed.

He went on. "In that case, this meeting is adjourned. I will send coded messages to each of you detailing when and where we'll meet next. Although by then, it may well be only for the purpose of celebrating."

He grinned and tried not to get ahead of himself. There was still much to be done, but his head swelled with confidence in his powers. His fangs showed.

Tucker nodded. "Sounds good, Gabe. There's only one problem, though...."

"What?" he snapped. He and Albert both glared at the Southerner.

The man shook his head sadly. "There's still a third of a bottle of this fine, excellent wine left. Are you gonna finish it?"

Gabriel frowned. "No. I do not drink...wine."

CHAPTER ELEVEN

Harrison, Westchester County, New York

Taylor was well experienced in the use of bait to spring a trap. Anyone or anything could potentially be employed in this useful—albeit risky—fashion, including herself.

The night was dark as they were only two days from the new moon. Her senses more than made up the difference, however.

She knew the rest of her neighborhood almost as well as her own house. Although she rarely interacted with her neighbors—they were largely diurnal—she'd still taken it upon herself to learn about all of them. She knew the names and backgrounds of every person in the household, their professions, their extended families, their extracurricular associations, and their human or preternatural status.

As a rule, she made no use of this information, except at those times when it might be needed for her own protection. Now was one of those times.

The vampire crept down the street as a silent shadow

and checked leftover letters and ads in mailboxes for any new or unfamiliar names. Nothing suspicious came to light, fortunately. She also scouted the roads and drives and the houses themselves, looking for tracks and spoor—anything unusual, any sign of new or unusual activity.

She moved in ways that, while invisible to humans, would still have been fairly obvious to most preternaturals. If someone was about to try something, they might as well get it over with out in the open. She knew she would survive against anything except the most unlikely combination of overwhelming force combined with the element of surprise.

But there was almost nothing tonight. Certainly, no one attacked her outright, nor did she see or hear or smell anyone who ought not to be there, sneaking around somewhere out of easy perception.

There were no blatant signs, either. A few ambiguous signs, possibly, but no red flags.

Presley reported that the vehicular traffic during the day had increased, but that could be unrelated to her situation.

And there were slight disturbances in the surrounding woods. If these had been made by a humanoid creature, whatever it was appeared to be good at disguising its tracks since all she found might as easily have been made by raccoons or possums.

And yet, she knew something wasn't right. A ghostly wisp of ill intent wafted on the night's breeze.

She climbed the hill toward her own property and stood in silence before the garage of her mansion to think.

The conspirators may have been moving during the

day. Based on the information she'd teased out of the dwarf's brain, they included at least one vampire. Werewolves preferred the night as well, despite not actually being harmed by sunlight.

Daytime excursions were unlikely but neither impossible nor unheard of. A vampire could walk under the sun with sufficient protection and sufficient will to withstand the pain and primal terror that the burning orb always brought. If that was the case, she might be dealing with a dangerous foe indeed.

Taylor glanced around one last time. Then, she pulled her phone out and called her new employee.

He did not answer. She waited for the voice mailbox to greet her and prepared to leave him a message. Even he didn't seem so unperceptive and irresponsible as to fail to notice a voicemail from her.

"Remington," she said after the tone, "if you're looking for more important jobs than merely delivering letters and cleaning toilets, I have an opportunity for you. It's something that will allow you to prove yourself if you can show up in the morning prepared for it and avoid tardiness."

For the simple joy of moving in the night, she reentered her house not by the front door but instead, leapt onto the garage and clambered up the rear wall toward the guest bedroom's window.

As she crawled along the shingles, a horrifying thought came to her. If her problem-child accomplished the task she had in mind, he might be able to say, in all truth, that he'd saved her life. Then she might owe him.

· · ·

Midtown Manhattan, New York City

David had awoken to the irritating blare of his alarm, having only slept through the first minute or so of it. As such, he assumed he'd have no problem with being punctual. Not this time. Taylor would have no choice but to praise him for how quickly he'd improved.

He had also awoken to an intriguing voice message from none other than the vampire herself. It seemed she'd already promoted him to doing real, actual private-detective stuff. This struck him as a definite step up from household maintenance and errand running. It never occurred to him to consider that he had no idea how to conduct an investigation.

Now, as he stood again in the foyer—at, he was proud to say, 4:42 am—it seemed that he'd at least get some answers.

Presley closed the door behind him. "Ms Steele should be along at any moment. Oh, and thank you for arriving in a timely fashion today. It makes all of our lives easier—including your own."

"No problem, Jeeves," said Remy. "Is life really the right term in Taylor's case, though?"

As if he'd somehow conjured her, Taylor's voice—soft and musical but with a cold edge—wafted out of a dark corner. "Close enough, young man. One day, perhaps, the deeper mysteries of vampirism may be explained to you. But for now, we have other things to discuss. I take it you received my message?"

She stepped out into the foyer and looked elegant in a black silk robe and matching slippers.

He turned toward her, his hands in his pockets. He

swallowed his snarky response barely in time. "Yeah, and I'd love to hear more."

The vampire glanced at the grandfather clock. "I only have a few minutes before sunrise, but I need you to investigate the activities of a man named James over the past few weeks. You will discover he went missing several days ago. Do you remember when, the second time we met, I told you of a werewolf who had decided the rules didn't apply to him? His punishment was death by my hands. I now need to find out who that werewolf spoke to in the days and weeks before then. You will find notes on the kitchen table, as usual. Look at them carefully and think about it before you leave. I also have a couple of other suggestions."

Remy rocked a little on his heels. Last night, he'd been sufficiently exhausted to sleep like a log. Now, he felt refreshed and even a little excited. He didn't feel even the slightest urge to comment on the fact that there were literally thousands of men in New York named James. How many werewolves would there be with that name, after all?

"I'm all ears," he quipped. "Metaphorically speaking."

"First," she said and extended one finger, "James came into a fair amount money quite recently. Use whatever sources of information are available, including your own contacts, to find out anything you can about someone by that name who might have recently appeared in the kinds of places frequented by the rich."

His mouth twisted to the side in a sour expression. "Most of my so-called contacts among the wealthy and beautiful elite hate me, but I'll keep that in mind, yeah."

"Do so." She extended another finger. "Second, go back

to the Fluttershire Fairy Colony. They'll be able to help you."

At this, his eyes widened. "Wait, do you mean the same little pricks who went all police-brutality on me a couple of days ago? Hell no. That doesn't even make sense. I doubt they'd want to so much as see me, let alone—"

"Do as I say," she interrupted. "They don't think the way we do. It's not as though I have zero experience with these matters, so I won't tell you to do something without good reason. Seek them out and explain the situation to them. That may well be your best bet."

He could only shrug. "If you say so."

"Thank you, Remington. Now, I need my rest. Good morning, and good luck."

He waved at her as she disappeared toward the cellar. "Sleep tight!"

Fort Washington Park, New York City

As soon as he turned into the park and began his search for a space for his car, Remy began to squirm with discomfort. Some of the bruises and abrasions were still healing. Simply being here triggered flashbacks of twenty or more of the little winged bastards crawling all over him and head-butting him in the nipples, armpits, ears, nose, and crotch while mockingly calling him "Reh-meeeee!"

He parked his vehicle, turned it off, and sighed. "Well, let's see if Taylor actually knows what she's talking about."

The park was busier today than it had been during his first fae experience. Still, he was reasonably sure none of the normies would be able to see the little critters, anyway, so he ought to be fine provided some passerby didn't see him talking to no one.

He marched off through the emerald grass toward the area under the bridge, which looked all too familiar already.

Perhaps twenty paces sooner than anticipated, two small forms with iridescent wings appeared in front of him.

"Halt!" two tiny voices said in unison.

Remy's gut clenched but he only smiled. "Hi," he said. "I'm Remington Davis, from the Moonlight Detective Agency. Sorry about that little misunderstanding we had last time. Taylor has informed me that I should talk to you about an issue which has come up—"

It was difficult to be sure, but he suspected that the two fairies before him—one blue-tinged, the other orangish—were the same two he'd originally seen arguing.

"Oh!" the blue one piped up. "You! Yes, Remy—Rehmeeeeeeee! We remember. That was a good fight. You made such ridiculous sounds."

They both snickered at the memory. He tried to show no expression whatsoever.

"We have forgiven you for your insult," the orange one said, "since we settled the score, anyway, and things have been smooth here ever since you visited us."

He nodded. "Well, that's good to know. Could you...uh, help me? I need to track someone down, and Taylor said you could be of help."

By now, a few other fairies had wafted out of their nests and begun to drift over to join them.

"Help?" one of them inquired. "Help, you say? This from the giant who gave us such good sport not long ago?"

"Indeed!" another replied and squealed with laughter.

The two guards turned to face the gathering throng, and he stood and waited awkwardly while they conferred amongst themselves in a language unknown to him. A convoy of joggers passed and apparently ignored him, but he pretended to admire the bridge anyway to be safe.

The two guards turned back toward him. The blue one announced, "It is decided, then."

"Yes!" the orange one agreed. "You shall have exactly one helper assigned to your person. But in exchange for these services rendered, you shall pay us one pound of honey per week for as long as your helper assists you."

The blue one smirked. "And the first pound must be paid in advance."

Remy had somehow assumed that the price would be far steeper. "Okay." He shrugged.

The nearest grocery store was, thankfully, only a few minutes away. It took a while to wander the aisles but he eventually found the honey, although it was all in the stupid little squeeze bottles. He'd hoped to find something more like a gallon jug's worth.

"Hmm." He pulled one of the bottles off the shelf and examined the label. "Twelve ounces…a pound is sixteen ounces, isn't it? Wait, is this fluid ounces or weight? Fuck." He sighed. "Two bottles ought to be enough. They feel like about a pound each, I think."

He grabbed another one while he considered whether or not he'd be able to charge this to Taylor as an expense, then flushed with shame at the notion that such a trifling amount of money would even concern him, to begin with.

As he started back toward the checkout aisles, someone came up behind him, grunting and muttering. A hand was planted firmly on his shoulder, right near his neck.

"Back off!" he snapped, pivoted, and stuck his elbow out before he lashed a blow with his fist. Both extremities connected with flesh and bone and the mysterious person fell back and released him in the same motion. Without even looking back to see who it was—probably some crackhead—he strolled to the express aisle.

Remy placed the two bottles on the belt near the scanner. The clerk, a young Latina, must have seen the little incident a moment before and looked at him with wide eyes.

"As you can see," he said to her, "I require honey."

Five minutes later, he returned to the park. It occurred to him that while he'd never been overly frightened of his fellow humans, to begin with, he cared even less about the fact that he'd almost been assaulted than he would have guessed—somehow, dealing with paranormal creatures of myth and nightmare had altered his perspective on mundane shit.

He passed an elderly couple walking a pair of tiny poodles, who glanced at the two honey-filled plastic bears in his hand but thankfully moved on with their business.

And that's what I love about New York—you have to be really crazy to ever get a second glance.

The fae guardians reappeared before him in the same position they had earlier.

The blue one spoke first. "How quickly you've returned.

What is that? Is that our honey?" She pointed to the bear-bottles.

"Yeppers," he said. "I think the two of them together are about a pound or slightly more. Don't worry about it. Keep the change. Both bottles are the same size and quality, so I assume one can go to the blues and one to the oranges. Does that sound good?"

"Ha-ha." The orange one cackled. "This will last us at least a week!"

Eight more fairies fluttered over to take the bottles from him. They struggled somewhat with the weight, but their wings were stronger than they looked.

"Now, then." He put his hands on his hips. "Keep your end of the bargain. Where's this helper of mine?"

The two guards looked at each other in what he now recognized as private and nonverbal communication, and they smiled. Together, they flourished their hands at a point behind the man's shoulders.

"Why, Remy," said the blue one, "she's right back there."

Remy turned and suddenly found himself face to face with a naked woman. Or, more accurately, face to entire body. She was about five inches tall.

"Whoa!" he exclaimed. "Uh, this isn't what I expected."

The woman—fairy—unfurled herself before him. She looked similar to the others but subtly different as though her appearance had somehow been tweaked specifically to suit human standards of beauty. She was both lithe and curvaceous, possessing the best traits of both late adolescence and the full bloom of maturity at the same time. Her skin had a slight bluish tint to it but it seemed more subdued than in the other fae of that color, and her hair was a pale silvery blond.

"Hello, Remy," she greeted him in a voice that managed to be sultry despite being pitched about where a small child might be after inhaling helium. "I'm Riley. And I'm yours for at least the next week. Maybe longer if you have enough honey."

She giggled and rubbed one shapely leg over the other. Her gossamer wings folded over her front but did absolutely nothing to disguise her bare breasts or pubis.

He adjusted his tie at the neck. "Well, uh...hi there, Riley," he stammered. "It's nice to meet you and all, but if we're going to be working together—in a professional capacity, like, as co-workers and stuff—you'll...uh, need clothes." He turned his head and coughed.

Behind him, the other fairies laughed uproariously. He'd almost forgotten about them for a minute.

"What?" Riley exclaimed and her tiny, beautiful face pouted with sudden rage and hurt. "Don't you like my body?"

Remy was confused. He recalled Taylor's admonition that the fae did not think like humans, but she had not bothered to elaborate on how they did think. He wracked his brain for any clues he might already have encountered as to how the hell he should react to this situation.

"Well," he began, "it's a little small but otherwise very, very nice...yeah. I simply worry that it will be...distracting. We have work to do so...uh, unfortunately, I can't...um, look at you all the time." He wiped his hands on the back of his pants.

The fairy narrowed her eyes and pursed her lips which,

if anything, made her even more attractive. He had not lied but the facts were that she was about the size of a lab rat and a member of a different species that officially didn't even exist. These were not things he could simply ignore.

"But," she protested, "you should want to look at me." She turned in midair to show off her perfectly shaped ass.

"I do," he responded quickly. "I guess. But I also worry about the effects of being seen with a bite-sized naked chick floating over my shoulder. Well, most people probably can't see you anyway, but still. Put something on and I'll be happy to look at you whenever I have time."

She crossed her arms over her breasts. "No. It's pointless. I made myself look this nice for your benefit and now, you don't even want me."

Terrified that she might start crying or refuse to help him track James the werewolf's final days, he said hurriedly, "Okay, okay…you can fly around naked for now, fine. But…don't be surprised if it takes a little while for me to get used to it."

She relaxed and posed for him. "So you do want me."

He nodded at her. "Yes, yes, absolutely. So, do you have, like, kind of tracking powers or something? I need to find out where this one guy spent his time in the days before he got himself killed."

Again, she tensed and pouted, apparently offended. "Of course I have tracking powers. Don't you know anything?"

CHAPTER TWELVE

Sullivan Street, Lower Manhattan, New York City

The nudist fairy, distracting and contentious though she was, had actually proven quite useful.

"We're almost there!" she exclaimed in fervent excitement. Fairies, Remy had already learned, were far beyond bipolar in both the frequency and intensity of their mood swings.

"Oh, good." He sighed. "Whatever this place is, at least it ought to get us out of fucking traffic. I envy those of you with wings."

All around him, cars honked mindlessly and probably out of habit. New York motorists didn't even need specific things to honk at. They seemed to merely thump their horns in idle moments as a way to relax their minds.

As he waited for the obligatory traffic jam to clear, Riley examined the care package Taylor had attached to her notes.

In addition to writing down all the pertinent information about James which she had been able to collect, she'd also included a tiny plastic baggy that contained a few pieces of dark-brown hair. He assumed it had originally belonged to James himself.

For obvious reasons, he also assumed it was best not to ask exactly how she had come to possess the werewolf's hair—especially considering that she said she had killed him. Still, it did raise all kinds of questions he wished he could ask. Had she simply ripped some from the corpse? And why would she even think of doing that?

The fairy finished sniffing the baggie on the passenger's seat and floated to the dashboard. "It's stronger up there. See? There!" She pointed through the windshield.

Remy leaned forward and squinted. Silvery-blue sparkles—probably invisible to everyone but him—had appeared in the air near a nondescript building about half a block past the light and on the right. They were deep in Lower Manhattan now and near the edge of the financial district.

"Excellent," he said. "So, we only need to get through this light, half a block down the street, and find a place to park. It should take thirty or forty minutes."

It ended up only taking fifteen or maybe twenty, at most. He impressed himself by managing to parallel park between two cars of approximately equal size to his own without incurring a civil lawsuit in the process. His diminutive companion helped by fluttering out the window and guiding him, shouting estimates of how much space he had.

With his car safely tucked between the bumpers of two other vehicles, he slid his credit card through the meter and advanced down the sidewalk toward the building that the fairy had highlighted. She drifted beside him and indicated that the trail seemed to be coming from underground.

"I see that," he muttered. "Another basement pub or something?"

He wasn't entirely correct. A staircase led from the street to a subterranean floor and only once he stood in front of the door with a few pedestrians walking over his head did he encounter the sign—Chattering and Chips Casino.

"Crap," he mumbled. "Not gambling. That's another one I'm trying to give up." He shook his head and knocked on the door. It struck him as an exclusive kind of establishment and he might be lucky enough to have some goon tell him to get lost.

A small portal—about six inches across—opened near the top of the door. A broad face scowled out at him. "You got a membership?" the man asked.

Before he could think of a clever response, Riley flew over his shoulder. To his surprise, the doorman's eyes locked on the fairy and he seemed to nod.

"Okay, then." The window closed and the door opened.

"See?" she proclaimed triumphantly. "You love having me around."

Remy stepped into a narrow, featureless hallway. "You do seem to be earning your honey thus far."

Behind him, the big guy shut the door and said, "I ain't seen you around here before though, pal—so mind your manners."

"Oh," he retorted over his shoulder, "I always do."

The hallway turned left and opened onto a large floor

that housed the actual casino. He realized at once why and how the mere presence of the fairy had gained him access to the place. Only a few of the patrons were human.

Gnomes made up a significant portion of the clientele. Like Porrillage, they could almost pass for diminutive humans, but to those who could see, their preternatural qualities were obvious.

There were also strange small furry creatures he did not recognize. One of them scuttled past his leg and he jerked aside and tried not to think about what the thing was or how dirty it might have been.

He saw, too, a few men who were taller than the gnomes but still rather short by human standards, while being broad and powerfully built with long bushy beards.

"Holy shit," he said. "Dwarves? What character class are they, though? Have they put any points into Charisma?"

"What strange things are you saying?" Riley asked. "But yes, they're dwarves. Of course they are."

They advanced onto the main floor. Remy saw something out of the corner of his eye and almost jumped in place. He managed to stifle the reflex before he made a complete idiot of himself but cold prickles ran down his neck and back.

"Jesus." He gasped and dragged in a breath. "Was that a frickin' ghost?" He thought he could still see a barely tangible shape hovering eerily around the edge of the room but refused to look straight at it.

She floated up over his head to look. "Yes, there are two of them on watch. Ghosts make good security guards because they can surveil people less obviously."

"Ugh, I see," he responded. "With Taylor, it's not so bad,

but I'm not exactly a big fan of the undead when they are actually dead. I hope we don't have any zombies barging in."

Riley tittered. "That would be most unusual. Zombies aren't very popular."

Remy adjusted his tie. "Good. Smelly bastards usually aren't very popular."

As he said this, a gnome who passed stopped and looked sharply at him. "What did you say, asshole?"

"Oh," he replied hastily. "I wasn't talking about you. Zombies."

The gnome grunted. "Fair enough." He wandered off.

They paused a moment to examine the scene. It wasn't a large casino but given its niche clientele and general bustle, it probably turned a good profit. There were two poker tables, rows of slot machines, blackjack, craps...all the basic essentials.

His gaze settled on an usher who approached them slowly, probably to offer a polite version of the standard "spend money or get out" ultimatum.

Remy's palms were sweating again. "Unless you have any better clues, Riley," he said in the moment before the usher reached them, "I propose that, in the interest of the investigation, I should...uh, try to fit in. Especially at that poker table. It looks like it needs me, really. Most people suck at poker."

"Whatever you say," she cooed. "But don't get too distracted." She drifted in front of his face and writhed sensuously for his benefit. He noted that her carefully groomed pubes were bluish, which suggested that platinum blonde was not her natural hair color.

In fact, he was already distracted, but not by her. He pictured four-of-a-kinds appearing in his hand while chips piled up in front of him.

The usher, who had a subtle bestial look and was probably some kind of shapeshifter, stopped two paces away. "Hello, sir. First, let me remind you of the House Rule that no magic whatsoever is allowed during play, as I'm sure you know. With that in mind, what will you play, sir?"

He smiled. "Poker."

"As you wish." The man glanced at Riley. "However, the fairy has to wait outside. We've had problems in the past with their kind peeking at other people's cards and relaying the information to their companions. And I'm sure you can appreciate that we have a zero-tolerance policy on cheating."

"What?" she squealed indignantly.

Remy fixed her with a sympathetic frown. "I'm sorry, but you heard the man. Go guard my car. Or more importantly, guard the meter and feel free to magically open the window and magically insert a couple more quarters if need be. This might take me a while."

She looked as though he'd slapped her. "You hobgoblin-fucker!" With that, she spun and rocketed out of sight.

The usher stared at him.

"Oh," he chortled and waved a hand airily, "don't worry. She'll already be over it by the time I'm done. You know how fairies are. Borderline Personality Disorder and all."

The man shrugged and escorted him to the poker table. He found a place between an especially dour-looking, iron-bearded dwarf to the left and a scrawny gnome to his right. Two or three of the other players appeared to be human.

The last hand had just ended and the winner, a red-bearded dwarf, smiled as he claimed his pot.

"Deal me in," Remy said. "What are we playing, anyway?"

The dwarf to the left turned toward him. "Five-card draw. Any objections?"

"None," he stated and beamed. "That's possibly my favorite variant. The essential poker. Pure and uncorrupted by excessive innovation or creativity."

It also happened to be the one he had the most experience with—and the best winning record. He could feel the power of luck hover around him like an aura. Casinos often seemed to prefer seven-card or Texas hold 'em or God knew what else. He could deal with any of those but nothing beat the elegant simplicity of five-card draw.

The passage of time lost all meaning as he found himself totally consumed by the game. He won nine out of fifteen hands.

The dwarf and the gnome to either side glared at him and most of the other players, as well as the dealer, did not look particularly pleased, either.

He fondled his pile of chips. "It's a natural talent, really, and runs in the family. Our above-average intelligence seems especially well-suited to games of chance. That's probably why we're also so successful in business. My father even said I might be the best poker player he'd ever personally met, and it's not like he was simply saying that because I'm his son. Once, this asshole I knew in college had a poker table at his twenty-first birthday party, and—"

Someone walked up and planted himself directly behind him to interrupt his monologue.

"Excuse me," the new arrival said in what was very much a New York accent, "but it seems you've exhausted the possibilities of this table."

All eyes were now on him. He breathed deep, betrayed no particular concern, and leaned casually around the edge of his chair to examine his new friend.

The man was human—or at least capable of assuming human form. He was tall and slightly overweight, but he looked muscular enough to carry it. He had a round, dark face and wore a pinstriped suit, a jacket, and sunglasses, for some reason. Remy would have been shocked if there wasn't a gun under the jacket.

"Well." Remy sighed. "I guess I won too much, didn't I? If that's the case, I suppose I can go quietly. Let me cash in my chips quickly and—"

"Actually," the goon cut him off, "the proprietor of the establishment wanted me to invite you over to the high-stakes table."

He cocked an eyebrow. "Well, that's interesting. I accept his invitation." He turned to the other players, who all looked relieved to be rid of him. "So long, gentlemen. It's been fun. You're all getting better, though, really. Keep practicing and one day, you might even be good enough for Vegas. Assuming they have a place for...uh, preternaturals there."

"Of course they do!" the scrawny gnome snapped. "You gonna keep talking shit or you gonna go play with the big leagues?"

Rather than reply, he merely waved and left. He followed the pinstripe-suited man to the far corner of the main floor, where there was a double door that he hadn't seen previously.

His escort held the left side open. "After you," he said and smiled.

Remy stepped through. In the back of his mind, it occurred to him that maybe this was some kind of trap or shakedown or something...but probably not. At worst, they might punch him in the stomach a couple of times, throw him out the back, and tell him never to return.

That had happened at least once that he could recall. Maybe twice, although substance abuse did odd things to one's memory.

More likely, however, they merely wanted to seat him next to the heavy hitters, humiliate him, and win their own money back. He couldn't wait for them to try.

The hallway beyond the corner door was dark aside from a single hanging lamp, which lit a choice of three blank walls and one corridor to the left. Looking down it, he saw a well-lit room beyond, where a few more men were seated around another, smaller table.

"Ah." He sighed happily. "I've come home."

The man stepped up behind him. "Don't keep the proprietor waiting," he advised.

He strode into the room. There were five players besides himself. One was dressed in a white shirt and tie with no jacket, and the others all wore charcoal-colored suits.

The individual at the head of the table stood and walked over to greet his guest. He was of average height, lean, and somewhere in his forties, with narrow, suspicious eyes that glanced constantly around the room.

"I'm glad you accepted my invitation," he said by way of greeting. "You can call me Albert. I run this place. Tony here tells me you're fairly good."

It occurred to Remy that the man's accent was slightly off—he sounded like a Chicagoan trying to imitate a New Yorker.

"Pleased to meet you," he responded. "I'm Remington. And yeah, fairly good is one way to put it."

"We'll see about that. Have a seat over there." He pointed to the foot of the table and returned to the head.

He settled into the chair that had already been set up for him—simple but comfortable leather, a definite improvement over the cheap seats at the rookie table. "So, tell me," he began, "how high are the high stakes I'll play for?"

The five men all regarded him with a kind of superior amusement. Tony, the guy in the pinstripes, waited in the doorway, conveniently blocking it.

Albert eyed him. "We usually start at triple what they were playing back there," he replied and gestured down the hallway with his thumb. "It gets higher, though. Depending on how the game goes, of course."

Remy tried not to smile too broadly. "Awesome. I love poker, honestly. They say it's easy to be good at things you actually enjoy. In fact, I should probably gamble instead of working. Work is a waste of time."

A few of the men chuckled at this but it was difficult to tell if they were laughing with or laughing at him.

Albert ran a knuckle across his nose. "That's an interesting perspective, Mr Remington. What is it you do for work, anyway?"

His elation ebbed slightly. Maybe he shouldn't give these people too much information about himself.

Noticing his brief hesitation, the man went on. "We merely like to know that someone has a nice steady source of income, you know? That way, if some scumbag loses at this table"—he pointed to the surface in front of him—"and tries to stiff us on his debt, we explain to his employer that we require their cooperation in garnishing his wages. It works out best for everybody that way, see?"

He rolled his tongue around his teeth but finally nodded. There was a certain logic to that and since he owned the company he worked for, any garnishments were technically his own money, to begin with, anyway.

"It's Remington Davis, not Mr Remington. I'm with Moonlight Detective Agency," he stated. "You might have heard of us. We do mitigations…cleaning up disputes between preternaturals and that kind of thing." He decided not to mention the other two M's. "Lately, the workload has been too intense for the existing staff to handle. Which, of course, is why they brought me on."

"That's very good to know, Mr Remington. Make sure you know what you're getting yourself into before we deal you a hand and hopefully, we won't need to contact your employers."

"Yeah, yeah," he said. "Deal me in. Maybe you guys can provide a real challenge, for once."

The men all chuckled at that. "He thinks highly of himself," one pointed out.

Remy shrugged. "I can't help it. I simply base my opinion on the evidence." He paused. "Speaking of evidence, have any of you gentlemen seen or heard of a werewolf named James? He seems to have gotten in some trouble and I'm responsible for putting a stop to any further problems that might arise. Of course, I doubt a reprobate like him would stop at a fine establishment like this, but it's worth asking."

"Never heard of him," Albert snapped. He glanced at the deck, then looked at Remy. "Need I even bother to state that cheating of any type will not be tolerated what-so-fucking-ever?"

He leaned back in his chair, smiled again and folded his hands behind his head. "Of course not. If I cheated, I wouldn't have the right to be this cocky. I'm not so sure I believe you about not knowing who James is, though."

The bristling silence that followed his remark made him regret his too-cocky words.

The man in the white shirt and tie shuffled the deck. The guy to his left cut it and handed it back. The cards became a blur as the dealer's hands moved with expert speed and grace. They were tossed out in a concentric ring and each player drew theirs toward them until everyone had five.

"Opening ante," Albert announced, "is one thousand dollars."

In the back of Remy's mind—far back—he knew this kind of game could rack up sums he might have trouble paying but he didn't expect to lose. He never lost anything he couldn't win back.

"Is everyone still in?" Albert asked with a smirk.

"Of course," he said and the others all grunted their assent.

He examined his cards and slid his face into poker-mode neutral.

Already, he had two kings—the spade and the diamond. It was a start. Otherwise, the others were honestly junk. He took a quick peek over the tops of his cards to check the faces of the other players.

None of them betrayed any obvious emotion or agitation, but one of the gray-suited Italians had subtly adjusted his posture in his chair. It was difficult to be sure, but he suspected this meant the man had a decent hand.

They all added another thousand to the pot, and he discarded two of his cards and kept a ten. Somehow, it felt lucky, despite being useless on its own.

His new cards came in. One was a ten. The other was the king of clubs.

Poker face, he reminded himself. He might still have to bluff a couple of these assholes into folding if they thought they had a good hand.

"So," Albert said, "Mr Remington. You said the workload lately was too much for the rest of the agency to handle. That sounds like some serious shit, if I may say so. You were, what, called in for special purposes?"

"Yes, indeed," Remy confirmed. "I'm the kind of multi-talented individual they need. I have certain skills that make me a nightmare for the assholes who've interfered with the agency's business. Already, I've handled three completely different kinds of jobs and will be on my way to a fourth soon. Not everyone can survive in this line of work."

"I see," the man said neutrally and glanced around the table. "Final bets, gentlemen."

It started at another thousand. One of the men folded. The others remained but Remy could have sworn that a couple of them looked distinctly nervous. "I'll raise you five hundred," he said.

The remaining players saw him but did not raise it further.

"All right, show your hands," said the white-shirted guy.

They all laid their cards down at the same time.

A straight, a flush—of hearts—and two pairs, all beaten by Remy's full house.

"Ha!" He laughed. "I knew it. I knew that ten was lucky. And I could tell that you"—he pointed at the dude who'd fidgeted in his seat—"were banking on the straight. Maybe with players of a lesser caliber that would have been a safe bet. But, as you can see, gentlemen, the game isn't the same with me in it."

They pushed their chips in his direction without speaking.

Albert stared at him. "That's some good luck you had, my friend. And maybe some skill as well. A man who's both skillful and used to being lucky...he'd be a major asset to a mitigation agency, I would think."

"Damn right." He grinned. "I'm basically their new secret weapon. Hell, I probably increased our stock value with that epic victory."

The men exchanged glances. Most likely, he assumed, they all agreed that he was a prick. He was used to it.

Their host paused the next round of the game with a hand gesture and said, "Mr Remington...you know what? I believe everything you say. It seems to me you really are someone with a certain amount of clout and the ability to get things done—someone to be taken seriously."

"Thanks." Remy brushed a fleck of dust off his shirt. "So, does that mean you'll actually tell me—"

"It means"—Albert raised his voice enough to cut him off—"that I'm gonna ask you a serious question. Do you wanna make this game interesting?"

He assumed this meant increasing the pot to something in the five-digit range, a prospect that was almost irresistible. "Sure thing," he replied.

Another brief round of eye contact followed between the other men. Albert looked squarely at him. "All right then. Here's the wager for the next round of the game— information on this James guy, which you seem to want fucking bad, against...hmm..." He pretended to pause to think. "Your life."

His smile froze in place for a moment and, as the import of the words sank in, it melted slowly off his face.

"Uh," he said, "that's not exactly what I had in mind. If it's money, then yeah, I'll wager anything. But in this case, gentlemen, it's been fun and all, but I really ought to get going—" He stood.

A rustle of motion startled him and he blinked. Suddenly, every man in the room, including Tony at the exit, aimed a gun at him.

Albert smirked over the barrel of his semi-automatic. "Sit down, Mr Remington. You're a lucky guy and a good poker player. Your odds can't be that bad, right?"

He returned wordlessly to his seat.

Nodding, Albert went on. "Smart man. Now, the rest of us are gonna lower our guns so we can play us some cards.

Keep in mind that Tony over there isn't about to let you leave until the bet's settled, though." He gestured with his head toward the pinstripe-clad goon.

"Yeah," Remy said, "it's kind of hard to forget that."

The handguns retracted. Tony's remained visible, and although he kept it pointed at the ground, his gaze never left the back of Remy's head.

Albert looked at the guy in the white shirt. "Deal us out, Pat."

Pat shuffled the deck before passing it to his left to be cut, and the game proceeded as before—aside from the fact that no one placed any monetary bets at any point.

He needed his poker face more than ever right about now and it was mostly functional, although he was sweating. Especially his palms. As cards appeared before him and finally reached five, he wiped his hands on the knees of his pants before he took them.

Everyone examined their hand.

Unfortunately, he had very little to work with, starting out. Three different clubs, so there was a chance he could manage a flush, but no matching ranks. If he only discarded two cards and made for the flush and that failed, his next best hope would only be three of a kind.

But something almost imperceptible in the air suggested that no one else had been dealt a stellar hand, either. He looked up, hoping to read something on the mobsters' faces. Nothing was immediately apparent. Even the fidgety guy managed to hold himself still.

They will definitely kill me if I lose, he reminded himself. The thought was not encouraging. But if he won, it would be, in a way, his biggest victory ever.

He discarded two cards and kept the three random clubs.

The guy in the white shirt tossed two more at him. Breathing deep through his nose, he picked them up and looked at them. The eight of hearts and the eight of spades.

Three of a kind it was, then. Three eights. It could be worse.

Albert cleared his throat. "Nobody folds this time," he ordered. "Especially not Mr Remington. But the rest of you don't stand to lose anything on the chance that he wins...so you might as well stay in the game."

This meant, Remy realized, that he would not be able to bluff his way to victory. He had already spent his one chance to strategize and win. Now, all that remained was luck.

Albert waved a hand. "Show."

Everyone threw their cards down at once. He raised his sweaty hands to his neck and adjusted his tie as he looked around.

Pat, the dealer, had managed to deal himself two pair. No one else had anything higher than a pair. The one exception was Albert, who had three sixes.

They all stared, hard scrutiny in their eyes. Glances were exchanged. Remy double-checked the cards again. The vibe in the room was like ice.

"Okay then," he said a little too loudly and swallowed. "It looks like another win for me. Like I said, luck and skill in tandem. It's a good combination to have. Sooooo...I get to keep my life, and I believe you owe me some information about this James guy." Within his chest, it was as though a flight of birds had been released from captivity.

Albert resembled a steel statue. After a moment of neither moving nor speaking, he ran a knuckle over his nose. "I don't claim to be a nice guy but I am a man of my word, Mr Remington. Therefore...yeah, James was in here a few days ago. I don't know the guy too well, but he'd come in every once in a while to lose money."

Remy did not cringe when the mobsters all stared at him with obvious disappointment at his continued existence. "That's good to know, but it's not much. It almost seems that, if you were willing to kill me over the issue of divulging info on him, you might know more. Like some other place he's been where I could learn something a little more useful."

Silence ensued and the proprietor turned to Pat and asked him for a pen and piece of scrap paper, both of which the man provided. He placed the paper on the table and wrote briefly, set the pen down, and pushed the scrap toward the foot of the table.

Cautiously, he took it.

James had a second house, nice place upstate by the Catskills, that he hid from the tax collectors. Maybe you'll find something that interests you there.

"Thanks," he said, folded it, and slipped it into his pocket. "So, I should probably go now. Do I get to keep my other winnings?"

"Your luck," Albert began and pointed the pen at him as if holding a knife, "is already stretched thin today. Don't push it, buddy."

Remy sighed. Typical. "Fine. Thanks for an...uh, exciting game." He turned and left.

Albert sat in silence and watched him depart the high-stakes table, step past Tony, walk down the hall, and turn toward the main floor and exit.

One of the other charcoal-suited men cleared his throat. "Too much piss and vinegar in that fuckin' guy."

"No shit." The proprietor pulled his phone out and called one of the three men he'd had tailing David Remington since dawn.

"Joe," he said as soon as the man picked up, "our boy just left the casino—hopefully, you noticed. He's headed to James's place in Windham. Either way, we're fucking sure this guy is the kind of problem we don't need. Follow him there and see to it that he gets a nice view of the place. From the floor."

CHAPTER THIRTEEN

Greene County, New York

Remy groaned. This had been a mistake, he decided. He'd never entirely wrapped his head around the sheer size of the world beyond the lower Hudson Valley.

As the freeway zipped by beneath his tires and stretched on without end through the towns and forests, Riley lounged on the dashboard in front of him.

"This is boring," she complained, "but at least you don't have to concentrate on all those other things and can look at me."

"It's true," he said, "you are lingering right in the center of my field of vision."

She extended a shapely leg. "Don't you agree that clothes would ruin the effect? Isn't my body beautiful the way it is, exposed for admiration?"

"Hmm," he mused and pretended to wax philosophical, "you might say that the tantalizing paradox created by a revealing outfit is more enticing than when a woman is either fully-dressed or fully nude."

She rolled and spread her legs. "That doesn't mean anything. You're only trying to confuse me while you get out of having to admit the obvious."

"That's nice, dear," he said and kept driving.

James's secret house, according to Albert's note, lay in a town called Windham, at the northern edge of the Catskill Mountains and a short distance west of 87, although south of Albany.

According to his mapping app, it was a two-and-a-half-hour drive from Lower Manhattan to the town in question. It had already been two hours and forty minutes when he saw his exit coming up, veered into the ramp, and slowed to bear west.

"Ugh," he muttered, "even if I find this place right away and only surveil it for half an hour, it'll still be dark before I'm even back past Poughkeepsie. I should have told Taylor that the investigation won't be completed until tomorrow. I found a lead and even a naked fairy sidekick already. That qualifies as a fair day's work."

Riley made a little unhappy coughing sound at this. "Are you implying that being with me is work? It's supposed to be pleasure."

"Oh, I'm not implying that at all," he retorted. "Every single moment of your company has been positively orgasmic."

She smiled at that, lounged back in satisfaction, and actually shut up and ceased to bother him for a few minutes.

He was unsurprised to discover that James's house was not located in the town itself but in the hilly area southeast of it. His directions led him quickly onto a winding back road that seemed to average one or two houses per mile. Finally, he reached a private drive matching the address on his piece of paper.

"There you are, you bastard," he said to the road. "Now, let's see what James didn't want the taxman to know about."

The drive took a sharp bend, and his tires kicked gravel up as he plunged between a dense strand of trees whose deep shadows turned the afternoon almost to night. When the trees thinned, a two-and-a-half-story saltbox house appeared ahead which, although it looked like considerable money had been dropped on all the bells and whistles, did not seem lived-in. The yard was neglected and the grass was long overdue for a trim.

Riley perked up. She stood on the dashboard and put her hands on the windshield like a kid looking through a bay window. "Wow, what a nice place," she cooed.

"Eh, it's all right. It clearly belongs to someone who isn't that rich. But it's not bad."

He glanced around as he approached the structure itself, looking for any sign of security cameras or alarms or that kind of thing. He saw none, so far. The drive encircled the whole front half of the property, and he drove from one end to another, checking for anything suspicious, before he finally parked in front of the garage and turned the engine off.

"Okay," he observed, "it's not like the front door will be open, but I can probably pry a window open or something."

"Oh!" she chirped. "I can open locks."

Remy nodded. "Right, you got into my car while I was

kicking ass at poker. I forgot about that. If you were bigger, I'd pat you on the head."

He'd half-expected her to take offense at that, but she smiled at him in a way that almost made him wish she were bigger.

They got out and approached the front door. "Riley, wait a minute while I look through the window to make sure he doesn't have...I don't know, a golem or a dragon or something guarding the place."

The fairy snorted. "That isn't likely."

"Whatever." He peered through the glass. The curtains were mostly shut although, in the small gap between them, he could see furniture and an end table. The place was dark within, and he could hear no sounds beyond those of the surrounding woods.

Satisfied, he gestured at the doorknob and nodded to Riley. She waved her hands and silvery sparkles erupted from them before the latch clicked open. He turned the knob and opened the door.

"Hopefully, I didn't trip one of those goddamn silent alarms," he mumbled. There were no stickers advertising a security company outside but then again, some people were smart enough to remove said stickers. Professional thieves, if they knew what company protected a property, would then know what they were dealing with and adjust their strategy accordingly.

Beyond the front door was a small foyer-type area that opened into a spacious living room. The kitchen lay off to the right behind an island-counter. Deep gloom and silence hovered over everything, and the air smelled stale.

"Hello?" Remy called. "I'm from the utility company. It seems you have some unpaid bills."

No one answered, so he shrugged, flicked the nearest light on, and stepped inside. Riley floated along behind his shoulder.

He paused when the overhead lamp came on and illuminated the scene around him. "Oh, dear God." He gasped.

"What is it?" the fairy inquired. "What's wrong?"

"This is awful." He shook his head in near disbelief. "It's like a textbook case-study in *nouveau riche*."

Having been around wealth his whole life, he had seen this kind of thing before, although the Chateau James seemed to be an especially horrendous example. The whole place stank of someone who, having come into large amounts of money for the first time ever, was over-eager to spend it on something—anything—regardless of how ugly or inappropriate it was.

The furniture pieces, on an individual basis, were expensive and of high quality. They failed, however, as an ensemble. No thought had been put into coordination or complementary colors, patterns, or themes. Nothing within the room had the slightest whiff of *feng shui*.

The place also featured an abundance of pricey electronics, much of which looked as though it had barely been used. Video game consoles looked right out-of-the-box yet were covered in dust. The games for them still remained unwrapped in their plastic.

A top-of-the-line television was so big, it hinted at compensating for something. Attached to the TV was an intricate surround-sound system of conspicuous black speakers, atop which the owner had mounted useless golden statuettes.

An exercise machine was stuffed into the corner, where it would be impractical to operate. In the kitchen, fancy gadgets gleamed like they were still in a store showroom.

Worse still, every flat surface contained random expensive knick-knacks which were neither beautiful nor even slightly pragmatic. A ship in a bottle was the most egregious offender, but similar garbage was everywhere, all of it the types of things that would be popular with trophy wives for a year or so as status symbols before slumping into the waste bin of decorating history.

Remy drew his hand slowly over his face. "Terrible. Absolutely terrible. It's like this place is a historical museum dedicated to preserving knowledge of the day when some tasteless asshole got rich."

"Well," Riley commented and stuck a pinky finger in her mouth as she took in the sights, "at least there's a ton of shiny things. I don't know why most of them are here, though."

He nodded. "The world may never know." He strode through the living room and glanced around for anything that might qualify as a clue.

"Hmm." He scratched the back of his neck. "I actually have no idea what I'm looking for. Still, we might as well explore and see what's here to find."

Still in something of a daze, he moved on through the house. Each room was a badly organized treasure trove rather than part of a classy home. This did not surprise him. Nor did the fact that he found little that was worth examining.

Riley, meanwhile, zipped to and fro to examine things from angles he could not and stuck her nose in places he would never have considered. Occasionally, she remarked on something that caught her attention, such as a dead mouse atop one of the cabinets or a part of the floor a foot or so from the toilet where the smell of wolf urine was especially strong.

It wasn't until he investigated the upstairs bedroom, however, that he struck pay dirt.

"Well," he exclaimed and narrowed his focus on the items spread out on the king-sized bed beside a plastic shopping bag. "This looks significant."

He stepped into the room to examine them more closely and soon realized the objects were mostly hotel stuff. A possibly stolen towel, complimentary bars of soap, a garment that may have been a bathrobe, and a small, mounted, framed picture of the hotel itself.

The fairy followed his gaze and flew over the collection. "It smells...fancy," she reported.

"For once," he said, "I agree."

The towels, the back of the picture frame, and the gift-shop bag itself all included the name of the hotel, The Gold Reveal. It sounded familiar—a fairly high-end establishment in Midtown Manhattan, if he wasn't mistaken.

Remy picked up one of the miniature soap bars, still in its untorn wrapper, and put it in his pocket. "I'm sure Taylor will find this highly interesting. She'll have something to go on—a place where there would be witnesses. Hell, I might even be able to review the guest list myself, assuming the Remington name still carries the proper clout."

He paused and smiled to himself. Given his talents at so many other things, it didn't surprise him that he was also shaping up to be a brilliant detective. The vampire would, at last, be forced to acknowledge his competence. No more scrubbing the toilets. She might even give him a raise.

While he fantasized about the various possible scenarios, he strolled downstairs and into the living room. The sound of a car's engine caught his attention. Someone was pulling up to the house.

"What the hell?" He froze. Any visitors were unwelcome right now—even less welcome than himself.

Riley darted ahead and flapped toward the window to peer through it. She turned and flew halfway back.

"It's three men." The fairy gasped and sounded alarmed. "I saw two of them at that casino, and I'm very sure they have guns."

"Shit." He hadn't yet moved a muscle and honestly wasn't sure he even could. This was, obviously, bad. At the same time, though, he still seemed buoyed by the mental high of his successful discovery and when that weighed in again, he did not feel as cowed as he might have under normal circumstances. If anything, he was curious what a gunfight might be like. He'd never been in one before.

As the fairy wafted beside him, he asked her, "What kinds of guns do they have? It helps to know how big the magazine is." Shadows closed in near the front windows, and he was sure he could see another guy move toward the back of the house.

"Um…" she responded, "the smaller kind that they hold in one hand, I think."

Remy sighed. "Does that mean an Old West six-shooter? Bond's Walther PPK? A Desert Eagle? A Beretta? A Smith & Wesson .40 caliber? A Colt Python Revolver? What?"

She shrugged.

They both retreated toward the staircase and found partial cover along the side of a tall oak cabinet with gilded fixtures. No sooner had the wood blocked them slightly from the view of the front windows when two gunshots cracked.

"Goddamn!" he snapped and winced. "I forgot how frickin' loud guns are in real life. Anyway, that's two bullets fired by that guy over there." He gestured toward the large hole in the window ahead of him and to his right. Fragments of shattered glass twinkled on the floor.

There were also a couple of holes in the lovely hardwood cabinet. Since it was damaged already, Remy—in the grip of a thrilling surge of adrenaline—grasped the cabinet and flipped it over and up onto its side edge to act as a barricade.

Riley gestured frantically toward the holes in the wood with her hands. "That won't protect us! The bullets already went through it."

"Well..." He shrugged. "It might slow them down, at least." He dropped to his knees and crawled behind the piece of furniture as the dark figures approached the edge of the house. One of them kicked the door repeatedly to try to break it down.

Riley seemed to charge herself—there really was no other way to describe it—with silvery light and flung a hand outward toward the cabinet. It immediately flashed the same strange color. "That will help."

The front door slammed inward and a man stepped in and immediately fired two more rounds. Remy was almost positive that the gun he wielded was a Glock with a fifteen-round magazine, so it meant he still had eleven left. He thought about simply finding the nearest heavy object and hurling it at the intruder but decided that might be a bad idea.

While he tried to decide what to do, the fairy pointed a finger toward the man as if pantomiming a gun herself. The air cracked and exploded from her hand.

His jaw fell open in shock and his eardrums rang. Beyond the edge of the cabinet, he saw the hitman dive behind a chair.

She flew up beside his face and spoke directly into his still-pained ear. "I can't directly harm humans but now, at least, they think we have a gun, too."

"Good." He shook his head to try to clear the ringing still present in his ears.

The other of the two gunmen who'd approached from the front hurtled through the damaged window and climbed into the living room. His partner must have signaled him since it sounded like he overturned an end table and ducked behind it.

Riley "fired" another couple of "shots" to keep them busy. They responded with a flurry of bullets directed mostly around the edges of the cabinet, and he had to jerk his leg back to avoid being hit.

All the while, he counted how many rounds were fired.

"Riley," he whispered, "you can't harm humans. But what about, like, putting them to sleep or something?"

"Oh, right!" she said brightly. "I can do that, actually."

The first man fired a couple more shots. He now had only two remaining before he'd need to reload.

Remy gestured to the living room. "Incapacitate that guy over there, then the second one. Once the first asshole runs out of bullets, I'll engage him in hand-to-hand combat."

"If you say so," she replied. Despite her compliance, she sounded confused and a little nervous.

Hastily, he flicked his hand upward and retracted it, only enough to tempt them to shoot. They did and the air blazed with pistol fire. In the instant he heard the first attacker's gun click empty, he signaled his partner to attack the second man.

He sprang up, charged, and snatched one of the cheap golden statuettes off a speaker. The mobster looked up from behind a broad chair and his eyes widened in sudden panic. He fumbled with the fresh magazine and managed to fit it into the grip of his gun as Remy bore down on him.

Off to the side, two more gunshots rang out before a dull thud signaled a man slumping heavily to the floor.

He swung the statue as the mobster raised his gun. The gold figurine struck the man in the side of the head and thunked against his skull, and his hat spun from his head. He sputtered and fell in a heap.

"Hah!" Remy laughed and whirled around. The other intruder, too, was unconscious. "Good work, Riley." He could barely see the fairy where she wafted on shafts of sunlight.

Upstairs, another window broke and heavy footsteps landed on the second floor.

Riley fluttered over but he spoke before she could. "Fly

outside and make sure there aren't any more. I think I can deal with this guy."

"Are you sure?" she asked.

"Yes." He hadn't felt this good about his personal combat skills since the heyday of his *Call of Duty* career.

The fairy flitted out the front door.

Remy stepped quietly over to the loveseat in front of the television and picked up the remote control. The last assassin was already coming down the staircase. With the gold statuette still clutched in his hand, he hid behind the overturned end table beside which the unconscious assassin lay slumped.

The approaching footsteps slowed. The man was being cautious and advanced one step at a time, probably scanning the whole house in an attempt to discover where he was and if there were any other unexpected hostiles.

When his quarry had taken a few steps across the living room floor—perhaps ten feet from the end table—Remy pressed the Power button on the remote.

The TV flashed to life and a canned laugh track from a sitcom blared from the speakers which projected sound from every direction.

"Fuck!" the mobster cursed and he pivoted toward the TV and fired his pistol at the screen.

The investigator stood quickly and hurled the statue end-over-end like an old German stick grenade. The man looked back in time to take the golden object directly in the face. He grunted and staggered back, his nose and mouth bleeding, but he struggled to raise his weapon even as the other man attacked.

Remy attacker grabbed his opponent's wrist and kneed

him in the stomach. He saw Riley float in beside him before he punched the man in the side of the head and felled him.

Silence set in, and he turned to stare at the fairy.

"Well," he panted, "that didn't go too badly. In fact"—he grinned stupidly and had a sudden urge to jump straight up and fist-pump into the air—"I kicked ass."

Riley stared coldly at him. "You would have been shot—twice—if I hadn't deflected the bullets, you know."

His gaze snapped toward her and his eyes narrowed. "Oh yeah? Prove it."

CHAPTER FOURTEEN

Harrison, Westchester County, New York

It had been a long day, Remy acknowledged. He'd been up since well before dawn and it was now a couple of hours after dark. When he arrived at Taylor's mansion, though, he felt good. To be able to tell her that he'd found a lead, not to mention survived an assassination attempt... the anticipation was almost overwhelming.

As he mounted the short staircase at the front with Riley in tow, the right door opened.

"Good evening," said Presley. "Ms Steele wishes to speak to you immediately."

He smiled. "I'll bet she does."

The butler frowned at him. "We were considerably worried since you did not bother to call to inform us where you've even been this entire time." His gaze drifted toward the fairy and the sight of her seemed to distract him for a moment.

"Aww, but I wanted it to be a surprise." He protested and made an exaggerated pouty-lips face. "And yeah, Riley likes it when men stare at her all slack-jawed and drooling, so feel free to do so as much as you want."

She giggled.

"My jaw," Presley retorted, "is not slack in the slightest. I was merely trying to ascertain if this particular fairy was known to me or what her purpose here might be." He closed the door behind them.

"Sure, Jeeves, whatever you say. Everyone knows that proper old gentlemen like yourself turn into the dirtiest perverts imaginable given any motivation. Riley, go on and hover directly in front of his face for a couple of minutes."

"Okay." She sounded cheerfully amused at the prospect.

"Stop." Taylor stepped into the foyer from the hall. "That won't be necessary. Remington, sit down." She pointed at the nearest chair.

Remy suspected she was about to try to chew him out and couldn't wait to destroy her with the news of all the useful things he'd discovered. He tried not to smirk too obviously as he lowered himself into the chair and noted the way Presley, behind him, sighed with relief.

The vampire stood before him and seemed to loom more than usual. "All right, why have you returned so late, and what have you been doing all day? You never sent word to us, so we were beginning to consider the possibility that someone had captured or killed you."

"Well," he retorted, "they tried."

She betrayed no great surprise. "Indeed? Start from the beginning. I want to know everything."

He took a deep breath and related the whole story, beginning with his purchase of Riley's services in exchange for honey. From there, he proceeded through his experience in the casino, his trip upstate, and finally, the shootout at James's second house in Windham.

When he finished—looking extremely pleased with himself—she folded her arms over her chest and nodded.

Riley piped up. "I helped," she pointed out. "He would have been shot twice if—"

"Yes, thank you," Remy interrupted her. "That still leaves all the other bullets that never would have hit me at all, though."

Taylor seemed to flick her gaze aside for a moment, but when she looked at him, she said, "Today, you have drawn a disturbing amount of attention to yourself, but I am impressed that you produced a viable lead. I will investigate this hotel directly."

He beamed and lounged back in his chair. "Ha! Yes! I knew you'd come around to seeing my true potential. We can forget all about that nonsense with the toilets. From this day forth, I am your equal in every way, aside from also being the owner of the company, of course. I—"

"Be quiet," she snapped with understated power. He flinched even as his jaw snapped shut.

She narrowed her eyes. "It's true you've not done too badly, but don't go getting delusions of grandeur. You are still the most junior person here and will be for the foreseeable future."

The fairy hovered between them and raised a hand. "Does this mean my services are still required, ma'am?"

The vampire answered before he could. "Yes, it would be useful to have you around. He bought you for a week, anyway, didn't he?"

"Yes," she confirmed and grinned. "He said I should wear clothes, though. That's completely stupid."

Taylor ignored her. "All right, I want both of you to stay here until I specifically give you leave to go anywhere else. And since I'm about to depart for this Gold Reveal Hotel, that probably means you'll spend the night. You may use the guest room upstairs. Presley will see that you have what you need."

Remy blinked in confusion. "Wouldn't it make more sense to take me with you? Granted, I am tired, but...well, after my sterling performance earlier—"

She shook her head. "No. There's no way of knowing what I'll walk into there. I can handle it myself. Some things become far more difficult if I also have to keep someone who doesn't know what they're doing alive."

He started to protest but she made a strange, sharp gesture with her hand and again, his lips seemed to seal themselves together against his will.

Presley walked up and looked at Taylor. "Madame, will you require full battle gear?"

She paused to consider the question. "No, light gear should suffice. They probably won't expect anything too serious yet. And if they do, I don't want anything heavy to slow me down on my way out."

The butler nodded. "Very well, madame. But please be careful."

She put a hand on his arm and strode past him toward the garage.

Remy snapped his fingers and shouted, "Presley!"

The old man turned. "Yes, sir? Oh, and thank you for finally getting my name right. I knew you had it in you."

He cursed. "I didn't eat all day. Order me a pizza, Jeeves."

Park Avenue, Midtown Manhattan, New York City

It took Taylor only thirty-nine minutes to reach her destination. She knew when and how to drive faster than most people could get away with, could locate obstructions before they occurred, and was able to use New York's myriad side-streets to her advantage. When she broke the human laws, she did so unobtrusively and without causing damage to either humans or their property. Her black Tesla slipped through the city like a thief in the night.

She arrived on Park Avenue in Midtown Manhattan about half a mile before the point where the hotel ought to be located. She intended to drive past it out front and, if necessary, circle to the back and surveil the place a little before she plunged in.

The building appeared on the right and she examined it quickly, using not only her eyes but the subtler perceptive abilities which she'd had centuries to hone.

It was clear to her almost instantly that something was not right.

There were no clear visual clues out front and it wasn't anything obvious. Something seemed to linger in the air, an off-kilter frequency of its electromagnetic ambiance.

The vampire found the nearest parking garage and left her car there on one of the higher levels, confident that the vehicle's considerable security systems would keep it where it was and in one piece. She slipped into the shadows that clung along the edges of buildings as she made her way back toward the Gold Reveal.

She wore a light bulletproof vest under her dress and had a few minor weapons and useful tools stashed elsewhere on her person. Despite her precautions, she didn't anticipate going to war. Not yet, anyway.

As she neared the tall, elegant structure, it occurred to her that she could try to fly or crawl to the top and work her way down through it, but even with her skills, there were many ways that could go wrong. More than anything, it was imperative that she not be sighted.

There was no other immediate threat so she resolved to simply walk into the lobby and speak to the staff. She could enthrall them if need be.

Unfortunately, she stepped through the glass revolving door and realized at once that doing that would be a total waste of time.

Someone else had already gotten to the hotel's staff—and very likely the same people she was looking for. There was at least one vampire on her list of prime suspects. Humans under a spell always gave off a disturbing uncanny vibe. There was something unnatural in their behavior and a subtle odor about them.

The doorman, the concierge, and the security guard all stared at her with placid intensity as she strode toward the reception desk. She would have to be careful, her instincts warned.

And, she resolved, if things did turn ugly, she would do all she could to merely incapacitate these people. It was not necessary to kill them.

"Hello," she said across the desk. A thin, friendly-looking man stood there. She looked into his eyes only long enough to give him a small jolt of her own influence. If she pushed too hard against the enthrallment he was already under, she could provoke a violent reaction and possibly break something in his mind.

"Good evening, madame," he acknowledged robotically. "Unfortunately, the hotel is closed to new guests this evening. The entire building has been rented out for a private gathering. I'm sorry. You are welcome to return in two days if you still need accommodation."

While he spoke, a pair of janitors, a maid, and a cook all wandered into the lobby to join the doorman and the security guard. All of them looked at her.

"Oh." She drummed her fingers on the desk. "That is disappointing. May I see the register to at least know who it is who's rented the hotel? I strongly suspect it's an acquaintance of mine, so if that's the case, I could speak to them and perhaps I could even change their mind."

She hadn't expected this argument to work. Rational discussion was a lost cause against the bewitched. The idea was to gauge his reaction and that of the six other people who'd begun to surround her.

The concierge flinched. "Madame!" he protested. "Absolutely not. We strictly respect the confidence and privacy of our guests. The individuals renting the building have done so according to the rules, and their instructions were quite specific. I'm afraid I must ask you to leave."

Everyone else took another step closer to her. The concierge himself, meanwhile, seemed to reach under the desk for something.

Taylor noted the way the man moved and also the sense

of rhythm she felt from the other six. One of the janitors would probably be the first to strike but the security guard would be the most potentially dangerous. None of them were a threat, but she did not need either the distraction or the commotion.

"Oh," she said again, "that's quite all right. "May I use your phone?"

The janitor was the first to move. She was already halfway into her reaction before he had even fully prepared. A black blur was all any of them saw.

"Stop her!" the concierge yelled.

The first man had tried to sweep a broom around her to pin her head against him with the handle against her throat. He had barely registered that she was no longer in front of him when she yanked his legs out from under him and he landed face-first.

The concierge and security guard both drew handguns while the other four still on their feet spread out, confused but alert. The maid tried to tackle her in what she obviously considered the moment of opportunity when the janitor fell. The vampire was already behind her. She flung the woman across the floor and her head struck the wall, where she lay unconscious in a heap.

By now, Taylor had already vaulted over the head of the security guard and seized the man's shoulders as he raised his pistol to fire. She swung him upward and threw him down as she descended and stamped on his wrist. The bones cracked and he screamed and relinquished the gun. She snatched it and crushed it in her hand.

The other three all attacked at once. She backhanded the cook across the face and he wheezed and coughed blood as he spun and toppled. Two quick kicks to the ribs felled the second janitor and the doorman.

The concierge aimed and fired. Taylor stepped aside and a bullet hole appeared in the opposite wall. Before he could shoot again, she was suddenly on top of him, yanked the pistol from his grasp, and punched him in the stomach.

The man doubled over and vomited. She pounded his head into the desk and allowed him to slump to the floor beside the puddle of puke.

The lobby was silent aside from a few groans of pain. The vampire examined the seven humans quickly. All of them would live and she didn't think she'd crippled any.

Footsteps approached and men shouted, and she cursed. Of course, her enemies would have surrounded themselves with as many enslaved protectors as possible.

She darted to the elevator, pressed the button, and stepped inside as the next group of would-be assailants rushed into the lobby.

"Stop!" she commanded, and they reeled. Their bodies experienced small, brief seizures as her impelling voice clashed with the brainwashing they'd already received.

The delay was all she needed, though. The doors closed and she thumped the button to take her all the way to the top—the Presidential Suite. That seemed the most likely place.

The compartment lurched and ascended.

Listening to the building around her, she could hear people moving on one of the higher floors and it didn't come as much of a surprise when the elevator stopped about halfway up, followed immediately by the sound of someone taking a powerful cutting tool to the heavy cable that suspended the compartment.

"Shit," she murmured, irritated by yet another hindrance. She vaulted up, pushed the ceiling panels aside, and swung her body up around the frame bars like a gymnast when the elevator began to tilt and sway as the cable started to fail.

Taylor crawled out on top of the compartment and jumped to the side of the shaft as the cutting process, somewhere up above, reached its end. Freed, the thick metal cord made a whining sound as it whipped loose and the elevator itself plummeted down the shaft to its inevitable ruin below.

She remained where she was for a moment, her nails gripping the steel girders and her body hidden in the deep gloom of the shaft.

Up above, someone asked, "Did we get her?"

"I don't know," another voice replied. "Call the dumb-asses downstairs and have them check the wreckage. Until then, we have to assume she might try to fly or crawl up here."

These people were probably higher-end security. It was unlikely that the conspirators had brought their personal bodyguards with them, so those on the top floor were either more hotel staff or third-party hirelings. Either way, they had no experience fighting a vampire.

Taylor climbed silently and carefully, knowing full well that the men above kept a close eye on the elevator shaft but also confident that she could be almost on top of them before they saw her.

Soon, light appeared from the doorway leading to the

Presidential Suite. Within it, silhouetted against the glow, were the heads of two men who leaned into the shaft to watch out for her.

She could pounce up, grab them, and haul them in to let them fall to their deaths. But it could also be done without any killing. It merely took more steps.

Lizard-like, she moved another yard or so upwards.

"Jesus," one of the men said, "I think I see something moving down there. Where's our report from the ground floor?"

That would be my cue.

Without a moment's hesitation, she vaulted up and flew the rest of the way. The walls of the shaft fell away around her and in an instant, she stared into the faces of the two security men.

They fell back, their eyes wide and white, and mouthed curses without speaking while the sub-machine guns they carried aimed toward her.

The vampire landed between them before they could fire and shoved them both in opposite directions, slightly forward and at an angle. Each guard tumbled into a wall. The one on her right managed to squeeze the trigger of his weapon as he fell.

Taylor leapt again as the gun flared to life. She avoided taking the full brunt of the burst but two bullets grazed her leg. The pain was sharp but not debilitating and the wound would heal quickly enough.

The man who'd fired was still conscious, so she darted toward him. At the same time, she registered the presence of four more men who raced toward her position from around the corner. She'd deal with them momentarily.

Smoke rose from the barrel of the man's weapon as she appeared before him. She was too fast for him to aim again, especially since his collision with the wall seemed to have injured his shoulder.

His face fell. "No!" he cried, certain he would die.

She merely swatted him hard across the face so his head bounced into the wall and he slumped limply, out of the fight.

The other guard had already passed out on the initial impact so she spun to face a new group of attackers. Like the first two, they were clad in paramilitary gear and carried sub-machine guns. Only one of them held his weapon, though. His teammates had them hanging from shoulder straps at their sides and brandished other objects.

One held a large wooden crucifix, another, a clove of fresh garlic, and the third, a vial of holy water.

Taylor let her eyes go wide and she stopped in place. She took a step back, held a hand up with the palm faced outward, and covered her face with the other hand.

"It's working," one of the men exclaimed. "Thank God. Close in on her."

The vampire dropped to one knee as the men encircled her. The one holding the SMG, she realized, intended to shoot her repeatedly in the legs to temporarily cripple her while the others black-bagged her head and zip-tied her wrists.

The nearest man smirked as she continued to cover her face and cower. "So the bullshit old legends were true."

Her gaze snapped up. "Not so much, actually." She punched him in the stomach hard enough to catapult him over and past his comrades.

"What the fuck?" another managed to get out before she seized the next two by their heads and pounded them together. Both men staggered and fell.

The last attacker attempted to open fire. She scuttled under him, moving beetle-like across the floor, and trip-kicked him hard enough to fracture his lower leg. Groaning in pain, he collapsed, and she yanked the gun away from him before she almost casually slammed his head into the floor.

Once again, she'd achieved victory with no death. Although none of them would remember this experience with much fondness, of course.

The halls were silent now. Taylor examined her surroundings. It seemed that the Presidential Suite took up three-quarters of the floor and the rest consisted merely of hallways on two sides and a couple of closets.

That was simple enough. She strode quickly to the door leading into the suite, kicked it down, and brandished her stolen sub-machine gun in case she needed it.

Beyond the doorway were fine, sprawling quarters, opulent yet tasteful and even cozy, with gold-plated fixtures that shone in the bright lights. Subtle signs of recent habitation were strewn about but no one was there.

The vampire moved in quickly and quietly and all her senses strained to find her enemies.

She checked everywhere and found nothing. The marble bathroom, platinum kitchenette, and leather-and-velvet sitting room had all been vacated—judging by the smell—within the last ten minutes.

Dammit.

And at the far end of the suite, a window was open. The

curtains billowed in the stronger wind that prevailed at this elevation.

She approached the window and peered out at the city, the night sparkling with manmade lights. No figures caught her eye. She could try jumping out herself and giving chase, but if her quarry had a head start of more than a couple of minutes—which was likely—she had little chance of catching them.

The extra time it took her to climb the elevator shaft by hand and defeat the guards on the top floor had given the conspirators time to escape.

"But not without losses," Taylor rasped. She'd driven them out of their hiding place and removed many of their minions from active service for quite a while to come. She had made her point.

They knew that she knew and now, they could either run away with their tails between their legs or commit fully.

Either way, she would kill them. The rules were the rules.

CHAPTER FIFTEEN

Harrison, Westchester County, New York

Remy awoke to someone rapping lightly on the door.

"Uhh…" He moaned, rolled to one side, and kicked the covers off. "Yeah, Mom, okay, I'm up." He did not get up.

The knocking came again, louder. This time, he opened his eyes but did not speak and clutched the ends of his pillow angrily against the sides of his head.

A male voice on the other side of the door said, "Mr Remington. I've brought your breakfast."

He blinked and rubbed his eyes. The bizarre dreams he'd had were already fading into oblivion, and knowledge of the real world returned. He remembered where he was —the guest room at Taylor's mansion. He sat up. This was as nonsensical as his dreams.

"Okay," he said, his voice hoarse and slurred from sleep. "Thanks, Jeeves. You can…uh, leave it—"

Before he could finish his instructions, the door opened and the butler walked in, carrying a tray piled with dishes. He set it on an end table next to the bed. "When you've eaten and dressed, please come down to the sitting room. Ms Steele wished for me to update you on her exploits last night and their ramifications for our continued efforts."

Remy cleared his throat. "Hey. You barged into the room before I gave you permission to enter. That's not how staff is supposed to behave."

Presley remained expressionless. "Very good, sir." He turned and shut the door behind him.

He sat up and examined the tray before he tucked in.

The butler—or someone, although he'd seen no sign of anyone—was, he had to admit, an excellent cook. The eggs were fried to a nice over-medium with unbroken yolks and the toast was the perfect shade of golden brown. There was also a tray of sliced fruits and a cup of strong but mellow coffee. He polished it all off, then stood to dress.

As he pulled his pants on, Riley suddenly appeared from somewhere overhead.

"I saw that." She snickered.

He scratched his stomach. "Saw what, exactly? The toast crumbs?"

She tittered again. "Of course not."

"Where," he inquired of the fairy, "did you even sleep last night?"

"With you," she answered and ran a tiny finger along the edge of her chin. "Under the covers."

Remy sighed. "You really ought to ask permission for that kind of thing. It's common etiquette among those of us more than a foot tall. Well, except for elves, I'd guess."

The two of them exited the guest room with him firmly instructing her to wait outside while he used the recently scrubbed upstairs toilet. They descended to the first-floor sitting room, where Presley wiped some of the vases and candlesticks with a cloth.

"Ah," the butler said, "how good of you to come so promptly. Have a seat, please. Would you like more coffee?"

He considered this. "Yes, I think I would. Now that I work mornings, I'm starting to understand why so many normal schmucks rank it slightly below oxygen on their list of priorities."

Presley fetched another steaming cup and also provided cream and sugar. Like any civilized human being, Remy took his with only a small amount of cream and did not touch the sugar at all. If he was going to drink coffee, he might as well do it properly rather than disguising it as a liquid dessert.

The other man seated himself in the chair across from him. "Now, then, sir. The mistress of the house requested that I inform you of what she discovered last night. However, she also asked me to remind you that you are not to leak this information in public, especially not while on duty and in the presence of others who may not be friendly to us. Is this understood?"

"Yes, yes, of course I understand." He sipped his coffee. "Any previous bragging on my part was entirely justified as part of my efforts to bluff people into submission, or something like that. But I can appreciate that it might be better to avoid saying too much now that we have some kind of actual lead. So, tell me, what did the old girl find on her little trip to the hotel?"

Presley grimaced, and there were steely determination and deadly seriousness to his sagging old face that he hadn't noticed before.

"The hotel's staff were under the mind-control effects of a rival vampire. Ms Steele was forced to disable them for her own safety and in order to investigate the building. Whoever had been holed up there fled before she could reach the top floor and deal with them."

"Damn that sounds...exciting, actually. Too bad she didn't allow me to tag along. She found some kind of clue though, right?"

The butler made a low sound in his throat. "Mm...no, not exactly. However, she had previously acquired three names from another source of persons she considers the most likely suspects. We have our dots but cannot yet connect them, you see."

"Too bad," he said.

The old man went on as if he hadn't spoken. "Ms Steele's hope is that her violent confrontation last night will throw them into panicking and force them to show their hand through hasty action."

Remington considered that as he continued to drain his cup. "Wouldn't a failed attempt to capture them—not that I'm accusing Taylor of failing, exactly, but you know what I mean—merely make them more careful? Or even run away?"

Again, the low humming sound emerged from the old man's throat. "Mm, yes, that is her fear. It would be such a bother to have to hunt them out of state. This evening, she hopes to brainstorm further action that might point us in the right direction."

He glanced aside at Riley, who was spread-eagled on the arm of the chair and lolled her head lasciviously. She reminded him of a particularly slutty state senator's

daughter whom he had known—in the Biblical sense—
about six years prior after meeting her at a party. They'd
broken it off shortly before the election.

"You know," he suggested, "I used to find that parties
were an excellent way to determine who my enemies were.
There is something about the inherently disgusting nature
of social gatherings that seems to bring out the worst in
people who already have the worst of intentions." He set
his now all too empty cup down.

The butler squinted as if thinking hard. "I will suggest
that to Ms Steele. It is very likely that she won't like the
idea due to the dangers involved, but you do raise a fair
point. Bringing our suspects closer under some innocuous
pretense would allow us to observe them."

Remy grinned. "Great! Another brilliant idea from me.
So, then, I'll go home—finally—and have Taylor call me
this evening once she's scheduled the festivities."

Presley frowned and tensed. "Now, wait a moment, sir.
Nothing has yet been agreed upon. You should speak of
this to Ms Steele yourself, preferably in person, before we
assume anything."

"Yeahhh, you're probably right. She might make me go
back to the werecats and change their litter box or something if we don't get her stamp of approval. What time is it,
anyway?"

While he pulled his phone from his pocket, Presley
glanced at a nearby clock. "A little after nine in the morning, sir. Would you like chores to occupy you while we wait
for dusk?"

The day seemed to take forever to pass.

Remy helped the butler with a few household chores

until this grew too boring and the old man finally sent him to buy groceries and toiletries. After he returned, he took a nice hour-long nap. Then they looked over some of the company's accounts and Presley explained the usual course of the agency's cash flow.

He honestly tried to pay attention. But mostly, he was excited to talk to Taylor about the party.

Finally, the sun began to set. He paced from one end of the foyer to the other while he reviewed the sales pitch he would use in his mind. As darkness settled in beyond the mansion's windows, the cellar door opened. He listened for the soft sound of feet on the floor but heard nothing until her soft voice spoke.

"David. You're still here."

He looked up. She wore her black robe once again. "Yes, I thought I'd help Presley get a few things straight around here. More importantly, though, he told me all about your adventure last night and—well, I have a brilliant idea for what to do next. When you're ready to hear it, of course. Feel free to have a cup of coffee—blood, sorry —beforehand."

Taylor managed a wan smile. "I'm ready now. The sitting room."

He told her about the party. She frowned her way through most of his spiel but allowed him to keep talking.

"It never fails," he explained. "The people who hated me always crashed the party—they showed up for the sole purpose of clogging my toilets and stealing my booze. It was a tremendously efficient way to keep my enemies list up to date."

The vampire drummed her fingers on the armrest of

her chair. "The idea intrigues me, I must say. It's quite devious. However, this house is my sanctuary. Inviting the people who most despise me into my home will lead to far worse than clogged toilets."

"Witnesses," he pointed out and raised a finger. "We'll invite your friends as well as our suspects. They won't try anything when everyone else can see, will they?"

She nodded. "You may be right about that, yes. I will confer with Presley on how we might go about this." She rose and took two steps toward the hall before she stopped. "Of course," she added, almost off-handedly, "anything that goes wrong is on you, Remington."

He beamed. "What could possibly go wrong?"

It was with mixed feelings that Remy took a sip. Although he knew it might sabotage his efforts to clean up, it felt good to have a cocktail in his hand again.

A stout, bearded dwarf marched up to him. "I have never seen this place before. It is a fine house and you seem to have requisitioned a very fine supply of beer."

"Thanks," he replied. "If there's one thing I know how to do, it's throw a proper bash at a nice place with a properly-stocked bar. Well, that and gamble. Especially at poker. Didn't I see you at the casino the other day?"

The dwarf squinted at him under his massive, bushy eyebrows and grunted. "No. I do not think so. Unfortunately, other species have been known to say that we dwarves all look alike, so you may have mistaken me for someone else."

"Probably, yeah," he admitted. "I could have sworn, though… In any event, have as much beer as you like. Uh… within reason."

The dwarf nodded and wandered off.

Riley hid under his shirt in the crook of his armpit. "That was a good idea," she whispered at him.

"What?" he asked.

"Saying 'within reason' at the end. Dwarves don't really get drunk so they tend to imbibe alcohol by the gallon if you let them."

"I see." He sipped his cocktail. "That sounds expensive. I'm already blowing a goodly chunk of the company's quarterly budget on this bash, considering all the esoteric provisions you suggested."

Taylor had been busy, so he had been forced to consult with the fairy—and, to a lesser extent, the butler—as to what kinds of things preternaturals expected at a good, high-class party.

In general, a party was a party for any type of being. But of course, different species had different likes and dislikes. Some of which were…unexpected. It had taken two days to get everything sorted out.

Preternaturals, Riley had explained, liked spectacle but nothing too showy. He had arranged to have half a dozen crystal half-globes suspended from the ceiling, mostly filled with water, and the main lights suspended directly above the liquid. It created a lovely refraction which sent light and rainbows to weave around the room as the liquid moved.

The fairy had also told him to stock a large quantity of good, dark, hoppy beer for the dwarves, make sure they had a supply of hard liquor for the werewolves, and to talk to Taylor's supplier about procuring the necessary ingredients for something she called a Historical Bloody Mary.

As for snacks, many of the attending species would eat almost nothing but meat, so that meant a hefty deli order. The ingredients also had to be carefully marked next to each dish. Remy had started to joke about garlic but Presley had told him to shut up.

Some of the more...metaphysical creatures like ghosts and such even seemed to expect a strange broth that he could only think of as "witches' brew." He couldn't picture anyone who was actually alive being interested in such gunk.

Music was a somewhat difficult affair, given the vastly different preferences he would have to consider. He finally decided on an unobtrusive light jazz playlist, which made itself conspicuously pleasant every few minutes but which he planned to keep at a low volume, anyway.

At last, only forty minutes before showtime, everything was ready. They'd cleared out the sitting room, kitchen, and foyer to provide enough floor space with the tables arranged along the sides.

And, of course, they had carefully barricaded off the rest of the house, save for the short stretch of hallway leading to the first-floor bathroom.

The guests began to trickle in, as guests were wont to do, about ten minutes early, and the remainder spread their arrivals across the next hour or more. Remy greeted them all as old friends, happy to introduce himself— although it took some effort in the case of the ghosts, who still creeped him out, and the obnoxious little gremlins.

The elves from Brooklyn arrived as well. Fortunately, he had ample experience in pretending that nothing at all was awkward.

Riley, meanwhile, had continued to offer him advice on what to say or not to say to preternaturals of different clans and species. He tried to listen but mostly simply went with his own instincts. The lack of fistfights or death threats suggested he was doing all right.

"See?" he said to his armpit. "I'm popular, as usual. They all seem to think I'm an excellent host."

"Maybe," the fairy admitted, "but I'm not sure how many of them like you and how many simply want to eat you. There used to be gatherings where the humans themselves were the party favors."

A particular man caught Remy's eye. He'd arrived late— one of the last guests, in fact—and he looked familiar. It took a moment to recognize him since he'd dressed up for the occasion, but Taylor had shown him a photo and this was undoubtedly the same person.

He was tall and heavyset, a little jowly, with big square hands and shaggy hair that he'd slicked back. Attire-wise, he'd chosen a white tuxedo in a style so old that Remy's brain had been forced to play catch-up. Finally, it clicked. It was the outfit one would expect of an antebellum Southern gentleman.

"Hi," he said and approached the man. "I'm Remington Davis, the agency's new partner. I'm proud to say that I was also the buyer for this party, so you can thank me for whatever it is you're drinking there. Mint julep?"

The man smiled broadly and raised his glass. "Yessir. How did you guess?" Unsurprisingly, he spoke with a pronounced Southern drawl. "Where the hell are my manners? I'm Tucker Bedford." He extended his right hand.

He shook it and managed not to wince. The man had one hell of a grip. "I have some familiarity with alcoholic beverages," he explained and nodded toward the drink. "Plus, the sprig of fresh mint seemed like a dead giveaway."

"Careful," Tucker retorted and lowered his voice, "some of the folks at a gathering like this won't take kindly to a man throwing that word 'dead' around so carelessly." His eyes twinkled and he could not decide if he was being charming or threatening.

"Oh, right, ha." Remy laughed. "Sorry! I'm new to all this preternatural business, although nothing I've seen so far is any more scandalous than what I've already gagged my way through while dealing with high-society New York humans. That gets simply terrifying."

The Southerner took a swig of his julep. "I'll bet it does," he conceded. "Still, in my time…well, I've seen nice boys from that other, mundane world wander into this world, thinking they could handle it, and one day, they put their foot down in the wrong place, and…" He snapped his fingers. "Gone."

He nodded and summoned an appropriate façade of wide-eyed naiveté. "Gosh, yes. I'm trying to be careful. It's true, after all, that you never know when someone's luck will run out. I used to encounter all these cunning old bastards, who'd been scheming behind the scenes for decades, and then, alas, they got overconfident. The old proverb about how there's always a bigger fish proved itself true." He shook his head sadly.

Tucker smiled in a grim way. "Ain't that the truth." He

moved his left hand in a circle to swish the ice and bourbon.

His gaze shifted to the drink. "Isn't it traditional, though, for mint juleps to be served in a silver cup?"

The other man, too, looked at the glass, then his gaze slid up to lock with his. "Glass, crystal…any is acceptable. The drink itself is what's important. Besides, if you organized this party, I'm sure you'd know better than to have silver around. Some species don't much care for it."

"Indeed," he said. "I gather that Taylor—and vampires in general—aren't particularly fond of silver, but it doesn't seem to really harm them much. So, in that respect, I imagine they have a clear advantage over lycanthropes."

Tucker took a long drink until the glass was almost empty. "Vampires don't have many weaknesses, it's true," he stated. "But, of course, every species has its strengths and, well, its vulnerabilities. Even the most powerful can end up in a bad way. Like you said—if they overstep their boundaries."

He let the pause after his last word stretch out ominously. A soft footstep intruded on Remy trying to find something to say.

"Hello," Taylor said and looked at the large Southerner with a pleasantly neutral expression. "I'm your hostess. I believe we've met once or twice before, Mr Bedford."

Tucker extended his hand. "Ms Steele. Nice of you to join us. Mr Davis here and I were discussing the things he's already learned since he joined up, and how—"

"The powerful," she interrupted, "can end up badly if they misstep. Yes, I heard. It's good that you're teaching

Remy here such an important lesson." She extended a hand and ruffled his hair.

He pulled away from her unwelcome display. "Remington, please," he grated. "I would think this was too formal an occasion for fond nicknames."

Taylor arched her eyebrows. "This isn't a formal occasion, exactly. It's a party. We can all speak our minds freely."

The other man chortled. "That's good to know, but it seems some folks are upset that we all can't act freely. Maybe you've heard the rumblings. A lady as smart as yourself ought to know that when things like that start happening...well, maybe it's time to enact some reforms and give the people what they want. Stave off the rebellion, as it were."

The intensity with which the man said the word rebellion brought a slight chill to Remy's spine.

"Oh?" the vampire inquired. She ran the tip of a red-nailed finger around the edge of her glass, which contained what looked like a Bloody Mary. "I was under the impression that things were quite well-balanced as they were. After all, 'the people' is a term that also includes the humans. I feel it's entirely reasonable to shut them out of our affairs in exchange for their safety."

He almost held his breath while he watched. The two stared into each other's eyes now, and the vibe had turned as cold as winter.

"That," Tucker began, "ain't exactly how it's worked for most of history. You're running a very strange experiment here, you realize. Experiments have a way of failing over time."

Taylor smiled. "It hasn't failed yet."

The Southerner raised his crystal glass in a mock toast. "True enough, ma'am. Maybe we'll get lucky and things will all work out well for everyone. Maybe." He drained the vessel of both alcohol and ice.

"I'll drink to that," the woman replied. She raised her glass, sipped at the red liquid, and nodded to Remy. "I'll be around. Let me know if either of you requires anything."

Tucker watched her leave. Remy was about to wander off toward other guests when the big man turned abruptly toward him.

"Listen, now," he drawled, and he could feel the man's drunkenness by this point. "I respect Taylor. She's not a lady to be trifled with and she plays by the same rules she enforces on everyone else—she ain't no hypocrite. But sometimes, even an admirable individual gets too comfortable being in charge. They think they always know what's best, they won't listen to anyone else's suggestions, and when change comes a-knockin' at the door...well, they simply check to see that the deadbolt's shut and won't budge an inch to open it. And at some point, that becomes a problem."

Slowly, he nodded. "I...see."

The Southerner extended his empty glass in a gesture of emphasis. "It's a regrettable problem—the kind that would be better not happening in the first place. But sometimes, things are set in motion that can't be stopped, even if regrets are involved."

"I will relay the message," he said.

Tucker nodded. "Do so, Yankee Boy. It's been nice chatting, but I ought to get going. I've about drank enough and said enough." He smiled. "I'll see you 'round."

"It's been educational." He extended his hand and again, it was crushed in that huge paw. The large man sauntered off and disappeared.

The rest of the evening's festivities passed by uneventfully enough, aside from one uncomfortable incident in which a ghost possessed a loudmouthed gremlin and forced him to leap into the sink and douse himself in cold water. Fortunately, Taylor stepped in to personally resolve the matter before it could lead to a brawl.

As the last of the guests filed out hours later, he felt a sharp ache in his bladder. He stumbled toward the bathroom and pushed his way through the door.

"Oh, for fuck's sake!" he exclaimed. "The toilet's clogged. It never fails."

He sighed. At least he knew where they kept the plunger and brush.

CHAPTER SIXTEEN

Fall Fair Demolition Derby, Middletown, New York
The early autumn sunshine was bright and warm, and the trees were barely beginning to show tints of yellow and orange. If you looked one way, it seemed like a perfect fall postcard, peaceful and soothing.

If you looked in the other direction, the place was anything but.

"I cannot believe," Remy murmured, "that I am actually, literally standing here in attendance at a goddamn demolition derby."

Riley, who floated over his shoulder near his left ear, turned to ask, "Why not?"

"Because," he stated. "It's not very...Remington-esque. That's the shortest and most accurate answer. Let me get my bearings here and maybe I'll give you a longer one, as well."

After the party, everyone—Remy, Taylor, Riley, and Presley—agreed that Tucker was, as the police would say, a person of interest. It was impossible to be certain that he was among the conspirators since he'd spoken in riddles and vague innuendoes and could have defended himself on the grounds of merely trying to warn Taylor of general discontent.

But given that she had already pegged him as a suspect following her interview with a dwarfish friend it seemed, Remy thought, a little too coincidental.

That night, after the party, they'd asked the fairy to sniff Remy's hand to pick up Tucker's scent and discussed all the pertinent information as to his recent activities and known whereabouts.

Today was a new day and Remy and Riley had spent the first few hours of it trailing the Southern gentleman across New York, much as they'd done their first day together while determining James' activities.

It hadn't taken long to find him. After leaving the soiree at Taylor's house, he'd simply gone to a hotel room in White Plains and spent the night there. In the morning, he had gone to Middletown, a municipality northwest of Tuxedo which apparently was big enough—barely—to qualify as a small city.

All along the town's streets were signs advertising the Fall Fair Demolition Derby. Even before Riley's tracking capabilities pointed him toward the event, Remy assumed that was where Tucker was headed. It seemed like his type of recreational activity.

He sought out directions to the fairground and as they drove toward them, his fae companion confirmed that they still had the big Southerner's trail. Finally, they'd parked and gone for a walk amidst the hastily assembled bleachers, the crowds thronging the concession stands and beer tents, and the avenues of trampled grass leading to temporary buildings where the organizers were set up.

"But," Riley asked, "what is a demolition derby? It doesn't seem to make any sense, from what I can see. Is it some kind of punishment ritual for people who are bad drivers?"

"No, but now that you mention it, that would be an excellent idea. I'd go door to door trying to elect the politician who vowed to put that into law. But no, it's a...sport, I guess. They put half a dozen idiots in glass-free cars, plunk them on a muddy field, and have them all deliberately crash into one another in an effort to disable their opponents' vehicles. The last one still operational is crowned the winner. While I could see it being fun to watch, even by my standards it seems a little...stupid."

The fairy circled his head as he walked and when he caught a glimpse of her face, he saw that she was squinting in confusion. "Why? What's stupid about it? I think it's interesting. And it does sound like fun. Humans can't fly, so why shouldn't they enjoy themselves by crashing cars into things?"

"Oh," Remy quipped, "some humans do that anyway but they typically get arrested and fined for it. Somehow, the laws don't seem to apply to rednecks at festivals, though."

"That's strange." She smiled in a curious way as she stared at the arena, where a couple of modified cars were already set up.

He thought of something in that moment. "Get back into my armpit, Riley. Since we're looking for a preternatural, he'll probably be able to see you and might get suspicious. I'm less conspicuous without a miniature naked girl flying around."

She sighed. "Oh, all right."

No sooner had she burrowed under his shirt than he caught sight of a familiar figure.

"Ha," he said and tried not to celebrate prematurely, "the bastard is out walking the crowd. I'll tail him for a while and see what he gets up to."

Tucker was about two hundred feet from where he now stood and faced away from him as he strolled the grounds. He had exchanged his antique white tuxedo for a less dignified but more appropriate outfit consisting of blue jeans, a red t-shirt, and a battered blue baseball cap. The man was barely distinguishable from half the other guys present.

Remy tried to avoid looking directly at the man's back and instead, swung his gaze from side to side to keep track of him, hurried to catch up, then fell into a more casual stroll before he increased his pace again. It seemed to be working.

The large man stopped abruptly and suddenly, a tidal wave of pedestrians appeared from a nearby beer tent and flowed between them to block the stocky Southerner from his sight.

"Crap," he grumbled.

He kept his eyes angled downward as he tried to push through the stampede. The bodies finally cleared and there, directly in front of him, was his quarry.

Tucker looked at him, his face largely neutral, but something about the expression reminded him of a man he'd once encountered who always glowered with low, seething contempt whenever his wife's poodle took a shit. His nostrils flared. Being a werewolf, he likely had an animal's olfactory superiority and might even have smelled his pursuer before he saw him.

"Mr Davis," he said. "What brings you here, if I may ask?"

Remy smiled to buy himself a couple of extra seconds. Now was the time to think on his feet because, quite frankly, he hadn't bothered to come up with a Plan B. He wasn't scared, exactly, but this investigation had already come so far—in no small part thanks to his own efforts—and he refused to screw it up now.

"Oh, well, to be honest," he responded, "I kind of always wanted to drive in a demolition derby myself. It looks like so much fun. I saw one on TV when I was a kid and of course, I immediately asked my father if I could grow up to be a derby guy. He was all, 'Absolutely not, young man. You're a Rem—er, Davis. We Davises don't do stupid, dangerous stuff like that. I can't risk you getting killed or injured.' But now, I'm an adult and can take care of myself, mostly, so I thought I might as well look into it. You wouldn't happen to know the owners or chief operators would you?"

If he was lucky, the answer would be no, and after a few more pleasantries, he could melt back into the crowd.

Tucker's subtle sneer widened into a grin. "Well, as a matter of fact," he began, and Remy's stomach felt much the way it did when an elevator first began its ascent. "The owner, promoter, and manager of this event is none other than Yours Truly."

"Ohhh," he said and maintained his bright smile with

some effort. "That's...great. Now that I think about it, though, there's probably a lot of paperwork involved, qualifications and licenses and all that rigmarole, which you probably don't have time to deal with since you're running a festival here."

"Nonsense," the Southerner responded cheerfully and hooked his big hands into belt loops. "You'd be amazed at what we get away with at these things. Heh, heh. All you need to do is sign a quick waiver—absolving me of any responsibility for injury, of course—and we'll have other people crashing cars into you in no time."

He clapped him on the shoulder with one hand and reached into a back pocket with the other. "I have one of those very forms right here, in fact." Some folded, crushed, and not very clean papers appeared in his hand. "Let me see if I have a pen..."

Riley had become agitated, which made his armpit itch severely.

"Uh," he stammered, "well, I almost feel like...isn't there a training course for this type of thing? It might be better to..."

He trailed off when he noticed that most of the men clustered nearby now watched him and listened unashamedly to the conversation.

Tucker laughed. "Nonsense," he said again. "All you need to know how to do is drive. And don't hit the driver's side—your goal isn't to kill the other guys, only to total their cars."

He peered sidelong at the younger man. "Say...you ain't having second thoughts, are you? I never met the man who said he dreamed of participating in a demolition derby and didn't actually mean it. Backing out now would be like a betrayal of your dreams." He shook his head with mock sadness.

Now, Remy's teeth clenched and his hands curled into fists. All the hicks smirked at him.

"And," the big man went on, "I might have to contact the agency, in that case, to make sure this isn't some kind of surreptitious effort to shut down this popular, family-oriented festival."

He took a step forward. "I'll do it. The sooner the better, in fact. I've already waited long enough. I might as well get on with living out my childhood dream."

Tucker, looking pleased with himself, extended the paper and a battered plastic pen. "Well, that makes me as happy as a dead pig in the sunshine. Sign at the bottom, please."

Remy skimmed the text of the waiver only briefly before he scrawled, *Remington Davis* into the blank space above the line.

"Right," he stated, "now show me which car I'll be using, and—"

"You provide your own." The man interrupted him. "In fact, it even says that right…here." He pointed to a place on one of the forms he had just signed.

He cleared his throat. "Of course. So…ah, show me where to pull up for the…uh, pit crew or whatever to look me over."

It didn't take long. Tucker produced a trio of underlings who personally accompanied him back to his car, stood and waited while he started the engine, and directed him to a makeshift garage.

"This," one of the men said with a huge grin, "is a Lexus, my man. Are you sure you want to enter it in a derby?"

Remy glowered. "It's three years outdated. And I have no sentimental attachment to it whatsoever." He tried not to grind his teeth, although the latter part was true. Of the three, the Lincoln was his favorite.

"If you say so." The man shrugged.

The pit crew explained that they needed to remove all the glass for safety reasons, which they did with stunning speed and an array of tools he had never seen or heard of before. That done, they slammed his driver's side door shut, spray-painted it white, and painted the numeral five in black atop the white.

"Thanks," he said and tried to think of all the maintenance costs he'd save as a result of never having to care about this vehicle again.

The lead mechanic nodded to him. "Buckle your safety belt and head right on over there."

Another guy directed him down a dirt path toward the big central mud-ring where four other cars were already assembled. Two more men quickly removed the blockade around the ring and motioned for him to drive in.

He complied with the greatest reluctance and a bright smile.

"Umm," Riley's voice said from her armpit lair, "this might not be a good idea, Remy…"

Before he could respond, a loudspeaker crackled and a familiar, Southern-accented voice asked everyone to pipe down. Silence settled in as the crowd shut up and took notice.

"Ladies and gentlemen," Tucker announced, "welcome

to the thirteenth annual New York Fall Fair Demolition Derby. Before we get on with the event, let me take a moment to thank our sponsors…"

As Tucker kissed the asses of the various companies who'd helped make this event possible, Remy examined the competition.

The other four vehicles consisted of two sedans, a brown one and a black one, numbered one and two, respectively, a red pickup truck numbered three, and a blue SUV numbered four. The drivers were a motley group but something in their expression and demeanor was shared among all four. They were members of the same tightly-knit subculture and he was an outsider.

The fairy wriggled her way up his chest and poked her head out the top of his shirt. "They're going to crash into us? Is this car made for that?"

"No."

"Well, I can probably enchant it to be more resilient—not invincible, but it ought to give you an edge."

Some of Remy's confidence came back to him like the manic boost of a sugar rush. "That…would be helpful, even though my driving skills are top-notch. What would I do without you, Riley?"

She giggled. "You'd be lonely, for one thing."

Tucker finally reached the part of his introductory spiel that everyone cared about.

"Now, let's get introduced to our demo drivers. In addition to four returning fan favorites, we also have some fresh meat on display."

The crowd reacted to this with a mixture of cheering

and laughter. Some of that laughter was good-natured and some definitely not.

The man went on to name each of the first four drivers and they honked their horns after he'd revealed their names. Remy paid little attention to them. He could always write them down later if he needed to for legal purposes.

"And finally, appearing here for the first time, Mr Remington Davis from Manhattan. Isn't that a fancy car he's driving?"

The crowd guffawed at this.

"Well," he said, mostly to himself, "I can't blame them for wanting to see something so expensive get smashed to hell." When he was six or seven years old, he'd deliberately shattered his aunt's crystal mirror, simply because he could.

"But wait," Tucker announced, "there's one other thing. Mr Davis has volunteered to motivate the other drivers to put in their best damn performance ever. He even signed for it. Heh, heh. Anyone who totals his car will get a bonus prize of ten thousand dollars, cash."

The crowd went wild. Now, Remy saw, his four rivals stared at him with something almost like hunger.

He glanced at the passenger seat, where Riley seemed to have settled. "How's that enchantment coming?"

The fairy twisted her hands in circles and subtle flashes of silver light erupted from different parts of the car's frame. He only hoped that Tucker, perched high in the observation building, wouldn't notice. The sun was bright and clouds moved over it constantly, so the spell's effects might be mistaken for natural glare when it emerged from behind cover.

She put such focus into her spell that she gave off a faint thrum. "Done." Her arms fell to her sides.

"Okay then." He breathed deeply, adjusted his tie at the neck, and wiped his hands on the car seat.

"Start your engines," Tucker bellowed, "and begin on my count."

Remy turned the key and the other drivers did likewise. The revving almost drowning out the announcer.

"...two, one, *drive!*"

With almost giddy abandon, he pounded on the gas and accelerated directly toward the nearest vehicle—black number 2.

"Ha, ha." He laughed. "Yeah, let's fucking do this. It's like playing chicken back in—"

Brown number one had started at an angle to his right and now veered toward his passenger's side, its souped-up engine growling with fury. Its front bumper rammed into his front side door.

"Shit!" he cried as metal crunched and the world shook. He was knocked off-course and the car rumbled through the mud in a broad arc to miss black number two by at least a yard.

When he glanced to his right, though, he saw that the sound of crunching metal had mostly come from the brown car's bumper. His door seemed...fine, mostly.

"Goddamn, Riley!" he exclaimed and grinned. "That actually worked."

"Of course it did!" she shouted back. She dove toward him and wriggled under his shirt.

In front of him, red number three and blue number four crashed into one another, their front ends colliding as each tried to force the other aside. He dodged them for now. They weren't trying to defeat the other, yet. They were fighting to get at him.

Dimly, he registered the presence of the crowd and the almost deafening noise, but mostly, his perception had narrowed to the derby itself. The wheel spun under his hands as he snaked his car around the perimeter of the battle arena in search of a rematch with the black car, which had outpaced the damaged brown one and now approached at speed.

"This time," he vowed, "you're going down."

The other three vehicles ground against each other as Remy and number two sought a head-on collision. Both pressed hard on the gas, although the mud slowed them somewhat. An awful lot of gunk had already splashed inside and ruined the interior, but he barely noticed.

The black car careened toward him and he scowled at the front of the vehicle that seemed to encompass the entire space where his windshield had been.

His jaw clenched. "Here it comes—"

The world exploded, or so it seemed. Everything shook and spun so much he could not even see what was happening. But he wasn't airborne. Darkness and weight bore down on the roof, which sank a few inches and actually brushed his hair.

Then, suddenly, he hurtled ahead with no obstacles.

"What the hell?" he gasped. He looked over his shoulder.

Black number two had flipped over its own hood, landed on top of him, and rolled onto its wheels. The crowd had gone completely wild. A fat guy in the stands jumped up and down and spilled a gigantic cup's worth of carbonated citrus all over the people next to him.

Riley laughed with mad glee from her place under his arm. "Wow. That was really fun," she all but shrieked.

He blinked as he turned. "It was, actually. It was."

Remy realized that while his car was still taking some damage, the other drivers, by now, probably wondered how the hell he held up so well—by rights, he should have already been totaled.

His four nemeses lined up to advance on him like a Greek phalanx. Slipping between them or going around all four in the limited time he had before impact would have been almost impossible. But he had another idea.

"Prepare to be disqualified, you pricks," he muttered and stamped hard on the gas.

He aimed directly toward them, then pulled a sudden U-turn, fishtailed his driver's side toward their front bumpers, and put himself in immediate risk of being crunched.

Numbers one, two, and four all applied the brakes while they jerked their steering wheels aside and scraped against one another as their wheels kicked entire sheets of mud into the air. His front end destroyed the front right headlight of number three, the red pickup that had been at the end of the column, and he cackled when he broke free of them.

The respite was short-lived. He saw the drivers exchange glances and nod at one another.

"Aw, hell," he said, "it looks like they agreed to split the pot."

All four of the rival vehicles burst into action. They

separated and made for, roughly, the four points of the compass.

Remy guessed their plan at once—a combined charge from four different directions, designed to trap him while they turned his car into a strange, S-shaped metal object.

"These guys," he admitted, "have some chutzpah, I have to admit. They'll probably total their own vehicles with this shit. I guess if that's how they want to play, then—"

The four engines screamed as wheels spun. There was nothing to do, he decided, but attempt a mutual kill.

He accelerated only a fraction of a second after his foes did. It would literally be only a second or two until impact.

A quick mental calculation presented itself. Black two and red three would collide with his front corners. Brown one headed toward his rear driver's side corner, and blue four was about to T-bone him on the passenger's side. He had one avenue of escape.

His right hand fell to his side and clicked his seatbelt off at the same time as his left hand opened the car door.

Riley's voice, barely audible amidst the din, cried, "What are you—"

He jumped.

The ground pounded into him, threw him, and rolled him like a piece of dough destined for spaghetti. Pain and shock followed, mud and noise were everywhere, and twisting, shattering metal howled in what almost sounded like pain. He somersaulted into a barricade and lay still but the earth somehow still rotated around him.

The crowd cheered in a downright frenzy.

Remy scrambled to his feet and identified a few places

in his legs and left shoulder that would probably need examining later. He felt giddy and half-nauseated.

In front of him was a Lovecraftian clusterfuck of vehicular abomination. All five vehicles had been totaled.

"Hah!" he cackled. "No one gets the bonus." He wobbled in place and braced himself against the barrier in an effort to not fall. A few people in the audience ran up and supported him on their arms while they laughed and shook his hand.

The loudspeakers crackled. "Well, I'll be damned," Tucker's voice began, "it appears we have a washout. Let's congratulate all five of our losers on their mutual failure."

A few spectators laughed at that but mostly, they seemed floored by Remy's sheer audacity.

He smiled and waved as they began to surround him. "Thanks…thanks. Is there a medical examiner on hand? You might want to check on those other guys, too. I think they're alive."

A hasty glance at the wreckage confirmed that the other four motorists stumbled out of their wrecked vehicles. At least they weren't dead.

Riley, who'd somehow remained lodged under his arm this whole time, shouted toward his ear through the cacophony. "We need to leave."

"Good idea," he whispered and smiled and waved as he shoved his way through the people around him.

He hurried away from the ring and ducked between milling herds of admirers—some of whom catcalled or patted him on the back—and tried to put as much distance as possible between himself and Tucker, whom he suspected would descend from his perch at any moment.

His legs and shoulder still hurt, but at least he was now out of sight—and reach—of most of the audience. A small voice emerged from within his shirt. "Now, please let me out of here. It's getting so hot and stinky."

Remy glanced around. No obvious preternaturals were in sight and he had no reason to believe that any of the normals would be able to see the Fair Folk.

"Okay," he whispered and raised his arm.

A small bulge moved up his chest before she burst out from the collar of his shirt, literally shaking sweat from her hair as she hovered in midair.

"Thanks, by the way," he said. "But yeah, let's get the hell out of here, shall we? Before I attract even more attention. Although I suppose the ship has already sailed on the whole low-key investigation secret-agent type shit."

And, of course, he no longer had a drivable car.

He pulled his cell phone out and called up the rideshare app. Idly, he wondered if his old pal Stanislaw drove this far upstate. Probably not, although he would have happily endured his life stories all the way home.

CHAPTER SEVENTEEN

Fall Fair Demolition Derby, Middletown, New York

Jenny Ocren, a reporter for the Page Six, stood gawking at the fiery, smoking aftermath of the derby. She had to write this down but before she was even physically capable of pulling her tablet out, she needed to wrack her brain to confirm what she'd actually seen.

Or, more precisely, who she'd seen—David Remington. It had to be him. She'd met the handsome, smarmy bastard once at some bland gala charity event his parents had hosted.

Her hand went into her pocket and retrieved her tablet. Feverishly, trying not to stick her tongue out the corner of her mouth—as she'd done far too often as a child—she added a ream of shorthand notes describing all she'd witnessed.

It was incredible—the gold-plated heir to a multibillion-dollar family fortune, mixing it up with these salt-of-the-earth types and risking life and limb in a contest of steel against steel.

Demolition derbies were something of a guilty pleasure of hers, to begin with. It was always fun to observe the devastation and pad out the storylines behind it. But she'd never expected to see him there.

David Remington did have a reputation as a playboy, bad boy, thrill-seeker, and so forth. She and her co-workers had helped leak some of the earliest rumors surrounding that infamous party—the one that had spawned all the lawsuits. The "respectable" press quickly picked up on the aroma of scandal and subsequently conducted their own investigations.

Jenny snorted as she finished writing. "Respectable press," she muttered. "I fail to see how they're really any different than we are. They simply do the follow-up and make it more presentable. We're the ones on the front lines out here."

Some guy whom she had tried to interview once had asked "What's it like, working for a gossip site? Your work doesn't even see print."

She had maintained her professional composure and explained to him that all journalists did important work by drawing society's attention to significant events. He'd merely taken another swig of beer, ignored her, and made his way to the dance floor.

The reporter drove this irksome memory from her consciousness as people jostled past her, heading to the outhouses or the concession stand now that the big match was over. Instead, she tried to think of why Mr Remington had turned to a life of automotive self-vandalism.

"Maybe," she said, softly, "he has...gambling debts. No. The lawsuits. Either they're negotiating an out-of-court settlement and the potential payouts are threatening him financially or the stress and attention are causing his mind to crack. Now, filled with unhinged aggression, he seeks relief in the crunching of car frames and the burning of rubber, his only solace the symphony of controlled destruction in which he must play the active role...."

It sounded good. Lacking any actual evidence, however, she would have to be careful about how she worded it. Page Six didn't have much budget for litigation.

Jenny looked around for the beefy Southern guy who seemed to be running the operation. She might be able to coax a quick interview out of him. But, browsing through the stands and the crowds and even poking around at the official buildings yielded no results. The man had vanished somewhere into the chaos.

"Dammit," she muttered. "Well, at least I have David. How difficult can he be to track? I bet he's been doing all kinds of other interesting things lately."

She grinned and pulled her phone out to call her boss. Without a doubt, she had a good feeling about this.

Harrison, Westchester County, New York

Remy slumped in his usual chair in the foyer and allowed his head to rest on one fist while Presley examined his shoulder and legs. He decided he ought to wait until the old man had checked him thoroughly for serious injuries before he attempted to flee.

"You idiot!" Taylor raged and her fangs showed beneath her upper lip for the first time since he'd met her. She swiped a long-nailed finger through the air in his general direction. "A quarter of the state of New York has now connected you to Tucker and his fucking bumper-car shit-show. What the hell were you thinking?"

"Well…" He shrugged. "At least I found him. We know he's connected to the…uh, demolition derby industry. I had to participate in order to keep my cover from being blown."

She threw her hands up and looked at the ceiling. "You already blew it. The instant he saw you, you were fucked and should simply have turned and left. Sometimes, we have to cut our losses. Instead, you had to keep losing, and losing, and losing."

The butler prodded his shoulder blade. "It doesn't seem to be dislocated, sir."

"Thanks, Presley," said Remy.

"Now," Taylor continued, her usually soft voice practically booming, "our enemies know we're onto them, which destroys our ability to take any stealthy or subtle actions against them. And"—she looked back at him, took a heavy step closer, and extended her finger toward his face—"while I'm trying to stop them from killing us, there is now the possibility that the Moonlight Detective Agency will be mentioned on the Internet and the goddamn evening news for everyone and their grandmother to hear about. Do you realize why that is a problem?"

He allowed himself to sulk, even though he definitely recognized the possible repercussions. Painful though it was to admit, he had fucked up. Still, he wasn't about to go down without a fight.

"In all fairness," he replied and looked squarely into the woman's wide, dark eyes, "you did beat up an entire hotel a few nights ago, didn't you? Wouldn't that have clued them in already?"

She snapped her jaw shut, straightened stiffly, and folded her arms over her chest. "Yes." Her voice was calmer again now. "But—and this is important—I knew exactly what I was doing. I sent them a message, but it's not the kind of message they can publicly acknowledge. To accuse me of attacking their hideaway is to admit they were meeting secretly to plot something, to begin with."

Remy frowned. She had a point there.

"And," she went on, "the press, not to mention social media, were not involved. I would be shocked if at least twenty people didn't capture your little stunt on their phone cameras and haven't already uploaded it to YouTube. Tucker might be able to turn this to his advantage, somehow—perhaps by directing too much human attention toward us for us to be able to act at all without getting in deep shit. He's not a moron. His dumb hick act is only a façade. You underestimated him and, clearly, all of us overestimated you."

It had been a while since he had been chewed out to this extent. Especially by someone other than his own family. He did not speak.

Presley seemed to have finished his medical exam. "You are not seriously injured, Mr Remington, but you'll want to avoid strenuous physical activity for the next week to ten days, I'd estimate. If you start to feel worse, you should see a proper doctor."

Taylor flipped a hand toward Remy again. "And you were hurt on company time. Publicly. You can't do half the things I might need you to do, and I don't have time for fucking around. I have connections that can defang most governmental organizations, but it takes time. Do you have any idea how much bullshit paperwork is involved with workplace injuries, workman's comp, and all that crap?"

He vaguely recalled his father discussing such things once, but he hadn't paid much attention. Sex, drugs, and rock n' roll were more interesting.

After a moment, he looked at Taylor and tried a joke. "So, then, it sounds like my promotion will be delayed. But...uh, seriously...I'm sorry. I'll try to deal with all the media stuff myself if I have to—that won't involve strenuous physical activity, anyway. And I can probably take the fall for my own actions. You can claim I acted on my own, not under your direction."

She put her hands on her hips and shook her head. "Go home, David Remington, and get some rest. Take tomorrow off. But think very, very hard about what you plan to do next. Because if this is how you intend to operate, you're better off not coming back."

The vampire turned away from him and walked down the hallway to vanish into the shadows of the old house.

With a heavy sigh, Remy pushed to his feet. "And here I was believing that she'd at least think the whole jumping-out-of-the-car thing was completely killer-bad."

Presley put a hand on his shoulder. "You'd best do as the mistress suggested, sir. Call a car to take you home and spend a little time recuperating."

"I think I need to, at this point." He groaned. "Maybe I'll even remember your name. What was it, again?"

The butler folded his hands behind his back. "Your

attempts at humor are appreciated," he commented, "but not particularly successful. Good evening, sir."

He wandered out the front door and into the cool night air. Presley shut the door behind him.

Riley had perched herself either on his head or his forearm during the whole dressing-down but had not spoken until now. As they descended the winding path through the estate's grounds toward the gate, the fairy detached herself from him and flew in front of his face.

"Hey," she said in what was probably intended to be a cute voice, "don't worry too much. I thought the car thing was awesome." She tittered and fluttered her tiny eyelashes at him. "In fact...it even makes me kind of...excited to think about it. I like men like you, human or otherwise."

She was so close to his face now that he was afraid she would try to kiss him on the mouth. Or, rather, on one tiny corner of his upper lip.

"Riley," he said and no longer even tried to fight the black mood that swelled out of him. There was no point in restraining it. He was born to be an asshole. "Why don't you give it up? Your sexual interest in me displays a fundamental ignorance of rudimentary physics, for fuck's sake. Think about it. Your entire body is smaller than...never mind. It simply won't happen so you might as well stop acting like a stupid little girl."

The fairy flinched. Her jaw dropped and eyes widened as if he'd actually slapped her. "That's it!" she shrieked, her chipmunk's voice surprisingly loud. Tears so minuscule they were practically water vapor flowed from her eyes. "I will give it up. I'm going back to my nest. Don't ever ask me for anything ever again!"

Sobbing, she flapped her wings and rocketed herself into the trees. In an instant, she was gone.

He stopped where he stood and looked at the ground for a moment. After a few breaths, he rolled his head in a circle and cracked his neck. It made him feel marginally better.

"Well," he said to no one at all, "I'd say it's time for a drink."

Por's Bar, Lower Manhattan, New York City

Remy pushed his way into the basement tavern and noticed immediately that it was far busier than it had been a few days before. Granted, that had been in the afternoon and this was the hour when New York's vibrant nightlife was reaching its full stride.

About half the tables were occupied, mostly by humanoids, but a few by strange creatures he could not identify right away. The lighting was dim and the angles of the shadows hid many of the clientele. Several forms mingled freely on the open space around the solitary pool table.

Conscious of how caked with sweat he was after his misadventure at the demolition derby, he ignored the other patrons and made a beeline for the bar. His purpose there was straightforward. He needed to kill some brain cells.

Porrillage the gnome stood upon a pyramid of boxes, his back to the bar as he filled a mug with frothy golden beer for another customer. When he turned, he saw Remy at once.

"You again?" he remarked in his thin yet gruff voice. He climbed down and handed the beer to a wan and grizzled-looking man who might have been undead. Remy couldn't be sure.

"Correct," he said gloomily.

The gnome wiped his hands off on his apron. "What does Taylor want this time? A shipment of liquid courage for her helpers with all the crap she's getting herself into lately?"

He mounted a stool and leaned forward on his elbows. "No, what she wants is for me to go away and leave her alone for the next thirty-six hours. I'm here purely on my own initiative. And what I want is...let's say, a whiskey and Coke on the rocks. Light on the Coke and ice, heavy on the whiskey." He sniffed. "Don't worry, I managed to total my car earlier so someone else will do the driving."

Por shrugged. "Whatever you say, pal." He turned to retrieve a glass and a bottle of nice blended Irish. "It sucks about your car, though. What the hell happened?"

Remy glanced briefly at the guy two seats to his right, who'd ordered the mug of beer. He did look like a corpse but he smelled kind of dry and spicy, which made him wonder if the man were an unwrapped mummy.

Turning his head toward the gnome, he explained, "Oh, you know, I was forced to enter it in a demolition derby. The other cars already did half the work the scrappers would normally have to do when salvaging the parts."

"Hah!" The bartender scoffed. "Yeah, that'll do it. I wasn't aware that anyone was ever forced to enter a demo derby, though. Are ya sure you didn't simply make a hasty-ass decision?"

"Anyone," Remy stated firmly, "would have done the same thing in my position."

By now, Por had filled the glass about two-thirds with whiskey over a cursory smattering of ice and was in the process of topping it off with fizzing brown cola. "Yeah, yeah, that's what they all say. Here ya go, buddy." He walked along the single wooden beam along the floor that acted as a step for him to reach the bar and pushed the glass toward him.

"Thanks." He raised it in a mock toast and drank about a third of it at once. "Ahh. Very refreshing in a burning kind of way."

Over the course of the next couple of minutes, he drank another third and grew pleasantly woozy while the gnome hurried around to tend to the other customers seated at the bar and dispatch a waitress to deal with the folks at the tables.

When the proprietor had a moment and was again within earshot, Remy said, "You know...if Taylor does want a shipment of liquid courage for her minions, she'll probably need a considerably supply, especially if she doesn't want me to help out. I basically won that derby, even though I have zero experience with crashing my car into others. Intentionally, anyway."

The gnome gave him a squinty look. "Hmph. What happened this time, Mr Bigshot?"

He told him the entire story in great detail and tried conscientiously not to slur his words.

"It's horseshit," Remy concluded. "Sure, I made more noise than I was supposed to, but I intimidated the hell out of that guy, Tucker. He knows, now, that Taylor has someone in her corner who he shouldn't fuck around with. And she yells at me and practically kicks me out. Now, I have to go sit in the corner and think about what I've done. For fuck's sake."

"Well…" Porrillage snorted. "What did you expect? You basically did the complete opposite of what Moonlight Detective Agency is supposed to do. Aren't you supposed to be on mitigation? Creating a gigantic media feeding frenzy isn't a very good way to mitigate much of anything."

He waved a hand flippantly. "It's only one battle. And it wasn't so much a loss as a strategic retreat or something like that. It puts us in a better position to win the war." He took a final swig from his glass, emptied it of liquid, and retained one of the ice cubes in his mouth.

"How do you reach that conclusion?" the gnome mused. "In any event, Taylor might have been more forgiving of your cock-up if you'd taken immediate measures to, you know, mitigate your own actions and approached her with an apology and a plan. Instead, it sounds like you kinda waltzed into her house expecting to be praised instead of convincing her you deserve praise."

Remy rolled his tongue around the melting ice cube as he considered this statement.

So what he's saying is that if I come up with a really good plan—which I'm sure I can—and work harder at persuading her of my value to the agency….

"Por," he proclaimed and slapped a hand firmly on the bar, "you're right. Someone of my talents has a responsibility to convince someone like Taylor that I'm not merely someone she can brush off due to a minor error. She told me to take tomorrow off, but I'll go back to her house an hour before sundown so that I can give her a piece of my mind as soon as she gets up."

The proprietor raised his eyebrows as he nodded very slowly. "Yeah. Good luck with that, pal."

"Thanks." He stood, smiled, and dropped a business card on the counter so Por could bill him for the drink later before he half-stumbled toward the exit. He pulled out his phone to secure a ride. To his amusement, one of the available drivers was a guy named Stan.

Riverside Boulevard, New York City Waterfront

Just beyond the warehouse, the first rays of dawn cast glimmering streaks of rosy crimson and sparkling gold across the choppy waters. This was the hour when most vampires would retire to their coffins if they hadn't already.

Gabriel, on the other hand, was still very much out and about.

He snapped his fingers toward a pair of men who carried a heavy wooden crate from the shipping ware-house to one of the trucks. "You," he intoned. "Bring that over here. I wish to inspect it."

Looking put-upon, they took deep breaths and hauled the crate in his direction to set it on a low, broad concrete ledge.

The man on the left looked at the vampire and seemed perplexed by the fact he wore sunglasses before the sun had even risen. "Do you wanna look inside?" He reached for a crowbar hanging from his belt.

As he stepped toward the crate, Tucker suddenly

appeared from somewhere off to the right. "Let the man have a look," he said. "'Course, he'll find that everything is exactly as it should be but I can't blame him for wanting to see with his own eyes." He hooked his thumbs into the lapel of his jacket.

Gabriel glanced at his partner before he returned his gaze to the cargo. "Thank you, Tucker." Ignoring the man's offered crowbar, he cracked his knuckles and tore the top off the crate with one hand. The workers stepped back, immediately tense.

Within, partially hidden by packaging materials, was a nice selection of automatic weapons. There were rifles elsewhere, but these were mostly high-caliber sub-machine guns—compact but powerful. A few riot shotguns ought to be in one of the other crates, as well.

All, of course, were highly illegal. But that wasn't a problem. They had managed to evade any unwanted attention from the Bureau of Alcohol, Tobacco, and Firearms, and the vampire had ensured that bribes made their way into the hands of any inspectors or NYPD officers who might get in the way as well.

"Good." The corners of his lips turned upwards. He replaced the crate's lid and used the flat of his palm to pound the nails back in place. "You men may proceed."

The workers nodded, hoisted the crate up, and took it to one of the trucks which would soon be bound for Gabriel's personal estate.

Tucker sidled up and smirked. "Yessir," he stated cheer-fully, "things are coming along nicely. They probably don't even realize how far along we are. Heh, heh."

Before his companion could respond to this, a few

sleek, old-fashioned cars pulled up along the edge of the docks. The men who stepped out as the doors opened wore suits and hats.

The werewolf chortled. "I see the Italians are fashionably late again."

Albert and three of his bodyguards wasted no time and strode over to where the vampire and the Southerner stood. Albert, as usual, seemed shifty and nervous. But once he satisfied himself that he'd not walked into a trap, he dismissed his henchmen and stood alone with the other two.

Gabriel cracked a single knuckle. "How nice of you to join us, Albert. Finally."

"Yeah, yeah," the mobster replied. "I had to do a little quality control on an operation that was making too much noise. I'm sure you gentlemen can appreciate the value of keeping things nice and quiet at a time like this."

"Indeed," said their leader dismissively.

Tucker grimaced and added, "I had to fob off some interviews with the dadgummit press over that little stunt Taylor's pretty boy pulled at my derby. But don't worry, my boys will handle it. If we're lucky, that idiot will traipse off to Connecticut or something and drag the reporters with him, while we—"

"He should," Gabriel interrupted, his voice loud and sharp, "be traipsing off to hell as we speak. But somehow"—he glared at the new arrival—"both of you failed to kill him. A mortal. A rookie in the preternatural world, no less. How is that, may I ask?"

Albert spoke first and rubbed his nose with a knuckle. "He had some fairy with him. One of my guys told the little bitch to get lost when he came into the casino, but he must have hooked up with her afterward—she's the only reason my guy Joe wasn't able to exterminate the bastard."

Gabriel turned to Tucker.

"Well, the boy has some talent for driving, and his car held up better than it should have. Hell, maybe that fairy enchanted the damn thing. It's purely his luck, though, that he bailed out of the car before he was obliterated."

The mobster snorted. "So you planned to derby him to death? That's not the way to do away with a man quietly, my friend."

The other werewolf narrowed his eyes. "People have been known to die in sporting events. Accidents happen. Murder by gun, on the other hand, tends to draw attention even when it happens someplace out of the way. I would have thought you'd know that."

Bristling, the mobster snarled. "Don't try to lecture me, fat boy, on—"

"Silence," Gabriel interjected sharply and raised his voice enough to shut them both up. "Think no more about it. We will let bygones be bygones. That Remington imbecile seems to have unnatural luck, but he is not the main target here anyway. He will be of little concern once Taylor is dealt with. And deal with her we shall. Today."

The lycanthropes calmed.

All three of them understood the ramifications of this. The limitations under which they'd been forced to operate would be removed. The natural order would return. Earth's most bounteous harvest was human flesh and blood—and all of it would be theirs for the reaping.

The vampire cracked the knuckles of his right hand

again. "Albert, I want you to personally stay out of the operation, but we will go ahead and allow some of your men to accompany Tucker and his group. It helps to have professionals on board and it's best your own hands stay clean."

The mobster swept the area around him quickly with his characteristic shifty-eyed glance, then nodded. "Yeah. I'll send top-level guys, though, but ones who can't be traced back to me if something goes wrong."

"Good," Gabriel said before Tucker could reignite tensions with some smart-ass comment. "Tucker, I understand that you've rehearsed this operation on your end several times over. My people and I will direct our efforts to keep the other preternaturals from interfering."

So far, everything was coming along precisely on that front. His agents had intercepted messages, sowed disinformation, disabled vehicles, and otherwise, done all they could think of to slow any response and create dissension in the ranks. Taylor's mansion was not even guarded, at present, except by a few basic security systems and her elderly lupine manservant.

Once the plan was set in motion, her sycophants would spit out their drinks, stumble over their words, and try to spring into action. But they would find that the rebel forces were more than prepared for them.

The vampire continued with his reminder to Tucker. "You, however, will handle the most important part of the entire mission. We rely on you to not drop the ball."

The lycanthrope chuckled. "The ball will remain undropped, Gabe. Don't you worry. We'll have that coffin out of there in a jiffy, kept so tightly under lock and key a fly won't be able to take a shit on it without us knowing."

Their leader leaned back, flexed his hands, and allowed a slow, smoldering grin to spread across his face. "Good. And then, while Taylor's allies flail uselessly and beat their heads against our defenses, or argue amongst themselves, or pretend not to believe what's happened…we kill her while she lies helpless."

CHAPTER EIGHTEEN

Harrison, Westchester County, New York

Remy pulled into Taylor's driveway, now behind the wheel of the Lincoln—his favorite. Driving it made him feel better and so much more in control.

He'd also decided not to wait until the hours of the sun's dwindling. Something about choosing high noon as the time to climb into his car and head north instilled a feeling of invincibility in him. He arrived in Harrison around one pm, exactly as he'd expected.

If he hung around the mansion for a few hours, it would make it harder to wuss out of confronting Taylor—and give him sufficient time to think of what he'd say. Presley would not persuade him to leave, either. He'd made his mind up.

When he arrived at the front gate, three or four minutes of buzzing failed to summon the butler.

"Well, that's odd," he murmured with mild confusion. "Then again, old boy Jeeves might be napping at this hour. It's not like he had any reason to expect me to come over."

He noticed, though, that the gate was ajar. When he pushed it with his hand, it swung open easily. The latch was broken.

"Ookaay. Something's wrong here." His hackles raised, he pushed the gate open himself and eased the car through. He drove slowly all the way to the garage and scrutinized the area. The door didn't open for him as usual. Something really was wrong.

The daytime there was so quiet. When he arrived shortly before dawn or after twilight, there were always birds and insects and reptiles making their night-sounds from whatever shadowed recess they happened to be hiding in. Under the sun, the estate seemed almost dead.

Remy saw nothing on his way to the front door. Not knowing what to expect, he knocked. He wasn't really surprised when he received no answer. After a minute, he knocked again with the same lack of response.

"Hmm." He adjusted his tie. "I hope they won't hold it against me if I have to climb in through a window."

Before he tried that, though, he turned the knob absentmindedly on the right-side door. He'd not expected it to work but it did. The door clicked and swung open.

"Old boy Jeeves is getting sloppy in his age." He tried to convince himself of the innocuous explanation, but his skin had begun to crawl.

Inside, he looked around. Some of the rugs were scrunched against walls, and a dirty footprint was visible in the middle of the hardwood floor.

He wished he'd brought a weapon. Not that he owned any guns—that was a no-no in NYC—but at least a knife or a baseball bat, or something.

His hasty glance alighted on an empty vase which might be a viable option and he grasped it by the neck. It was about the size and shape of a thirty-two-ounce beer bottle—a well-respected instrument, in certain circles, of violent blunt-force trauma.

"The cellar," he said to himself. "I need to check on Taylor."

Remy had never been down there before, but he knew where he'd seen her emerge from in the evenings and where she went after she said, "Good morning." He crept slowly down the hallway.

When he reached the door, distinctive cracks in the wood near the knob's base suggested that someone had used excessive force to overcome a lock. It was one he hadn't opened before, but he was not surprised to know it had a lock. And by now, he was not surprised the lock had been damaged.

He gave it a tentative shove. Slowly, it creaked inwards.

The staircase beyond descended into thick darkness. It was not totally black but close enough that he could see nothing at first. He felt along the wall for a switch and fumbled overhead for a chain or string but found nothing.

She probably doesn't even have lights in here. Which makes total sense. She can see in the dark and this is where she hides from the sun, so why would she need them?

Until now, he had simply reacted without any real thought. Fortunately, his brain had begun to adjust to the ominous situation and produce some constructive ideas. He pulled his phone out and turned on the flashlight app.

Along one wall, wrapping around behind the staircase, were wooden shelves piled with round casks and barrels.

Wine, undoubtedly. He wondered vaguely if the old gal had any Amontillado. That would be all too appropriate.

A large, antique wardrobe stood against the other wall, shut tight against the damp subterranean chill. That would explain how Taylor often seemed to emerge from her slumber fully dressed.

Finally, in the center of the floor was a stone rectangle that Remy at first mistook for a well or something. After he squinted at it for a moment, he recognized it as a sarcophagus raised on stone slabs like a high bed. The lid was propped alongside it.

It was surprisingly cold down there, and he shivered as he advanced toward the room itself. Within was nothing, only shadows and dust. In the outline of the grime, a smaller coffin-shape made a shocking statement.

His shoulders slumped and his stomach almost dropped out of him. "Oh, hell. They stole her goddamn coffin!"

He spun and raised the vase instinctively over his shoulder in case anyone leapt out at him. To his relief, he heard nothing and saw only darkened earth.

"No," he whispered. "There is nothing to suggest they're still here. They're long gone by now. But where to?"

He raised a thumb to his lips and brushed them absently while he wracked his brain. It occurred to him that he'd seen detective shit on TV and in movies. They consulted with experts about stuff like that, didn't they?

"Okay, uh..." He looked for a trail—any kind of trail. It did look somewhat like the vampire-abductors had dragged a large, heavy object across the dusty basement floor and to the stairs.

"Well," he muttered hoarsely, "that's about the only place they could take it."

Confirmation came in the form for a long, thick splinter of dark wood on the third stair up. He hadn't noticed it on the way down since he hadn't had his lightbulb idea of using his phone for illumination at that point. Now, however, the light caught the dark stained wood against the dull stone. Was it from her coffin? It seemed very likely.

Grimly, he continued upward and through the house. There were a couple more vague footprints here and there, indications that a group of men had walked through. But outside, there was nothing. The vamp-nappers must have been pros and they'd almost certainly had a vehicle waiting for them.

Remy stood out in the driveway, his hands on his hips, and stared at nothing at all.

He had no idea where to go or what to do.

"Think," he told himself. "They could have taken it to...uh..."

Middletown? The site of Tucker's derby? *No, that makes no sense. And it's too far.* He also considered Albert's casino briefly. That seemed slightly more likely, but barely. It didn't feel right.

That merely left the entire remainder of New York City and its surrounding environs spread across three or four states—the mother of all haystacks.

Remy's shoulders slumped again and the air drained out of his lungs. "Fuck. I'm in way over my head here. Where the hell is the butler? Who else might be able to help?"

The Fluttershire fairies. He had to find Riley and woo her back.

He practically hurled himself toward his car and wondered how far their enemies had already traveled and how close they might be to destroying Taylor's coffin or whatever other awful thing they had in mind.

"Wait." He gasped and stopped his hands before he opened the car door. "I'll need a sample for her to sniff."

Assuming Riley would even speak to him again.

He rushed to the kitchen and rummaged through drawers before he found some plastic sandwich baggies. With those in hand, he returned to the crypt and found the long jagged splinter, which he assumed was from the coffin which now held Taylor conveniently captive for their enemies. He slid it carefully into the bag and tried not to touch it with his hands, exactly like he'd seen on TV.

"Now," he whispered, "transportation. And not my own car. The bastards might already know what else I drive. Besides, no one's here to tell me no, are they?"

The door from the house's interior to the garage was not locked. The intruders must have forced it open while securing their perimeter or whatever. Remy hoped they hadn't trashed all the vehicles.

He flipped the light on and stepped into the sprawling structure. Everything looked fine. The attackers might have searched the area, but they'd left the vehicles alone. It did, he surmised, take valuable time to destroy a collection of vehicles when you probably only planned to kill their owner, anyway.

The keys were not difficult to find—they lay behind a false panel on the wall, similar to a device that one of his mother's friends had. He wondered why Taylor didn't keep them in a safe or something and under a combination lock, but that was really irrelevant in that moment.

As he clicked the fob to find which of the Teslas went with the key he'd selected, it occurred to him exactly how confident she was.

Her mansion was not a fortress. It wasn't easy to find and it had basic security, but she did not possess all the state-of-the-art tech she could have afforded. Her estate was not prowled by a private army of hired guards.

For a moment, he almost dismissed this as naïveté on her part. Then it occurred to him that the Moonlight Detective Agency was, in itself, her protection. It and the connections she fostered and the information she harvested.

It suddenly began to make sense why she'd damn near fired him.

"Aha," he said as the third car beeped and unlocked. "There you are, you bastard. Now, let's see if a mere mortal can drive this damn thing."

Fluttershire Colony, Fort Washington Park, New York City

After his initial nervousness, Remy had to admit that cruising in the Tesla was actually fucking fun. He'd never even considered purchasing one of the company's vehicles before. The fact that they were good for the environment impressed him the same way as the information that a particular food was healthy. It honestly sounded like having to eat one's green vegetables as a child and suggested that neither was enjoyable.

Now, as he eased into the nearest convenient parking spot within reasonable walking distance of the George Washington Bridge, he realized how wrong he'd been.

"That was such a smooth ride," he commented with a small sigh of satisfaction. "It almost makes New York's traffic tolerable. And removing the speed barriers...that was clever. If I get Taylor out of this in one piece, she has to tell me how she pulled that off."

It was also impossible not to wonder if the car included an anti-radar device since he'd managed—remarkably—not to get pulled over. Some of the Remington luck was still in effect, perhaps.

He was almost sorry the drive was over. It had given him time to relax and think. Now, however, he had to face the music with regards to the fae and their notorious fickleness. His plan might well fail and they might kick his ass again for good measure.

"Nonsense," he said and surprised himself with the sudden force and volume of his voice. He adjusted his tie. "I'm Remington Davis. If anyone deserves forgiveness and another second chance or two, it's me."

Remy opened the door, stepped out, and touched the door handle to secure it against his fellow New Yorkers. He double-checked to be sure—it was bad enough borrowing a forbidden vehicle without having it stolen as well—and set out across the grass of the park toward the colony.

There wasn't much sunlight left. It was not yet dusk but it would be in perhaps an hour, maybe two. He never paid much attention to the specifics of such things. If Taylor's kidnappers planned to murder her, it would make sense to do the deed before she woke up.

That thought prompted him to increase his pace.

He looked at the bridge and listened to the steady rush of endless cars that streamed over it. The George Washington was the single busiest urban causeway in the world. He recalled hearing or reading that somewhere once. Leave it to the Fair Folk to hide in plain sight of the entire Eastern Seaboard.

A cawing voice suddenly split the air to the left. His head snapped toward the sound.

"Aww, well look who it is," the high-pitched voice jeered. "*Rehhhmeeee*. And he doesn't even have any honey to offer."

Remy adjusted his tie. "Hello. Yes, I've come to apologize for my...uh, behavior toward Riley and to request your help. Taylor is in serious danger, so it's not only about me."

"Hah!" The fairy scoffed. He squinted at it. The little guy looked familiar—not one of the usual guards, but he'd seen him before somewhere. He might have been one of the various fae who'd taken turns head-butting him in the scrotum.

A few others also floated out of their well-hidden holes, blue-tinged and orange-tinged alike and all seemingly on the same wavelength of skepticism and affronted hostility.

"What is he doing here?" an orange-ish female demanded, shrill with indignation. "He has balls, I'll give him that. Maybe we should take one of them since he clearly has extra."

"That," he retorted instantly, "won't be necessary. I can, you know, buy you guys more honey if you want. But please hear me out. This is about Taylor. She's been kidnapped and the assholes who took her will probably kill her."

A portly bluish male fluttered to the front of the throng. "Nonsense. No one would dare do that. Besides, even if they did, how would that be any of our business? We look after our own here."

"Yeah," a few others chimed in.

He clenched his jaw and raised a hand to emphasize his words. "Taylor protects you, both directly and indirectly, all right? She maintains a balance of power among all the preternaturals in this region and keeps the strong from preying on the weak and that kind of thing."

They still looked skeptical, so he pressed on. "Furthermore, from what she's told me, her enemies want her out of the way so they can slaughter and enslave humans at will. Maybe you don't care about what happens to us, but here's the thing. Too many mysterious acts of violence against mortals and those mortals will start to investigate. They'll find you—and they might well blame you for what this gang of dickheads is planning to do."

One of the fae responded immediately with, "Is that a threat? You don't scare us. We can handle angry, stupid humans with ease."

However, a few others seemed to at least consider what he had said.

The shrill-voiced orange-hued female spoke up next. "Perhaps you have a valid point, Remy. But you haven't bothered to address poor Riley! She's been by herself, crying and sobbing nonstop, ever since she came back. And we all know why she's so heartbroken."

Remy cursed in his head. He most definitely would

have to offer a public apology, which wasn't something he wanted to do in the slightest.

But if that was what it took to save Taylor...

"Yes," he admitted, "it's my fault. She's heartbroken because I snapped at her like an idiot because I was bummed about Taylor chewing my ass. It wasn't even her fault and she only wanted to cheer me up. She tried to be nice because she likes me. I...shouldn't have done that."

He hung his head a little as he spoke. It was partly an act but he also knew that everything he'd said was true.

The female fairy stroked her chin. "Well...."

"And," he continued quickly, not giving them time to concoct reasons why his penitence wasn't good enough, "I probably wouldn't even be alive right now if it wasn't for her. Most of my recent accomplishments were due to her aid—hell, she virtually did all the tracking by herself and I followed around in my car."

The fairies listened intently now.

So, for a moment, did an old man who jogged at the speed Remy usually walked, who had turned his head toward the younger man as he passed.

"Hey there," he said and waved to the old boy. "I'm rehearsing my speech to my girlfriend. You know how it is."

The old fart shook his head and labored on through the park.

Remy turned back to the fae. "Ever since I started working for Taylor, I've tried to be a better person. To learn gratitude and empathy and stuff like that, which I don't have an entirely firm grasp on, admittedly, but I'm doing my best here. At the very least, I know that I was wrong. I wronged Riley, and by extension, I wronged your colony."

His face blushed cherry-red, which made it all the worse, but he made himself shrug it off and said again, "I'm sorry."

Somewhere in the back of the crowd of gossamer-winged forms, a gentle sob transformed into a cooing sound. "Remy!" a familiar voice piped up. "I forgive you."

He hadn't realized she would hear the apology. "Riley? Where are you?"

An apparently male fairy floated above the others. "Here," it said in Riley's voice before it flashed silver quickly and his companion hovered in its place. "I was in disguise."

The entire crowd made an "aww" sound, and most of them clasped their hands together, smiling now.

"Oh," he said. "Yes, I guess you were. It worked, anyway. And I meant all that. I really am sorry. None of it was your fault. Also—wait. Are you wearing clothes?"

"Yes," she concurred, grinned, and spun to show herself off. "I thought about what you said—about how it's more erotic when a woman only suggests her body, rather than shows the whole thing at once."

She'd put on a kind of semi-translucent, sparkling dress of a material that almost looked like the same stuff her wings were made of. It was brief enough at both ends to be tantalizingly unprofessional.

"Well." He cleared his throat. "It does certainly complement your cleavage and your legs, I must say."

"Thanks!" She flew in a curling loop in the air.

The fairies all giggled like a classroom of children who'd heard a naughty word.

"Hey!" one of them protested to shut the others up. "Wait a second here. If he wants her to help him again, he has to pay for her services."

Remy held a finger up. "I still have at least one day left on the week I already purchased," he insisted. "And as a sign of good faith, I'll pick up another pound of honey while I'm out. Right after we save Taylor. It will be the second thing on my to-do list."

Riley darted over to him and hovered beside his shoulder. "Don't worry," she said to her people, "I'll hold him to that."

CHAPTER NINETEEN

Riverside Boulevard, New York City Waterfront

The fairy had again climbed onto the dashboard and now peered out the windshield with her hands on the glass like a kid looking out the window. Most of her ass peeked out from under her ridiculously short dress.

"Yes, that's the place," she said in a hushed voice. "I'm sure of it."

"I'll take your word for it," Remy replied, "but we can't exactly drive in without them probably shooting us a few hundred times. I don't want this car to suffer that kind of fate, anyway, since Taylor would probably send me a bill for the goddamn thing." He sighed. That meant he would have to look around for somewhere to park. "Oh, New York...why do I love you so?"

"What?" Riley asked and almost gasped with excitement.

"New York," he repeated. "I was talking to the city."

The fairy's wings drooped. "Oh."

"You're rather nice, too, though, don't worry. And less of a pain in the ass than this town is, most of the time."

They had finally arrived—after Riley sniffed the splinter and directed him around half of Manhattan—at the battery of piers extending into the Hudson from the vicinity of Riverside Boulevard.

Being close to finding Taylor was one of two things that alleviated some of the tension that boiled in his chest. He made every effort to keep a tight rein on his emotions, but it was difficult not to collapse in relief and hope.

If the conspirators had brought her coffin to a warehouse by the pier, it meant that, rather than intending to kill her, they might simply try to ship her somewhere and hold her hostage. He seemed to recall something about how vampires couldn't cross running water but then again, he was also sure she had been driven over multiple rivers already. She'd not yet informed him which of the old legends were true and which were bullshit.

The other thing that improved his disposition, in conjunction with the first, was the setting of the sun. If Taylor was still alive, she might be able to break out on her own and deal with these fuckers herself—although even then, the hopeful rescuers' help couldn't hurt.

He turned down a side street and found a parking area another block away from the river. That ought to be far enough to avoid any immediate suspicion of him trying to surveil the warehouse. They would need to finish scouting on foot.

Soon, they reached the edge of the warehouses. With a grimace at the thought of what it would do to his clothes, he dropped to his hands and knees and crawled forward until he came within a couple of yards of a metal fence.

Someone with a flashlight patrolled the outside area but moved away from them. He waited until the sentry was a safe distance before he crept right up to the fence and peered through it.

Twelve or thirteen guys were gathered out front. He guessed that half or so of them were human mercenaries or similar such people. Every once in a while, his parents had dealings with private security firms. These men looked similar but somehow rougher and less reputable. Some of them also looked like mobsters or simply hicks with guns.

One of the men—who seemed to be in charge of the group—raised a phone to his ear and spoke a few brief words in a hushed tone. He motioned to a couple of guys who stood near the main front door to the warehouse. They raised the large, garage-like door and, together with two other men, disappeared into the building.

"I think," Riley said softly, "they're bringing Taylor out."

She was right. The four men emerged carrying a rectangular wooden box—an old-fashioned casket. A long gash in one side matched the splinter Remy had given to the fairy. A fifth man trailed them closely and beamed a battery-powered grow-light onto the head-end of the coffin.

Clever. They're using full-spectrum light to keep Taylor trapped within and possibly even keep her asleep by tricking her into thinking it's still daytime. In fact, it was now almost full dark.

They watched for another couple of minutes while most of the men assembled in formation as if awaiting a superior. A few others cracked a crate open and distributed what looked like automatic weapons and magazines. Remy suspected that most of the crates and boxes in there contained guns and ammunition.

"Wait," the fairy whispered in his ear, "who is that? He seems important."

It took a second for him to see who she meant. His gaze caught sight of a large man—both taller and wider than most of the other men—who strode leisurely down the pier toward the area by the coffin with a gunman at each elbow.

The figure passed under one of the lamps and the light illuminated his face. It was none other than Tucker Bedford.

He grimaced. *Him again.*

"Sir," one of the guards said, "so far, there's been no sign of activity from the coffin. We wanted to check inside but the orders we got from Mr G. stated that we were not to open it under any circumstances. We can only assume the lamp is working."

"Yessir," the man's boss acknowledged in his drawling accent. "You done right. We've got things all squared away with the box itself. You men only need to see to it that no one tries to take it away from us. Have y'all scouted around the perimeter here?" He motioned with his hand in a semicircle.

The guard nodded. "Yes, sir. We don't have enough men to keep the patrols as thick as I'd like, but any attack by more than one person ought to be easily detectable. And we have more than enough ammunition."

"Good." Tucker rolled on his heels. "We only have to

wait for another half-hour before Mr G and that other SOB will be right along. Then we can move on to the terminal phase of the operation. Heh, heh. Get it? Terminal?"

One of his bodyguards chuckled at this but the man who had given the report only nodded.

"Uh...yes, sir. Half an hour shouldn't be a problem. It's been quiet so far. We've had no word from Mr G or his messengers, either, about any of the target's allies moving against us. Although he said he's not sure where that one guy is—the human assistant."

The Southerner snorted and flapped a hand in an almost dandified motion. "Him? He probably crawled off to the bar for the night. It's the preternaturals on her side we need to worry about. Any sign of them and we go right to Code Red. Understood?"

"Yes, sir!"

Tucker ordered them to return the coffin to the warehouse and he and his two elbow-men sauntered out of sight to allow the other guards to resume their watch.

"Remy," Riley whispered, "let's get out of here. We need to either leave or...do something."

"Hmm," he mused. "How about both? Leave first and then do something."

They crept to the car. No one stumbled onto them or accosted them, although they did see one of Tucker's sentries come uncomfortably close for a moment. When he was distracted by another guy hundreds of feet away who gestured to him, they slipped past him and made their way toward the black Tesla.

He stood beside the car and studied it to examine its structure and aerodynamics more closely.

The fairy floated in front of his face. "Okay, you said you wanted to do something. What? We can't simply stand here—"

Remy smiled evilly. "Actually, I was thinking about the demolition derby."

She stared at him in confusion.

"That spell," he went on, "that you put on my poor, poor car…it worked quite well. Do you think you could do that again?"

"Of course," she replied. "But how will that help us to—"

"Ram them?" he said. "Obviously, it will offer us protection as we run over some of these pricks and batter the front door down. Fun stuff like that. And it looks like they have a large number of guns laying around anyway, so after we crash, I'll grab one of those while you deflect the bullets." He nodded to himself. "Yes, it ought to be a piece of cake, really. Even if Taylor does make me pay back every penny of repairs, probably for the rest of my life."

Riley frowned. "I'm not so sure about that, Remy. There are so many of those guys, and they have the bigger kind of guns that fire faster. And if you crash through the door, you might even drive into Taylor's coffin and kill her. We don't know exactly where it is in there."

He shrugged in an irritated way and retorted, "Well, we only have about twenty minutes until Tucker's friends show up—this Mr G guy, whoever he is, and probably that prick Albert and his minions as well. At that point, they might kill her anyway. We have to do something. Do you have any better ideas?"

"Not really," she admitted and frowned as she pulled her mouth to the side in resignation. "Let's do this. I will do all I can to help you. I don't want you to get hurt."

"Thanks." He retrieved the remote device, unlocked the car, and slid into the seat. Riley fluttered to the dashboard and he closed the door. "You might as well do the enchantment right now and get it out of the way."

She nodded, flew around the perimeter of the vehicle's interior, and waved her tiny arms to trigger sparkling flashes of silver light that erupted all over the car's body. When it looked like she was about done, he shifted into reverse, backed out of his space, and pulled onto the street, looking for an entrance to the area beside the warehouse and the pier.

He found it after less than a minute. The downside was that it was blocked by a tall chain-link fence held shut by a heavy cable secured with a padlock. There was also a small, lighted booth from which a security guard had already emerged.

Remy sighed. "I hate to crash a party too early," he commented, "but if I must, then I must." He stamped on the gas.

The guard's eyes widened and he leapt out of the way as the Tesla barreled directly toward the barrier.

He grinned as the rush he'd felt during the derby came back to him and he accelerated even more. The car's front sheared through the metal and thrust the gates inward. In the next moment, he hurtled across pot-holed asphalt with the warehouse ahead.

Men shouted in alarm and four or five guys with guns

appeared from behind the barrels and out of the shipping containers stacked along either side of the long yard.

His grin still in place, he yanked the steering wheel to the left before he reversed the motion immediately to fish-tail the vehicle into the two men who were closest. The first thumped into the rear window and rolled over the car's roof before he could even react. The second managed a short burst of sub-machine gunfire before the car plowed him aside to leave a noticeable blood splatter on the trunk.

Remy was vaguely aware of the stream of profanity that poured from his lips but it almost seemed to come from someone else. He veered right and clipped another of the mercenaries, whose body crunched before he screamed and catapulted into a cluster of barrels.

Two guys remained behind to fire at the vehicle's rear, but Riley's magic seemed to do an excellent job of deflecting the bullets. The only thing that made any real impression was the noise. He allowed his jaw to fall open as his skull rattled and his ears rang.

Now the warehouse door—which was shut—loomed in front of them. It appeared to be made of heavy sheet metal. The car might not break through it but he made his mind up to try anyway.

"Hold on!" He pushed down on the gas pedal. Speed was necessary to bust the door down, but he also had to hope the weight of it would slow him down enough after-ward that he would be able to avoid Taylor's casket within.

The world seemed to explode with tremors and relent-less noise. Metal screamed and tore apart, the car lurched and rocked, and suddenly, they were driving ahead again into a dark space.

"*Boo-ya!*" He laughed. "Ugh, I actually said that."

Another hired gunman disappeared beneath the bumper and the tires, and the wheels spun as they crushed him. More gunfire generated sparks along the sides of the vehicle.

He stamped on the brakes when he saw a mounted platform on which the coffin rested ahead. The car squealed and began to spin. His seatbelt dug into his chest and forced the air out of his lungs.

Thankfully, the vehicle finally stopped. The rear bumper was about three feet from the head of the coffin.

It was a long moment before he remembered to breathe, and Riley, hanging onto the slats of the air vent, stared at him with terror in her eyes.

Remy looked over his shoulder. Several more guards had assembled near the warehouse entrance and aimed their guns—preparing to shoot at them but trying not to hit the coffin, he surmised.

He had an idea. "It looks like we need another repeat from the derby, I'd say," he remarked. "Riley, we bail on three."

She nodded and burrowed into his shirt as he wheeled the Tesla around and revved it. "One!"

He pressed the gas pedal again and unhooked his seatbelt as the mercs opened fire at the vehicle, to no avail. "Two!"

The men began to stumble away from the entrance. The car picked up speed.

"Three!" He flung the door open, jumped, and rolled. The concrete pounded into him, but a silver glow surrounded him as he rolled aside and he knew that Riley had softened their landing.

The Tesla powered through the line of men, flattened one, and scattered the others. Its front end deflected off a shipping container and the car, driverless and slowing down now, swerved to the right and out of sight.

Remy scrambled to his feet, confident he wasn't injured unless adrenaline had masked the pain. He'd care later. He flung himself behind a crate a second before a few bullets pinged off the floor behind him.

The crate was partially open already. "Riley," he snapped. "Cover me."

She squirmed out from under his shirt and flapped above his head to create a sheen of light in the air before them that threw sparks when bullets struck it and veered off-course.

Remington leaned into the crate and hoisted out a newer-model Deutsch SMG, along with four spare magazines, which he shoved into his pockets. "Is that deflector shield two-way? I'd like to fire through it if you don't mind."

The fairy glanced at him and opened a narrow hole in the sheet of light. He thrust the gun's barrel through it and fired half a magazine while he wheeled the weapon to spray bullets as widely as possible. The fire directed at them stopped as the remaining mercs took cover.

He glanced quickly toward the coffin. Unfortunately, a couple more men had emerged from somewhere deeper within the warehouse and now tried to cut him off from their cargo.

"Riley," he snapped, "shield us from those guys for a

minute." He gestured at the two near the coffin. She increased the translucent silver barrier barely in time to deflect their opening barrage.

Something caught his attention and he grinned. Their adversaries stood in front of another crate, one with orange tape on it that said *DANGER* in bold black letters.

"Oh, this is rich," he quipped. "I think that's an explosives crate. Watch this—" He aimed his sub-machine gun.

"Remy, you idiot!" Riley protested. "We're too close—"

He ignored her and fired. Holes appeared in the crate.

Then, it exploded.

The blast knocked him off his feet and drove the fairy down beside him.

Remy looked up. One of the two guys who'd guarded the coffin had been blown to charred pieces. The other lay sprawled to the side of it, his legs in bad shape. He was dazed, but alive.

With a sigh, he jogged toward him and motioned with his hand for the fairy to follow him. She complied, still busy deflecting bullets from the men at the door who had regrouped.

The wounded man's unfocused gaze drifted toward him and sharpened. He twisted his torso to reach for his gun, which lay on the floor beside his hand.

"No, you don't," Remy snapped, raised his SMG, and fired.

Three bloody holes erupted in the man's chest and shoulder area. Shaking and groaning, he fell back and was still.

Something about the knowledge that he'd actually killed a person—several people, rather—disturbed him deep down, but there were too many important tasks to focus on for him to dwell on it. He had to get that coffin.

A few flames from the explosion were burning themselves out as he strode up to the cargo. He saw, with some annoyance, that the lamp was still functional despite the blast and blazed directly on the coffin.

He reached out and clicked it off. Nothing happened. Behind him, he thought he could hear Riley shout something.

As he turned, he saw the fairy rocket through the air toward him, still maintaining her translucent force-field against the gunfire of the last two guards. He aimed around the edge of the magical shield and fired the remainder of his magazine.

The guards ducked into cover behind large boxes. In the ensuing silence, he said, "Riley—can you levitate this coffin to the car?"

One of the guards took a potshot at him as he said this, but she deflected it.

"Yes," she answered, "but how will I protect you? I can't do both."

"I can manage this." He ejected the empty magazine and slid a fresh one in. "Luck and daring seem to go a long way, I've noticed. They have a kind of magic of their own."

While he spoke, he aimed at the crate that the closer of the two men had hunkered behind. As if on cue, the guy darted up.

Remy squeezed the trigger. The gun flared and four rounds sheared the corner of the crate off and also felled the guy behind it in a spray of blood. His target's gun fired aimlessly into the air as he fell.

The fairy bit hesitantly on a finger but agreed. "If you say so. Please be careful, though." She turned to focus on the coffin. Silvery sparks erupted from the base of the oblong box and it shuddered slightly before it rose, slowly at first but with increasingly smooth momentum.

He ducked when the other guard fired at him. At least one of the bullets pierced through the nearest crate and ricocheted off the floor. He couldn't rely on cover to protect him for much longer.

Meanwhile, Riley had brought the coffin almost fifteen feet above the floor. The remaining henchman, looking alarmed at their cargo literally floating away, aimed at her and fired. She managed to evade them in time, but the coffin rocked alarmingly.

To draw attention away from her, Remy returned fire at the man, who tried to jump away but wasn't fast enough. Blood spurted from his back and sides and he crumpled in a heap.

The fairy took the coffin out of one of the warehouse's high windows, which had already shattered in the explosion. He only hoped their car hadn't rolled into the goddamn river. In a moment, she was gone from his sight.

CHAPTER TWENTY

Riverside Boulevard, New York City Waterfront

"Okay." Remy breathed deeply "I'll...uh, make my way back on foot."

He stood and walked across the warehouse floor. For the first time since he'd begun the assault, the place seemed quiet. Somehow, he didn't think they'd killed all the guards, which meant either that the remaining ones had fled—possibly to fetch reinforcements—or that they waited in ambush.

There was also their hulking, rebel-flag-waving leader to consider. Although there had been no sign of him since the attack had begun, it didn't mean someone hadn't called him back.

Something stood out as he passed a large, undamaged crate and immediately caught his attention, but it was only a bunched-up tarp. He stood for a second and aimed his gun at it before he turned to the shattered main door.

There was, he decided, a possibility that he might make

it out of this alive. He broke into a jog with the exit only about twenty feet away.

Three men appeared in front of him—two more sub-machine-gun-toting guards at the far left and right sides of the door and a third man who stepped casually from behind a metal girder in the center.

"Hold," the third man commanded. "I say, hold your fire. Don't shoot him—yet."

Remy pointed his weapon at him. "Tucker. I can't say I'm surprised to see you here. I didn't realize you were involved in black market coffin-trading, however."

The big man chortled and hooked his thumbs into his lapels. "Black market coffin-trading...that's a good one, Remington. I'll have to remember that later. But for now, I'm afraid I have to ask you to put that gun down or else this might get ugly."

He was fairly sure it already had gotten ugly, so rather than lay his gun down, he fired it. Two bullets erupted from the barrel and sank into the other man's chest. The two henchmen, alarmed, raised their guns to fire in retaliation, but their boss raised a hand to stay them—again.

The Southerner looked at his torso. The impact of the bullets had done little more than push him back about half a step and now, the ragged holes were already weaving themselves together.

"Uh..." Remy gawked. "Well...I admire a man with resilience, I must say."

His adversary smirked but there was a savage gleam in his eye. "Who said I was a man?"

Not quite sure what to make of that, he blinked and in the split second his eyes were closed, something changed. The heavy figure had begun to literally bristle with hair, the gleaming eyes had turned yellow, the ears had elongated, and claws sprouted from his fingers.

He threw his head back and howled.

Remy's jaw dropped. "Shiiiiiiit!"

Operating on some primitive instinct, he hurled himself aside toward a stack of boxes. A dark, furry blur careened through the space he'd vacated, snarling viciously.

Tucker's two bodyguards opened fire.

He landed between two stacks of containers and scraped the sides of both, and pain flared through his body as he tried to go straight from collision with the floor to his feet. His tumble from the car might not have seriously injured him but it had bruised him in places and put unusual strain on muscles and tendons he didn't normally use. He had worn through his adrenalin and pain now began to become a factor.

Bullets streaked past or cracked through wood or chipped off concrete.

His focus now on staying alive, he pulled himself behind the boxes. Between two more crates, stacked about head height, he could see Tucker. And, unfortunately, his adversary could see him.

Instead of a big, beefy Southern gentleman, he was now a monstrosity. Most of his clothes had shredded and fallen away when he'd grown even taller and heavier. His entire body was covered with fur. It was a mixture of dark black-ish-gray and dull brownish-red, matted and bristly. His eyes shone, reflecting the hanging lights of the warehouse, and yellowed nails protruded from his huge, grasping paws.

Worst of all, his face had become a snout, and the mouth hung open to reveal a long, drooling red tongue and rows of jagged canine teeth.

"You," the werewolf literally growled, the sound inhumanly low and gravelly, "should have died at the derby. It would have been quicker and less painful."

Remy was not the type to panic easily, but hearing Tucker's awful new voice and seeing the beast rear in preparation to pounce, his heart leapt into his throat. He scrambled over the box beside him.

In the same moment, Tucker launched into the attack. The werewolf moved with such speed and force that the boxes and crates behind his quarry burst and the displaced air and kinetic force drove the human forward in his escape. He tumbled and rolled over the top of the next container before he landed flat on his back on the concrete.

"Shit." He gasped and hauled himself up on a metal railing next to a yellow-marked walkway. "Shit, shit, shit, shit!"

The two henchmen opened fire again. The guns' reports echoed deafeningly, and sparks rose where the lead struck.

While he bobbed and weaved between crates and sprinted toward the rear of the building, Tucker roared behind him.

Remy raced across the floor, swung himself around the base of a crane-type device, and ducked behind it as he heard the sounds of an enraged werewolf moving closer.

Air rushed and, out of the corner of his eye, he saw a hairy claw swipe at him. He scuttled forward to put the crane between him and it.

Tucker growled again in frustration. He seized a crate and threw it.

The man ducked, moved low to the floor, and tried to also keep count of the bullets as the two gunmen now took individual potshots at him. They were attempting to break his nerve to force him into doing something stupid, he assumed.

He caught a glimpse of something moving near the warehouse's ceiling and glanced up.

Riley floated there and pointed emphatically toward a pile of crates in the northwest corner. She practically bounced up and down in midair in her enthusiasm. A faint silvery glow emanated from the area she indicated and seemed to encompass four different crates.

Remy looked at her, nodded, and ran northwest.

"Yes, run, human! There's nothing I like better than catching my prey while it runs away." The werewolf laughed, a horrible rabid-dog sound that contained enough human mirth to imbue it with evil. He cleared a third of the warehouse in one leap and crashed atop the elevated platform where Taylor's coffin had stood.

His prey, meanwhile, had torn off the lids of the first two crates, both of which contained more guns. He struggled to get the covering off the third and broke half of the wood as he heaved it off. Within were more standard magazines.

"What the hell were you trying to tell me, Riley?" he said under his breath and gritted his teeth. His gaze swung upward but the fairy was gone. There was more gunfire outside, so she must have retreated to the coffin to defend it.

A lupine growl sounded behind him now and it was far too close.

"Hold still," Tucker jeered. "Get ready to be dinner."

Remy reached the final crate and kicked the lid off. He stared at it for a moment, his mouth agape. In his adrenaline-charged haste, it took a moment for his brain to comprehend what he was looking at.

Within the container was a long tray lined with red velvet that contained twelve individual bullets. They looked different from the other bullets he'd seen today. A piece of paper lay folded beside them.

The lycanthrope made a gasping, gurgling sound. "What? What the fuck!"

Unbelievably, the powerful hind claws retreated. Tucker was now backing away from him.

Curious, he unfolded the piece of paper. It was a handwritten letter and even before he could read most of it, he recognized exactly what it was—a death threat. He'd received more than his fair share of those in his day. His various infidelities with other men's girlfriends and wives and daughters, his snotty attitude, and his general misbehavior had all combined to make him familiar with written promises of doom.

He cleared his throat and read the letter aloud.

"My friend Tucker, you may have run your share of successful businesses, but you don't belong here. Running a few errands for Mr G isn't the same thing as running a family business with generations of history in both New York and Chicago.

Please accept this as a parting gift for your trip back to South Carolina, or else accept it as payment for the funeral expenses incurred by your next of kin. Your one-time associate, Albert.'"

The werewolf almost choked on his snarl of rage. "Shoot him."

Remy ducked behind the crates and snatched the velvet-lined tray along with an empty revolver. Quickly, he loaded the weapon.

Anxious not to lose his opportunity, he stood hastily and aimed the weapon. Tucker had backed away across the floor toward the large metal containers on the west side of the warehouse, but he had caught him before he could reach cover.

"Gosh," he said to the werewolf, "it really is a shame when the people you thought were your friends turn out to be assholes because you screwed them over. Anyway, you'd best be going now." He pulled the trigger.

Tucker tensed and cringed but nothing happened.

"Goddammit," the man cursed. "I'm out of practice with revolvers. I don't suppose you'd be willing to come closer?"

The words had not even left his mouth when the werewolf bounded forward in one last desperate offensive.

Remy stepped to the side, aimed the gun, and fanned the hammer like he'd seen in one of his grandfather's Clint Eastwood movies to fire another three rounds.

The charging mass of fur suddenly sprawled and uttered a high-pitched yelp like a dog that had been kicked in the ribs. While his adversary erupted in a long, sustained howl, he ran into cover behind the nearby crane-like equipment and peered around to examine his handiwork.

Tucker, locked somewhere halfway between man and

beast with tufts of wolf-fur sprouting from random places along his body, lay on his back with two bright red craters in his chest and stomach. His face grew pale.

"Ha, ha," he laughed through ragged breaths, although his voice and the crooked smile on his face were almost good-natured. Blood dripped from the corner of his mouth. "Your luck really is something, I must say. Mine, though"—he coughed and spat more blood up—"ain't been so good lately..."

His head lolled back and he became still and silent. The last of the fur had melted away.

One of the two bodyguards had frozen in shock at the sight of the werewolf's death. Remy aimed and fired the last silver bullet at him.

The round did not strike the man but did catch the SMG magazine in his hand. It knocked it away from him and also made him reel back and lose his grip on the gun. As the man tried to regain his balance, the other guard finished reloading and aimed.

Thankfully, Remington had the presence of mind to snatch a fresh weapon from one of the other opened crates and slap a magazine in. He aimed as the other guy fired. The first of the enemy barrage missed him again. His head swelled with crazy elation and he simply ran forward and yelled at the top of his lungs while he fired on full auto.

The guard panicked and leapt aside to barely avoid the spray. Remy bolted past him, out the front door of the warehouse, and into the night.

The Tesla—badly scratched and dinged but amazingly, not totaled—rolled down a slight incline and stopped in front of him.

Riley appeared out of one of the windows. "I can't drive this at all, but I made the wheels turn so it rolled back here."

"That's good enough," he said. A quick glance assured him that she'd managed to fit the coffin into the back once she'd worked out how to fold all the seats down except the driver's. The box barely looked big enough to hold even Taylor's petite frame, which was a good thing in this case.

He opened the door and slid in as the remaining bodyguard jumped out from behind his cover and fired again. The bullets ricocheted off the driver's side door.

"It's time to leave," Remy announced, started the engine, and pressed the gas pedal. He drove back the way he'd come toward the damaged gate. Halfway there, another thug poked his head and shoulders out from behind a shipping container and fired a shotgun. The buckshot sparked off the windshield but left only a faint crack.

Irritated, he flipped him off as he passed and they accelerated out onto the street.

"What a rush. I basically owned all those guys. and even slew a goddamn werewolf. I knew I had it in me after how good I was at video games. They really can teach you a thing or two that ends up being useful in real life. In fact, I can't wait for Taylor to hear about all this—"

The fairy sighed. "About how you did all of this on your own, you mean. Without any help."

CHAPTER TWENTY-ONE

Harrison, Westchester County, New York

When Taylor awoke, she knew at once that something was wrong. What it was, exactly, remained to be seen. But something in the air—the vibe and smell of it—was off.

She refused to panic or to do anything hasty. That would be worse than doing nothing at all. Instead, she lay where she was and noted the subtle signs of her predicament with all five of the senses she had retained from her mortal life as well as the vaguely defined sixth sense she had gained in undeath.

At first, when she'd come to live in the old house in one of the oldest parts of the New World, she had, with her own hands, dug out a neat rectangle of earth at the bottom of the spiraling caverns beneath the estate.

In this sepulchral alcove within her natural tomb, she had slept. Not every day but often, and especially during times of trouble, for many, many years. She knew the cave inside and out—every detail, every nuance of the air quality and electromagnetic balance, and faint seismic activity.

The vampire rested a moment, still and wide-eyed in the darkness, and her mind identified the disturbance at last. There were too little weight and pressure above her—above the ceiling of the cave.

That, she knew, could mean at least two things.

One, it might indicate a strange weather event—a powerful thunderstorm or a tornado or some such thing. But it was early autumn, not prime storm season, and tornados were exceedingly rare in this part of the country.

The other possibility was that her coffin was missing. And if that were the case, there were many explanations. None of them were particularly encouraging.

After a moment's thought, she raised her arms from their folded position over her chest and curled her fingers over the edge of the open grave. When she pulled herself upward, she'd already begun to float and now drifted through the stale air and pitch-blackness toward the top of the cavern.

Taylor extended a hand and felt the rock ceiling. Yes— her coffin was gone. She could not ascend to the cellar the quick or easy way.

She wanted to curse but held her tongue. There was the chance, both frightening and infuriating in its implications, that her enemies had struck and that this was their doing. They might be waiting for her even now, keeping a close vigil over the basement, alert to the existence of the hidden vault beneath it.

But more likely, her casket's truancy was the result of some stupid fucking thing Remington had done.

The thought brought with it a surge of irritation. She wafted down at an angle to the crude ramp-staircase hybrid she had carved into the rock walls of the cave. Her feet touched on the surface some ten feet above the cavern floor. From there, she walked softly and silently upward. The steps encircled the dark space and came to an end in a narrow gap which abutted the extreme rear corner of her wine cellar.

There were no sounds—no noises of movement, no breathing, and no pulse. Unless others among the living dead awaited her, the cellar was empty.

Satisfied that there was no immediate danger, she pushed the heavy stone trapdoor open and climbed into her basement, racks of wine casks to either side.

After a quick glance assured her that nothing lay in ambush, she hurried around the corner and beyond the steps that led to the ground floor and examined the sarcophagus built into the floor.

The space within was empty, as she'd expected. There was light scuffing on the stone of the enclosure and the clear outline of where her casket had rested on the lid. And footsteps, almost invisible to any but her, showed in the thin layer of dust on the floor and steps. It looked as though four or five pairs of feet had come through several hours before and another pair more recently than that.

"Dammit," she whispered and her small hands rolled into fists. "One way or another, someone will pay for this."

Careful to make no noise, she ascended the stairs and opened the door cautiously. Her senses did not warn her of anyone lurking nearby. The whole house was still and silent.

Except for a single, faint heartbeat from somewhere in the kitchen.

"Presley!" she called. "Are you all right?"

"Yes, madame," the butler's voice responded, muffled by the wood of a closet. "I look forward to being released, to be sure. But I've not been harmed."

"I'll be back for you," she promised.

But first, she needed to check outside. She could hear a car approach. The enemy might be out there even now.

Taylor crept into the foyer as a form approached the front door. She lifted her arms and immediately elevated up and back into a shadowed corner of the ceiling. At the same time, she applied all her powers of invisibility and obscurity.

The door burst open.

"I got you, Taylor." Remington gasped and struggled to drag in a breath. He was red-faced and thoroughly winded and struggled as he heaved her coffin to yank it foot by foot over the threshold and into the foyer. "Don't worry. I got you."

Taylor gawked while she watched him from on high. He wasn't speaking to her but to the casket.

"I'll make sure you're safe until you can get up, finally. We've made it this far. I only have to get to the cellar now." He patted the wooden lid.

Well, that clarifies a few things—the bastards plotting against me must have stolen it and somehow, my new employee brought it back. She decided not to reveal herself yet, though. Remington might have more to say.

"And once you get up," he went on, his voice ragged, "I guess it's more of the other two M's. We're beyond mitigation at this point, ha, ha. We have some murder to do. And then I think I could use a mindwipe. Don't want to constantly see all this stuff in my sleep at night."

What did he do?

Remy dragged the coffin across the floor a few feet, bunched one of the rugs, and gave up for the moment. He was breathing heavily and needed a rest.

"You know"—he patted the casket again—"I really have learned all kinds of useful things from you. I almost wish someone would have taught me some of this crap sooner. Like, why was everyone so nice to me when I was a kid? I didn't deserve it. They only taught me that I could do whatever I wanted. I wish someone had kicked my ass a little more."

Riley, the fairy from Fluttershire who'd been with Remy before, flew up to the doorway. "Is everything okay?" she asked.

"Yes," he told her. "Wait at the car for now. I need a couple of minutes alone."

"Okay." She shrugged and flitted out into the night.

He took a deep breath. Taylor didn't think her coffin was that heavy but it had been a long, long time since she'd been cursed with merely mortal strength.

"And the trust," he went on. "You actually trusted me to do things. Now that I think about it, my family only trusted me to...I don't know, be a Remington and collect dividends, I guess."

At that, he laughed and looked into the distance for a moment before he returned his attention to the oblong box. "Not that I didn't think you were kind of a bitch with that fairy assignment at first, of course. That was an intentional hazing, wasn't it? But maybe it's what I needed. I was...ignorant. And, you know, that which does not kill me, uh...well, it didn't kill me."

Taylor began to wonder if maybe he were back on drugs. She didn't smell any but he wasn't usually this emotional.

"And you know," he continued, "really, you're the only friend I have now. And I mean that. Well, besides Riley, but I'm not sure someone only a few inches tall really counts. Anyway, it's been a while since anyone wasn't using me for what little is left of my money...or because I know the good dealers...or because they were hoping the Remington fame would rub off on them. Hell, you want less attention, not more. I respect that, dammit."

The vampire had to admit she was enjoying this.

Remy wiped the sweat from his brow and rubbed his hands on his pant legs. "Okay, yeah. In a way, you're using me to deflect attention from yourself, so no one realizes that you're old enough to draw a pension multiple times over. What decade did they start pensions, anyway? Or century? I forget. But, whatever. I can't complain. You've paid my account damn well for the privilege of using me. If any of my other friends did that, I wouldn't be in this place."

He exhaled and calmness settled over his face. "Not that I entirely mind being here."

Finally, he again tried to hoist the coffin up but it seemed he was having even more difficulty than before.

A smile crept onto Taylor's face. She floated from the ceiling, landed soundlessly behind the young Remington, and said, "Need any help?"

He spun with a tense, jerky motion, stared at her with eyes like tea saucers, and dropped the coffin.

She slid past him, caught the casket's bottom edge with one hand, and easily supported it to prevent it from crashing into the floor. "You know, David," she chided, "a little more situational awareness might do you some good."

He cleared his throat and impressed her by regaining his composure in about a second.

"Yes, situational awareness," he drawled, straightened his tie, and smoothed his hair. "I've heard of that. And I suppose you heard everything I said. Not that I have any idea how you got out of the coffin so fast when I wasn't paying attention. But aside from the bitch comment, nothing I said was particularly scandalous, anyway."

"By all means," Taylor remarked, "keep telling yourself that. First, though, might you be able to tell me why my coffin was not in my cellar? And why it is damaged?" She had seen the long, jagged slash.

His nostrils flared. "It was Tucker," he stated. "No great surprise there. And Riley and I overheard and saw enough to know that he definitely wasn't working alone, although he and his men pulled the heist off. The...um, stealing you heist."

She nodded. Deep within, she seethed with rage. A bonfire had flared in the core of her being but no one looking at her would have been able to guess this. Her exterior was not of fire, but of ice. "Who else was working with him?"

"Oh, you know," said Remy, "a number of mercenary types, some good old boys, some mobsters...that guy Albert, who runs the shitty casino in Lower Manhattan I was at before I investigated James's house, was apparently in on it as well. Although he and Tucker obviously hated each other since I happened to stumble across a little gift he left for our Southern friend."

The vampire cocked an eyebrow. "Oh?"

"Silver bullets," he explained. "I suppose amongst werewolves, that's the equivalent of putting a horse's head under the covers. It was intended as a message. I, however, actually used them, so that worked out nicely." He smirked a little. "Tucker won't be a problem anymore."

"I see. That saves me the trouble of having to rip his spine out. However, once it gets out that you have killed a werewolf, your position in the preternatural world will change. We had better prepare you for it."

It looked at her like he was about to make some ridiculous comment about how much of a hero he was for overcoming the lycanthrope, so she spoke again before he could. "Now, tell me the rest." She put enough command into her tone to ensure he responded.

"Uh, yes," he stammered, somewhat disoriented by having his nascent boasting cut off. "Tucker mentioned someone he called Mr G, whoever that is. I got the impression he was working for him. And Albert's letter referred to the same person."

She nodded. Her eyes narrowed and she knew they were on the verge of emitting a faint red glow.

"Gabriel." She all but growled the word.

"Who?" Remy asked. "Well, obviously, you think that's what the 'G' stands for, but—"

"Gabriel Joshua Simons. The third of my three main suspects. A rather young and moronically arrogant vampire. He's always struck me as the vicious, hotheaded type—Precisely the kind who gives my species a bad name with humans."

He massaged his throat. "Another vampire. I'd almost started to think you were the only one."

"I'm not." She started to pick her coffin up. Remy, apparently suffering an attack of chivalry, stooped to help her even though she could more than support the weight. She allowed him to hold the foot-end, nonetheless.

As they marched down the hallway and sought the cellar door, she continued. "I cannot be one hundred percent certain that it's Gabriel yet, but I would be surprised if it weren't. Unfortunately, I don't know where he is. But I'm sure some of his allies or lackeys do."

"That makes sense," Remy agreed.

She supported the casket with one hand, opened the cellar door, and descended the staircase with Remington trundling along behind her, still holding his end of their load somewhat awkwardly.

When they reached the bottom, Taylor guided them toward the sarcophagus and directed him to circle to the other side. He complied and they lowered the box into its home.

He cleared his throat. "I have to ask, though...where the hell were you? We all assumed you were in the coffin, including Tucker and his pals."

"Obviously," she responded, "you were wrong. I never sleep in it. It is what you call a misdirection. And you don't need to know where I do sleep, either."

If he had examined the stone coffin in detail, he would

have found the trapdoor built into its bottom and surmised that she slept somewhere deeper underground.

The young man nodded with a sour frown. "To be honest, I thought they would take the coffin to a foundry or something and stuff it into a blast furnace. Anyway, if you had been sleeping in the damn thing, I would have actually saved your life." He attempted to smile.

Taylor finished adjusting the box's position within the sarcophagal enclosure. She flicked her gaze at him. "If. But true enough. Thank you, Remy."

"The fairy helped too, of course," he admitted. "I left her in the car, but I'll go fetch her in a minute so you can thank her yourself. First, though, where's Presley? And what do you plan to do next?"

"Presley," she said and brushed her hands against each other, "is in a closet upstairs. He's fine. I'll release him presently. And as for what I am about to do..." Her voice dropped to a low and icy register. "Think of everything you've heard about what happens when someone tips a motorcycle belonging to an outlaw biker. Now multiply that by seven, and you have some idea of what happens when someone fucks with a vampire's coffin."

CHAPTER TWENTY-TWO

Harrison, Westchester County, New York

Taylor crushed the severed zip-ties in her hand and threw them into the trash. Presley nodded to her and rubbed his sore wrists.

"Thank you, madame," he said. His voice was weak and scratchy, probably from thirst.

She went to the kitchen sink and filled a glass with water. "You know you don't have to thank me for freeing you, Presley. I'm only glad they weren't stupid enough to kill you."

"Indeed," the butler acknowledged, accepted the glass, and tipped it toward his mouth.

Remy watched them from the kitchen doorway. "Ah... I'm sorry I didn't check the house for you, Jeeves," he said and scratched the back of his neck. "I suppose I simply assumed that either they took you with Taylor, or that you were already under a few tons of wet cement somewhere. No offense."

The old man stopped drinking for a moment to respond. "None taken, sir."

He continued. "Pardon my asking, but why didn't they simply kill you?"

The vampire answered the question herself. "My enemies are not particularly smart," she began, "but they are not utter fools, either. Presley, too, is a werewolf. He's no pushover."

The young man blinked in surprise. "I did not know that."

The butler smiled as his mistress admitted, "We should have told you sooner. We were half-hoping that you might spread misinformation about him being human, in which case they wouldn't dare to kill him. The authorities turn a blind eye to most incidents involving preternaturals, but all bets are off when it comes to mortals."

"Well," he interrupted, "they tried to kill me." He put his hands on his hips.

"That," she retorted, "is probably because you attacked them, in the first place, and they assumed they could pass it off as a well-known substance abuser getting in over his head at a drug deal gone bad."

His gaze went distant as he considered this. "Yeah, true." He was glad that Riley had returned to her nest. Taylor had already spoken to her and he feared that if she were present, she might embarrass him.

"Furthermore," she continued, "Presley has a great many friends and connections by now. If he were murdered, no one in authority would seriously believe that he'd brought it on himself by some misbehavior. The DA might be personally involved in no time. You may not have seen Presley at swanky charity events, but I guarantee you that he knows half the servants and vendors and security people your family has had dealings with, Remington. And they would miss him."

Presley smiled wanly. "You're too kind, madame."

Remy could recall a few people like that—individuals who were not exactly famous but who seemed both beloved and indispensable wherever they went or wherever they were known.

"Presley," said Taylor, "contact our allies immediately. If the enemy hasn't already moved against them, they need to be prepared for what's about to come."

Remington felt a surge of excitement at the way she said that. He clapped his hands. "Okay, so now we go kick some ass, am I right?"

The vampire pulled a pitcher from her fridge that contained something that almost looked like tomato juice. "You're mostly right, aside from the 'we' part. Both of you will stay here—the enemy might well try a counterstrike. And before you protest, think back to what you said about not wanting to deal with some of the ugly memories you got from your first taste of real violence. I'm about to create several memories of that kind. It's better if you simply let me handle it."

He allowed his hands to hang at his sides. "Yes, Mom." He groaned. "I suppose you're right, though."

After drinking a glass of her scarlet provender, Taylor showed him to the mansion's safe room hidden in the interior of the house on the second floor. It had its own crude but serviceable facilities—water, food, weapons, and cots. It was fireproof, bulletproof, and climate-controlled. She opened it with her palm-print and explained that only her hand could open it again—or program the time-lock.

"I'll set it," she informed him, "for ten o'clock tomorrow morning. I intend to return by dawn, for obvious reasons, but I can survive past sun-up if need be. That means if I'm not back by ten, you may assume me killed in action, at which point, Presley will take over the agency's affairs and you will continue to work under him."

Remy's gut tightened at the matter of fact way she said this. "Do you expect to get killed?"

"No," she replied immediately, "but it's always possible." She turned to look into his eyes, her own black and deep. "Thank you, again, Remington, for providing me with leads and for trying to rescue me, even if I didn't actually need rescuing. You have more mettle than I thought. Assuming I return, we'll need to temper you a little more. Much more, actually. But still. I am pleased."

She turned and left, moving so fast he was surprised to find her simply gone and the safe room's metal door already closed.

"Bye, I guess," he quipped halfheartedly.

Presley stood beside him. "Don't worry too much, sir. While it's true there is real danger, she's rather experienced in this kind of thing and not one to be easily pushed over."

He rubbed his eyes and sat on the nearest cot. "I'll try to take your word for it but I can't help worrying. Don't tell her I said that, though." He stretched and made himself comfortable. "Don't mind if I pass out here. I was in a battle myself recently, and you'd be amazed how tiring it is."

His brief attempt to relax was interrupted by what

sounded like the blasting-off of a jet engine. He jerked himself into a seated position.

"What the hell was that? I didn't know she had an F-16."

Presley's mouth twisted with what almost looked like amusement. "Only a car, sir. Although not a Tesla."

Outside, Taylor's huge black muscle-car roared up and out of its subterranean compartment, which lay below and beside the formal garage that housed her other vehicles. It careened out of the driveway and surged down the winding residential streets before it reached one of the main roads leading toward New York City.

As it rocketed down the avenues at speeds normally reserved for professional racecar drivers, a deputy of the Westchester Sheriff's Office saw it streak past in his cruiser.

"What the flying fuck? Was that even a car?" he sputtered. By the time he checked his time-lapse camera, the vehicle was already long gone.

He called it in with the intention that someone farther south could deal with it and read the license plate number. There was silence on the other end of the line for a moment before Officer Larkin—who was usually as monotone as hell—spoke again in a confused tone of irritation.

"Sit where you are," she said to him, "and let it go. That's what they're telling me. I repeat. Do not pursue. This comes directly from the commissioner, apparently."

The deputy shook his head. "Cloak-and-dagger shit, man."

Sullivan Street, Lower Manhattan, New York City

The vampire's nose and sixth sense identified the Chattering & Chips Casino before her eyes did. The place smelled, as it always did, of preternatural activities, but the vibe of the air around it was tinged with warning.

Her black mechanical warhorse naturally tended to force other vehicles aside and she quickly found a parking space that was close to the sub-level entrance. A couple of drunks wandered down the sidewalk and stared at her.

She ignored them as she got out. The muscle-car was not a subtle vehicle but she was beyond the point at which subtlety was advisable. What she needed now was speed and power—considerable power.

Briskly, she circled to the trunk, opened it, and exposed her arsenal to the harsh white lamps that stood vigil against New York's darkness. The two drunkards glimpsed all the weapons, made slurred "whoa" sounds, and hurried away into the night.

Taylor knew that momentarily, the proprietors would notice her and take an interest in her. She outfitted herself rapidly. The idea was to get in and choose the battlefield herself before they could engage her on disadvantageous terrain.

She had already strapped a Kevlar vest on under her suit, one customized with extra protection over the heart. Now, she retrieved a modern update of the medieval gauntlet—a glove reinforced with steel and titanium that could stand up to major stress such as, for example, being jammed into the mouth of a creature with powerful jaws. She slid the gauntlet onto her left hand.

A couple of pistols loaded with silver-tipped bullets strapped onto the belt at her waist. The presence of silver nearby made her feel slightly sick but it wouldn't kill her. She had trained herself to ignore the feeling. It would do far worse things to her main target.

Finally, she added a sword in a reinforced scabbard, which hung on her back with the hilt within easy reach. This weapon, too, was a modernization of an old classic— something of a cross between a katana and military-grade machete. Its cutting power was fearsome, and she'd sharpened it before leaving the house.

Thus armed, she examined the building. A door at the rear was almost certainly an emergency escape. She started the car and drove it directly in front of the exit to block it effectively. Satisfied, she slid out again and locked the vehicle.

Before anyone could emerge to challenge her parking, the vampire leapt and floated upward to clear the entire building and waft down onto the staircase that led to the main entrance. She knocked on the door.

Eyes appeared in the slit. Even before their owner could ask her the password, she kicked the door down.

It crashed inward, its hinges ripped loose from the concrete in a spray of debris, and the man guarding the door collapsed beneath it. She hurdled over him, confident he wouldn't get up anytime soon, and strode down the hallway into the main floor.

The whole establishment had heard her entrance and had gone quiet. Everyone stared.

There were faces there she recognized and that recognized her in turn. Analyzing their expressions, those subtle betrayers of thought and emotion, she concluded that most of them were neutrals—they weren't specifically her friends but neither were they in on the plot against her. They would stand aside.

In fact, most of them had already begun to inch toward the walls.

Other faces were less friendly by far. "Hey," a rough voice behind her demanded gutturally, "listen, lady, you can't come in here and—"

Taylor spun. In the split second before her foot landed, she saw a large man in a ridiculous pinstriped suit bearing down on her while he reached into his jacket. Her boot struck his arm, crushed it, and sent the impact through it and into his stomach. Bellowing like a frightened cow, he careened away and spewed vomit in his wake until he pounded into the back wall and slumped.

Another guy—a mob enforcer like the pinstriped asshole—appeared from behind a slot machine, already aiming a Magnum at her. The vampire moved too fast for him to even see, seized the gun, turned its barrel upward, and shoved the butt into his forehead. His grip on it released and it stayed in her hand, but before he could fall, she caught him by the shoulders and threw him onto the poker table.

The dealer and the players sat frozen in horror. Taylor strode past them, grabbed the half-conscious man again, and dragged him to his feet. She hauled him to the door in the back corner and used his head to open it.

By now, he was almost completely out of it. Hauling him like a rag doll, she stepped into the corridor, threw the door shut behind her, and shoved him forcibly through the large, loop-shaped handles. They'd have to saw through him to escape via this route.

Exactly like they'd have to smash through her car to get out the other way.

There was a T-intersection up ahead, where a single light bulb hung from the ceiling. A dark-suited mobster lunged from the side-branching hall and fired a handheld sub-machine gun. She stood her ground, took a couple of bullets to her Kevlar-protected chest, and drew one of the pistols from her hip to fire it in the same motion.

The gunman's knee exploded with blood. He screamed —the sound high and wailing for such a burly man—and dropped, already on the verge of passing out with pain and shock. Behind her, the clientele could be heard stampeding toward the front entrance. They'd obviously wisely decided to get the hell out of there.

The vampire advanced. She took a long, floating step over the sprawled gangster. He wasn't a lycanthrope, but a bullet to the knee—silver or not—was more than sufficient to disable a mere human.

She turned down the side hall. It ended only a few paces beyond at a room where four men had been playing poker at an expensive table. Now, their cards lay flat before them and their hands held guns which were all aimed at her.

Three of them wore charcoal-colored suits like the guy who'd tried to shoot her. The last man wore a white shirt and tie with the sleeves rolled up. All four stared intently. They, unlike their friend, were smart enough to realize that she wasn't there to murder them all...unless they convinced her to.

The guy in the white shirt spoke for the group. "Whaddya want, lady?"

"Where is Albert?" she asked, in a calm, measured tone. "Is he with Gabriel?" She took a step forward.

These men, being poker players and all, were fairly good at hiding their reactions but not quite good enough. There was a definite trace of "Oh, shit!" in their expressions. Albert and Gabriel were her main targets, and all these men knew exactly why.

The spokesman shook his head. "I don't know who you're talking about, ma'am. I run this establishment and my name's Pat O'Reilly."

"An Irishman in charge of an establishment that otherwise has clear Italian-American proclivities. That's truly fascinating. You strike me as more the consigliere type. Why don't you tell me where Albert is right fucking now?"

She took another step and crossed the threshold into their poker den.

A small form dropped from overhead and claws scrabbled around her neck and face. The mobsters raised their weapons as her hand jerked up to deal with the attacker. She found a small, dense arm and snapped it like a dry twig.

The gremlin howled in agony and lost his hold on the silver-plated dagger he'd intended to use. She hurled him into the wall. It cracked, and the creature, now unconscious, stuck there within the impact hole.

The four mobsters stood frozen with their fingers on the triggers of their guns.

Pat swallowed. "Don't mind our little friend, ma'am," he said and tried to smile while sweat rolled down his brow. "He gets a little over-excited sometimes."

Taylor nodded. "So do I."

She kicked the table over. Pat and one of the other men, who'd been seated on the side opposite her, were driven hard against the back wall and the edge slammed into their stomachs. The two at the head and foot stumbled back. Their gun arms raised.

The vampire had already closed on the fat guy on the right, crushed the pistol in his hand, and shoved him between her and the other man. His cohort on the left fired and the fat man took the bullet in the hip. He grunted and fell.

The last gunman standing looked about ready to piss himself in terror, but he squeezed off another shot, now aimed at her face. She swung her head aside to evade it, drew her sword, and threw it in the same motion.

The blade flashed and barely slowed before suddenly, it embedded itself in the opposite wall. Her target stared at the bloody stump where his gun hand had been and screamed, his eyes wide with shock.

Taylor leapt gracefully over him to retrieve her sword.

The two men she'd thrust the table into were recovered now. The first, another grey-suited Italian, merely glared at her. She smacked him in the face hard enough that it probably put a hairline fracture in his jaw and drove his head back into the wall. He sagged and did not bother her further.

That only left Pat. He winced, and his hands trembled. Quite possibly, he had a hernia.

"Pat," she said softly, "let me ask you one more time. Where's Albert? And where's Gabriel?" She flicked the sword toward his face and brought the blood-streaked point to a stop about half an inch from his eyeball.

A shudder ran through his whole body. "Goddammit." He moaned. "Albert's with Gabriel, yeah. You have that part right. They're in Chappaqua. I don't know the address—" He tensed as though expecting her to drive the blade forward. "Really, I don't, lady. Uh, Campfire Lake. It's near someplace called Campfire Lake. That's all I know. I swear."

The vampire whipped the sword aside. Pat shuddered again, this time in relief, and closed his eyes.

"Thank you," she said, confident he'd told the truth. "Do not warn them that I'm coming or I'll come back here after I deal with them."

Behind her, the fat guy with the hip wound had struggled to his feet by bracing his back against the wall. "Bitch," he gurgled. "Do you really think you can get away with treatin' made men like this? I'm gonna—"

She spun and lashed out with the sword as she moved. Half of the fat man's head fell away from the rest, and his one remaining eye lolled stupidly as blood leaked onto his tongue. He collapsed in a heap.

"Jesus..." someone gasped. Evidently, one of the other disabled men had regained their wits.

Taylor turned to face them. "I do not fuck around, gentlemen. I was generous in allowing your petty machinations to proceed this far. But it's over and I will not be insulted. Don't make me come back to this shithole again. And next time, if someone raises a hand against me, you might as well cut that hand off yourselves—or I'll simply make chum out of you all and sell you to an aquarium."

She sheathed her sword in total silence. Calmly, she strolled out, through the deserted casino and over the fallen door, and returned to her car. No one bothered her.

CHAPTER TWENTY-THREE

Chappaqua, Westchester County, New York
Her first idea had been to leave the black muscle-car in the most obvious public place she should think of—directly in front of a big-box store in the middle of town. It wasn't the kind of locale where either preternaturals or human mercenaries would dare to try to blow it up, even at night.

However, that left the problem of how to move, on foot, all the way to Gabriel's hide-out, heavily armed and armored, without being seen by anyone. There were some things that would have been a stretch even for her abilities.

Instead, Taylor drove around a few back roads until she found a nice stretch of woods where she could safely hide the vehicle for a couple of hours. The area around New Castle and Chappaqua was not exactly heavily patrolled by police and her vehicle had little to fear from stupid teenagers who might try to carjack it.

She parked amidst black shadows cast by tall trees. Her warhorse would be almost invisible unless someone walked up and shined a light on it. Satisfied, she pulled her phone out to check the satellite photography of the area.

Campfire Lake wasn't far. It was almost funny—her deadliest enemy in years had his headquarters only about a twenty-five-minute drive from her own home. Officially, she could not seem to find any evidence of a vampire-worthy estate near the lake, which meant that her destination probably lay in the blank area of the map.

Satisfied that she'd found the location, she slid out and locked her car. In the silence, she paused and took a deep breath to steady her mind for the stealth and silence she'd need at first—and the violence she would commit afterward—then ran under the trees and into the deep of the night.

Soon, she sensed the lake ahead and before it, a clearing with a building. And many people and creatures around the structure.

They were expecting her.

At the first sign of a flashlight's beam cutting through the darkness, she floated into the nearest tree, a pine, and hid amongst its branches. She looked down and expanded her consciousness to its maximum breadth.

Before her was a three-story mansion, larger than her own although newer and crasser in its design. Only one or two electric lights were on within, on the second floor. A dozen men in black paramilitary outfits prowled the grounds and swept it with their gun lights.

The vampire paused to consider her strategy. She needed to send a clear message and slaughtering everyone there would accomplish that. But getting Albert and Gabriel was the most important objective. With that in mind, the risk of failure increased with every moment she wasted. They might use the delay to slip away.

She jumped and landed like a feather before she sprinted directly toward the house.

One of the patrolling guards came too close for comfort. She deviated slightly toward him and he noticed her when she came within arm's reach.

"What the—"

Taylor lashed out with her gauntleted left fist and punched him in the head hard enough to crack his helmet and turn him off like a light.

A few of the others seemed to hear the crunch and they moved to where their comrade had fallen, but she was already past them. She pulled the pins from a couple of grenades and dropped them behind her.

Twin explosions lit up the night with blazing orange fire, shaking the ground and burning the grass. Men shouted in alarm and rushed toward the blast and away from her.

A short jump brought her to stand before the front door of the mansion. It was locked, of course, but she kicked it down.

Wood splintered and metal screamed as the door hurtled inwards. She was already ten feet within, her sword brandished, but found no immediate adversary. The lights on the second floor indicated that Albert and Gabriel were probably there.

To her right was a staircase leading up. She ascended almost without touching the steps and could hear and smell the crowd waiting for her. Her nose gave no indication of a vampire, but Gabriel might have ways to disguise his scent.

She reached the landing and the trap sprung.

A device, halfway between a piston and a trebuchet, unleashed a powerful, spring-loaded metal arm which struck her with the force of an oncoming car. She heard her own left hip and ribs crack as she catapulted to the right and tumbled into a small, brilliantly lit room. Taylor struck the far wall and spun in time to see the mechanical door slam shut and lock.

Shit.

The piston-hammer device had only been the first half of the trap. The room itself was the second. The ceiling and walls were covered with vents, which had already opened and now discharged streams of brownish-yellow vapor that filled the chamber with a smell like a delicatessen.

"Mustard gas," she whispered. She trembled with anger and loathing. It wouldn't kill her but it would hurt, and the awful blisters on her skin and lungs would make it harder for her to fight if, for example, they broke the door down and came in with gas masks and guns—and stakes.

She had no intention of allowing them the time to accomplish that.

"Gabriel!" she roared. "You had your chance." She braced herself against the far wall and used that to launch herself toward the door and pound it with both fists. The metal dented.

"Urgh!" she bellowed and drove her arms and shoulders against it again. "You know this won't work. Come and fight."

The door, and even the surrounding wall, made

grinding and shrieking sounds as she assaulted it, and the exertion plus her furious shouts meant she drew more of the gas into her lungs. She could feel the tissues boiling, even as her regeneration capabilities strove to counteract it.

With a final, wrathful charge, she broke the door in two and the thick steel plates careened in opposite directions when she burst out into the hallway.

An armored guard rushed toward her with a crossbow. She stepped to his side and shoved him down the stairs. Screaming, he tumbled and left cracks where he landed before he rolled out of sight.

The vampire raced toward the chamber where the lights were still on. She demolished another door and pushed through into an elongated parlor, almost a private museum filled with reproductions of Classical statues and Renaissance paintings.

It was also filled with mobsters.

"Shoot!" a voice commanded.

The very air became a cacophony of noise as ten or eleven men opened fire with rifles and SMGs.

The worst of her wounds had already healed. She snatched a six-foot statue by the elbow, whipped it around as if it were a child's doll, and flung it into the middle of the throng. It absorbed some of the bullets and also felled the two men in front.

By the time they'd realized what was happening, she was already among them and so was her sword.

Two more men went down screaming in a spray of blood when the blade flashed through their bodies. She vaulted easily from wall to wall between strokes. Three more died in another leap as she slashed them in half at the waist.

She'd absorbed at least ten bullets, she realized. Pain seared through her and her left leg didn't work as well as it should. She used the right leg to provide thrust to somersault over the heads of the next few gunmen and swung faster than they could shoot to slit throats and faces as she twirled back to her feet.

Three more adversaries pushed in front of her, and a fourth at the rear had ducked behind a statue in the corner. She skewered the first two with quick thrusts to either side that pierced their hearts and spines. They fell, gurgling while their guns fired uselessly over their heads.

The third man stood frozen. Taylor swept her sword diagonally upward from right hip to left shoulder, and the mobster's body split beneath the sharp blade. Some of the blood spurted into her mouth and she swallowed it gratefully, electrified by the rush of combat and slaying and death.

No. I must not lose all self-control. There was still one man left and he smelled different than the others.

His voice carried a vestigial Chicago accent beneath its New York patois when it echoed from behind the statue. "That was real clever, Taylor, very fuckin' witty," he said. "Turn my guys into chum and sell them to an aquarium."

"Oh." The vampire sheathed her sword, drew her pistol, and made sure the gauntlet was secure on her left hand. "They disobeyed me and did warn you, after all?"

"Nah," Albert retorted. "The casino is bugged everywhere. You'd be amazed by what you can hear. Like this time. You're wrong though, lady. You are the one who's gonna be sleeping with the fishes. By dawn."

His voice changed at that last word. Dawn. It was no longer a human being who spoke.

Taylor stepped out as the werewolf launched into his attack.

She was already firing her pistol but Albert was smarter than she'd expected. The beast hurtled through the air and held a riot shield in front of him, which he'd concealed behind the statue. The silver bullets either flattened against it or ricocheted off.

Her one advantage was that the riot shield slowed him down. She darted aside, evaded his sudden lunge by at least a yard, and aimed her pistol as he landed heavily.

Briefly, she studied her opponent. She vaguely recalled that Albert was a wiry, weaselly-looking man. As lycanthropes went, he was noticeably slender and his fur was a whitish-silver streaked with black. Although not as powerfully built as some she'd seen, there was a lithe agility to him that gave her pause. When he operated at his peak, he was potentially as fast as she was.

He whipped the shield around in time to intercept her next two shots and surprised her when he threw the object like a discus at her hands and face.

Defying gravity, she spun to raise her feet skyward but her hands were too slow. The edge of the shield dislodged the gun from them. As her feet touched the ceiling, she drew her sword.

Albert glared at her, his lupine eyes a venomous yellow-green. "Get back down here," he snarled. He kicked her pistol toward one of the floor-length windows, shattered now by the gunfire and chaos, and it toppled out of the building. With her disarmed of her pistol, he leapt at her.

The vampire plummeted as her attacker vaulted up. She whipped her sword down, intending to simply skewer him in midair, but to her surprise, he managed to hurl himself aside, seize her by the wrist, and twist it sharply. Her forearm cracked and the force of the maneuver made her twist to land hard and painfully. The sword clattered away from her.

The werewolf landed next to her. He'd put himself in a corner but given that she was sprawled on the floor and the killing urge was upon him, he probably didn't care.

Taylor gritted her teeth and allowed her fangs to show as she scrambled to her feet and cradled her right arm. It would only need a few seconds to heal. "You might be the fastest werewolf I've fought, Albert," she conceded. He grinned and took a step toward her. "But you're not the strongest. Or the brightest."

Rather than lunge or jump, she simply walked toward him. He hesitated for a second in confusion before he raised his claws. She ducked under them and pounded him with a body-slamming bear hug, heedless of the pain it caused her right arm, and drove him back against the wall.

Faced with this kind of brute force, he reacted exactly as she thought he would. He tried to bite her head off. Her left hand, sheathed in its gauntlet, was ready.

Albert's jaws closed around the hand. She growled in response to his, leaned back, and shoved her metal-clad fist deeper between them and down his throat. His jaws clamped down, but she was too well-positioned for him to break her other arm and his teeth were useless against the steel-and-titanium armor. He made a horrible gagging sound as her limb vanished up to the elbow in his mouth.

By now, her right arm was back in commission. She used it to hold the werewolf's thrashing arms and braced herself as he tried to kick her in the stomach with his skinny hind legs. She shoved her left arm farther down his throat. By now, his teeth had begun to rake the flesh of her upper arm, but his jaws were too immobilized to do much damage.

Grunting with strain, she used the leverage she now had to hoist the entire beast up and bring the center of his back down on her knee. His howl of pain when his spine cracked was muffled by her fist.

She punched all the way down and her gauntleted hand burst through the flesh and bone of the back of his neck. When she ripped it to the side, his jaw came loose while the rest of his head rolled to the side and hung next to his shoulder as gore fountained from the wound.

The vampire pushed away to leave the ravaged lycanthrope whimpering in a heap while she retrieved her sword. He'd barely had the chance to start regenerating before she pounced and drove the blade through his heart.

A feeble howl escaped him. She twisted the sword and ripped it free, taking the heart with it. She pulled it off the blade and crushed it.

After a final, gurgling sigh, Albert fell still. The silver hairs faded from the body of a broken, half-decapitated, and otherwise mangled human.

"Prick," she muttered and tossed the crushed organ aside. "I have an arrangement with the Family. Splinter factions like yours only fuck things up for everyone."

Now, she needed to find Gabriel.

She heard something—faintly, distantly, the kind of thing mortal ears would not have picked up. It was someone, probably a security officer, speaking into a headset.

"Blow the floor," he ordered.

Taylor bolted toward the window but didn't quite make it.

Bright light and deafening noise filled the whole world in the same moment that her foot stood poised on the windowsill, ready to jump. An ancient and primal terror of the sun—the only other thing that was that bright —filled her.

And then she fell and all she could see was fire.

CHAPTER TWENTY-FOUR

Chappaqua, Westchester County, New York

The blast had scorched about a third of Taylor's skin off and the fall had broken her shinbone and thrust it out of the flesh. She slid it into place and lay in the grass, making no sound. They might assume she was dead already and burnt to a crisp. Hopefully, the hesitation of their uncertainty would provide her with the time she needed to regenerate.

The pain was intense but she knew it wouldn't kill her. They hadn't managed that, not yet. Knowing she could recover in minutes made it far more bearable. She recalled, dimly, her past life as a human and the fear she'd had that any great pain was a harbinger of death. That kind of fear applied to very few things anymore.

She'd also learned something useful. Sacrificing the top floor of the house meant that Gabriel was not there. Either he was on the ground floor or, more likely, underground.

And with his lackeys trying to decide if they'd eliminated her, she had a window of opportunity to sneak in and finish the job.

Once the worst of the pain had subsided and her leg was mostly mended, she found her sword beside her and levitated slowly from the grass and toward the nearest tree. Once hidden within its branches, she surveyed the mansion.

The planted explosives had wrought massive havoc and the third floor effectively did not exist anymore. The second was also badly damaged, but whoever had placed them had been skilled since the first floor had barely been touched.

Most vampires, when threatened, sought refuge in the earth. Taylor peered through the shattered windows, her keen perception seeking out the fastest path that might lead to the basement.

There—beyond the window toward the left side was a hallway leading into the center of the house. That seemed like her best option.

By now, a few paramilitary guys were fanning out into the yard, searching the grass with the flashlights attached to their guns. There were two of them between her and the window she'd identified.

She waited until their attention was focused earthward before she leapt, silent and graceful, from one tree to another and cleared both of them before the first of the men was beneath her. He started to turn and looked upward.

Taylor snapped a heavy branch off and flung it at the guard. He saw it too late and tried to stumble back but it came down on his head and pinned him to the ground.

His teammate a few yards ahead heard the noise and saw what had happened immediately—although he did not see Taylor. "Wilkes!" he hissed into his headset. "Ramirez is down. A fuckin' tree branch fell on him."

The vampire drifted into the night sky as the man's light panned the tree she'd recently occupied. Then, when she was directly above him, she allowed herself to plunge straight down.

He looked up, his face frozen in shock behind the glossy visor of his helmet, and she collided with a soft thump. Her feet came down on his shoulders, crushed the bones, and drove him into a crumpled heap. Other men—some of whom almost sounded like dwarves, she realized—exchanged fearful chatter over their headsets while she raced across the lawn and vaulted at her target window.

Fortunately, the explosion had already shattered the glass, even on the first floor. She soared through the aperture like a dolphin through a hoop, somersaulted and landed on her feet within. The house was dark but this was no impediment to her. She streaked into the central hallway.

Three creatures in paramilitary gear waited for her, guarding a doorway that gave off a slight whiff of subterranean air. The one on the left was definitely a dwarf, judging by his build.

"Kill her," he ordered.

They opened fire with their automatic rifles and sprayed a fusillade of silver bullets. She vaulted up and ran along the wall, then the ceiling, and barreled into them. At least four of the bullets struck her. The two that caught her torso were absorbed by her Kevlar vest, but the two in her legs sank into her flesh.

She ignored the nauseating pain and hurtled forward with a massive sweeping hook-kick. The two humans catapulted away, crashed into the walls, and groaned with pain. The dwarf, however, merely lurched back a step or two.

Taylor bounced off him and turned the motion into a rear handspring. Her adversary aimed his weapon again and fired, this time discharging what looked like a short-range flamethrower blast. Her feet were singed but she dodged most of the flame.

When she stopped in a three-point crouch, he had already begun his advance. She flung the sword at him like a javelin.

He cursed and fell back as the blade sank into his chest. His arms fell and the flamethrower discharged another fiery blast at the floor before his legs gave out and he toppled.

The vampire hurdled the flames and dragged the sword free before she aimed another kick at his head to be sure he wouldn't bother her any further. Finally, she turned to the basement door.

Her enemy was somewhere within. "It's time to finish this."

She breathed deeply and paused for a moment to wrestle the nausea under control. Already, her body was squeezing out the silver bullets and cleansing the residue from her bloodstream. Too much silver could have incapacitated her for entire minutes, but these guys hadn't been good enough shots for that.

The door was sealed with a heavy mechanical lock.

Taylor drew her fist back and punched the mechanism twice with her gauntlet. It shattered and the door creaked inward to reveal a concrete staircase leading down. She detected no sign of living things there, but she did sense electronics.

Quickly, she knelt and cut the thick bulletproof vest from one of the human troops she'd battered. She also took his rifle for good measure. The man started to stir, so she thumped his skull hard into the wall and knocked him out again. With the vest held in front of her as an extra layer of protection, she crept down the stairs.

At the second-to-last step, something whirred in the split-second before all hell broke loose.

A barrage of heavy gunfire pounded into the vest, which slowed the bullets but it quickly began to shred apart.

Drone gun, Taylor thought. She hurled the vest toward the weapon and flitted to the side, her sword already out, and slashed upward toward the muzzle flare. Metal sheared metal and the gun made an off-kilter whining sound as it faltered and died.

She inspected the sword. The blade was slightly warped and the edge had taken a few chips from all the punishment she'd put it through, but it was still functional. It would kill, and that was what mattered.

The cellar before her was immense and filled with all manner of useless junk—consumer technology, expensive trinkets, extra furniture, and the like. Her gaze slid over these items and instead, sought Gabriel's refuge of last resort.

She found it soon enough in the center of the basement.

Looming like a lost elevator car, a steel box formed a room-within-a-room. She strolled toward it.

"Stop," a voice snapped, electronically magnified. It was thick with the imperative tone of her species but the power of command did not work on her. She stopped anyway, though. She wanted to hear what this son of a bitch had to say now that he was cornered.

The vampire looked toward a tiny glinting circle, which she assumed was the lens of a camera that watched her and transmitted the information to the safe room's interior. Beside it was a speaker and a microphone.

"Yes, Gabriel?" she inquired.

"You might as well give it up at this point, Taylor," he replied, and she had to admit he sounded smoother and more confident than she'd expected. "Even before I remind you of all the other forces arrayed against you. There are currently four inches of steel between us. Not even you can punch through that. Ha, ha...Taylor Steele. It's fitting that you'd meet your demise as a result of it. Unless, of course, you take the hint and leave New York forever. You're no longer wanted here."

She frowned, unamused. "No," she stated.

Gabriel started to say something else but she directed a spin-kick at the thick metal door. Her leg stung and the very bones vibrated but the steel was dented only slightly.

"See?" He sneered. "You've been skipping leg day, haven't you? In the time it will take you to break through, my numerous allies will converge on you. For starters, Albert and his coterie of professional killers will be along at any moment, adding their strength to my own men."

Taylor scoffed. "They were upstairs. I already disposed

of them. And your own security personnel are currently all dead, disabled, or guilty of desertion now that they've seen what I'm capable of. Anything else?"

Before he could answer, she picked up a heavy oak table and threw it at the door with all her strength. It shattered and filled the air with brown splinters, but the steel caved a little more.

"Tucker," her adversary continued, but a trace of agitation had crept into his tone now, "is also on his way with a highly impressive arsenal. Not even you can come back from simply being shredded to pieces, which is exactly what will happen once he and his men arrive."

"Oh," she retorted cheerfully. "Tucker once again underestimated my assistant. He won't be a problem anymore—for either of us or anyone else. Ever." She punched the door in frustration, inflicted far too little damage, and looked around for something else to use as a battering ram.

He pretended to laugh, and Taylor answered it immediately. "Didn't you know that, Gabriel? That was hours ago. Have you been hiding in there all this time? Or was that merely an inept attempt to bluff me?"

"For your information," he went on, "there was also an impromptu vote by several important local figures after I convened them to talk. Nine out of ten agreed that you need to get the hell out of town, Taylor. Continue with your rampage and you'll soon have the entire preternatural community against you, along with half the humans."

The vampire retrieved the severed half of the drone gun and charged the door with it. The weapon crumpled on impact, but the steel barrier dented further and even sprouted a tiny crack.

"Now," she said toward the microphone, "you are flat-out lying. No such conference ever took place, and most of the influential people here still support me."

"I would support you," Gabriel countered, his words hurried now, "if you would amend your policies only slightly. Think of it—I was able to arrange all this. That proves I'm capable of making things happen. Your organization could benefit greatly from my help. Ha, I could be your youth consultant. You are getting somewhat long in the tooth, even for a vampire."

She saw a spare refrigerator in one corner of the basement, picked it up, whirled quickly, and launched it at the safe room as she came out of the spin. It struck the door head-on with an impact sound almost as loud as a gunshot. The top half broke into its component chunks while the rest buckled and clattered to the floor.

When she walked toward the chamber, she saw that the door was now distorted to the point that a sliver of air and light was visible around the edge.

"Your offer," she told him, "is appreciated. Thank you for your interest in employment with Moonlight Detective Agency. However, at this time we are unable—"

"One day," he interjected, his voice twice its previous volume, "you'll step on the wrong dog turd and slip into an open manhole. Maybe not today. But no tyrant reigns forever." A faint noise issued over the speaker which she recognized as the sound of knuckles cracking.

She thrust forward and kicked the door in. The thick steel slab detached itself from its bracings and crashed inwards. By then, she was already through, her automatic rifle raised.

Gabriel had flattened himself against the wall, as she suspected, and aimed a sub-machine gun, probably loaded with silver-tipped ammo. She fell into a somersault and avoided the first deafening shot as she aimed quickly and fired.

A stream of lead burst across the small space and perforated his bicep, armpit, and shoulder to spill blood across his black turtleneck. He stumbled and dropped the gun.

Taylor launched furiously into the attack, surged at her foe, and jump-kicked him in the stomach. He grunted and careened into the far wall. When she moved in, his left hand snaked out and caught her sword in mid-swing.

The blade arced back toward its owner but she caught his fist and for a moment, the two of them stood locked against each other. She squeezed but the bastard had strong hands...the knuckle-cracking, she remembered. He must have been among those vampires who gained especially powerful claw-like nails upon undeath. When he grinned, his fangs seemed almost impossibly long.

Sooner than she would have liked, Gabriel's injured right arm lashed out toward her. Five knife-like talons raked through her abdomen and his left hand overcame her strength to hurl both her and the sword across the room.

"Ha," he jeered. "You're strong but at the end of the day, I'm still bigger than you. That always counts for something." He lunged.

She rolled aside and her enemy's claws raked through

the air over her head. Seizing her fallen sword, she threw it up into the ceiling, where it stuck.

Her opponent pounced in another vicious attack. She avoided the bulk of his assault and kneed him in the gut, but one of his huge hands grasped her right thigh, ripped through the flesh, and cracked her femur.

Taylor gritted her teeth against the pain, shoved him back, and launched herself up with only her left leg. She used her preternatural power of flight to remain airborne long enough to seize hold of the sword and kick him in the face.

As he spun from the blow, she yanked the blade free and lashed it down as she fell. It split the other vampire's back from the base of his neck to his waist and severed the spine in the process.

"*Gah!*" he cried, the sound strangled and undignified as he flopped forward into the corner.

She moved in for the kill.

"Wait!" Gabriel gasped and looked at her with crazed reddish eyes while he held one of his impressive claws out. "Haven't you considered that—"

She swung the sword with every ounce of strength she had. It sheared through the four fingers of the outstretched hand seconds before it passed through the flesh and bone of his neck. His final comment was left unsaid and his head toppled from his body and rolled to the center of the floor.

"No." She gulped a breath. "You stole my coffin and tried to murder me while I slept. That act said it all. Anything else you might want to monologue about is a waste of both our time."

The decapitated corpse had nothing further to say.

The vampire sheathed her weapon and limped to the middle of the chamber, where she picked up the severed head by its short brown hair. She rested a moment while her body healed itself.

"What a night." She sighed.

Once her legs were back to full capability, she climbed to the first floor and tossed the unconscious human guards out onto the lawn. When she was satisfied no one remained alive inside, she returned to the dead dwarf and borrowed his flamethrower. With it, she set fires in a few key locations that would allow for maximum conflagration.

The entire mansion—or what was left of it after the blast on the third floor—grew brighter as the blaze spread to engulf its foundation, the roaring flames drawing sparkles off the lapping waters of the nearby small lake.

Taylor was already back at her car before police cruisers and fire trucks began to converge on the burning estate. She waited in the shadows as they passed. Gabriel's head rested within a black bag at the foot of the passenger's seat. She always carried an extra bag or two, just in case.

In peace and quiet, she drove the short distance to Harrison and her home. Gabriel might have had a few other lackeys around, but she highly doubted that any of them had the capability or the will to cause her further trouble. She—and Remington—had destroyed all three of the conspiracy's leaders.

When she arrived at her house, she left the muscle-car parked in the driveway and took the black bag with her out to the backyard. The night's blackness was turning, by now, to the dim ash-lavender of pre-dawn. She'd finished her work barely in time.

"Now," she said, "so no one tries to get this little trophy...."

She and Presley had dug a fire pit in the rear of the property on one of the slopes of the rocky hill that rose above the trees with clear exposure to the sun. She pulled Gabriel's head from its bag and set it in the middle of the pit, facing east.

"Goodnight, sweet prince." She turned and walked to the mansion, looking forward to her rest.

The vampire's head did nothing. Its face remained frozen in a bestial expression of cornered-animal fear and anger. It did not react until the amber blaze of the sun crept over the horizon and its deadly rays first scalded and blistered the white skin before the entire skull was engulfed in a wreath of flames.

CHAPTER TWENTY-FIVE

Harrison, Westchester County, New York

"No," Remington insisted, "three of a kind beats two pair." He planted a finger firmly on the central card of the trio.

Riley made a high-pitched scoffing sound. "That's nonsensical. Two pairs consist of four cards, and you only have three."

He put a hand over his eyes. "It's not the number of cards"—he sighed—"since we both start out with five, anyway. It has to do with the mathematical probability of how they match. Three of a kind is statistically less likely than two pairs, hence it's more valuable. Don't you know anything about market forces?"

Behind him somewhere, he thought he heard gentle steps coming up from the cellar.

The fairy made a little "uh" sound in her throat. "I know, for one thing, that beautiful young women are always highly valued. Why aren't you interested in me? I even wore this dress for you after you suggested it."

Recalling that he still hadn't picked up the next batch of honey, Remy said quickly, "Oh, you look lovely in the dress, and I mean that. But poker is serious business. Now, please acknowledge defeat."

She protested again that the game's rules were absurd, and he again tried to explain the basics of mathematics to her until a woman's voice, gentle but firm, interjected.

"Enough," Taylor proclaimed. "Listening to you two bicker is giving me a headache. Remy, I can't believe you, of all people, are trying to explain maths. Also"—she gestured to the fairy—"I appreciate you bringing her here, but I really don't need a snack right now, thank you."

Riley gasped. "What?"

Remy flapped a hand toward the fairy. "Ignore her, she's fucking with you."

The vampire floated through the foyer and over their game but left the cards totally undisturbed. The two watched her pass and shrugged at each other.

"Oh," she said, paused at the kitchen doorway, and turned, "there is one other thing, though. Riley, could you please give us a demonstration of your magic powers?"

He thought that odd since he already knew that the fairy could do a wide variety of helpful things. Hastily, he glanced at Riley. She still looked nervous at the prospect of Taylor taking a bite out of her, so she floated up and spread her arms.

"What would you like me to do, madame?" she asked.

Taylor tapped a finger to her lips, extended her hand, and spread it wide in the air. "Show Remington your ability to grow…say, to my size, and to hide your wings. He might find that…useful, at some point."

She turned away from the two of them and walked into the kitchen, where Presley was waiting for her having finished the preparation of her cup of red salt tea.

"Madame." He handed her the hot beverage upon its saucer.

"Thank you, Presley." She accepted it and after a few sips, she said, "I'd best check on the excitement in the foyer. When is the tow truck coming to deal with the Tesla that Remington borrowed?"

The butler folded his hands behind his back. "Tomorrow. Shall I make funds available or will you simply mind-wipe them?"

"The latter," she replied. "I can't have the poor fellows blabbing about my modifications."

She turned and walked over the threshold.

David Remington stood there, his mouth agape, and practically drooled on the floor. Across from him stood a beautiful young woman, totally naked and wingless, about five-foot, only a few inches shorter than Taylor herself.

"See?" the fairy said and twirled to show off. He shuddered as her buttocks came into view and when, as she stopped herself while facing him, her breasts gradually ceased jiggling.

She looked at the man across from her and frowned with concern. "What's wrong with him, though? He stopped talking when I changed."

"Oh." The vampire sipped her tea. "Don't worry about it. I'll snap him out of it momentarily and he can drive you home. First, return to your usual form."

"Okay." A few silver sparkles flashed where the woman had stood and a tiny fairy fluttered in her place. She was still naked, the miniature dress she'd worn having fallen to the floor when she transformed. Her laugh tinkled as she fluttered down to retrieve it.

Taylor walked closer to Remy, who still resembled an abnormally fresh zombie, and slapped him. "Wake up, Remington!" she ordered in her command voice.

"Ow!" he exclaimed, stumbled back a couple of steps, and raised a hand to his reddening cheek. "Yes, I'm awake. What the hell? Why did you do that?" He glanced frantically across the carpet and saw, with obvious disappointment, that Riley had returned to her natural form.

He cleared his throat, suddenly self-conscious, and sidestepped toward one of the big easy chairs. He grabbed a pillow and placed it on his lap as he sat and pretended to rest his elbows on it. "I'll...uh, sit here and rest for a moment," he mumbled.

Riley floated toward him. "Are you okay, Remy?"

"He's fine," said Taylor. "Remington, you'll be pleased to know that I have no intention of actually paying for the repairs to my car, which means I won't have to garnish your wages."

"Oh! Well, thank you."

"However," she continued, her tone more strident, "please do not do that again. Even if you think I'm in danger. You could have easily used your own car for the job. And, of course, you wouldn't be down to your second car if you hadn't totaled the first one by your own actions. Still, I appreciate your concern for myself and my coffin. At least you thought you were helping me."

The bulge under the pillow was shrinking by now, and Remy had begun to act like himself again. "Think nothing of it," he blustered. "It made for fascinating on-the-job training."

She nodded. "Now then, would you be able to drop Riley off at her nest on your way home? It's only a short detour, and there are certain creatures that sometimes prey on stray fairies the way hawks do upon sparrows."

He glanced at Riley, who stared at him with big dewy eyes.

"Oh...I suppose. She has been rather helpful. And besides, we can stop along the way for the honey."

The vampire finished her tea, and Presley appeared to accept the empty cup and saucer. "Good. Keep up the good work, Remington."

The butler nodded toward him. "Indeed, sir. Keep up the good work."

He set the pillow aside—a little nervously—and stood, collecting both Riley and his deck of cards on his way out. The two waved a brief goodbye before they disappeared out into the night.

Watching him, Taylor shook her head. "Males.... No offense, Presley."

"None taken, madame," he rejoined. "At least, not at my present age."

Por's Bar, Lower Manhattan, New York City

"Yes," Remington went on after a short pause for a swig of his Bloody Mary, "ultimately, everything went off without a hitch. And it would never have worked out so well without me. Taylor even acknowledged my indispensability to the agency, albeit in a tactfully indirect sort of way."

Porrillage nodded and occasionally remembered to raise his eyebrows and look interested. "Oh. Yeah, good job." He pulled the lever to dispense beer into a mug for another patron, who ignored Remy's spiel.

"At this rate," he continued, "I'll be up for another promotion in no time. The company will be a joint partnership—as it was always intended to be. And, of course, that will come with a pay raise attached. I always knew I was destined to be a proper, successful businessman. And somehow, it seems right that I'd turn out to have a talent for mitigation projects. Even of the more dangerous variety."

Por continued to nod about once every five or six seconds as he rushed around the bar doing his job.

He stopped talking long enough to drain his beverage down to about a quarter of its original volume. When the bartender climbed up to offer a martini to a sullen-looking male elf who'd wandered in, the monologue resumed.

"Yes," he said, "I'd only been working there maybe a week and already, I pulled off a truly epic rescue, retrieving Taylor's coffin from all those guys. And a werewolf. Not many men would have been capable of such a thing, even with an attractive fairy sidekick at their beck and call."

The gnome looked at him, his gaze steady and even. "Didn't you say a couple of minutes ago that she wasn't actually in any danger? How does that work?"

Remy recalled that Taylor had ordered him not to divulge the secret of her sleeping arrangements, and he had to bite his tongue to keep from blurting it out. Instead, he responded with, "Oh, right, but that's not the point. If she had been in danger, my actions totally would have saved her in an extremely heroic fashion."

Por patted his hand. "Whatever you say, buddy. Do you want another Mary?"

"Nah," he replied. "I probably ought to get going soon." He sipped the last of the vodka-spiked tomato juice and even thought about eating the stalk of celery. In fact, that reminded him of something.

"Also," he announced, ignoring the way the proprietor's shoulders slumped a tad at the continued sound of his voice, "I finished cleaning my apartment by myself and have kept it orderly and spotless ever since. Half my friends said it couldn't be done, but they clearly underestimated the Remington resolve. And my recent attempt at cooking my own food—for the first time ever—was largely successful. I only burned the edges of the spaghetti. The majority of it was perfectly edible. I couldn't recycle the can, though."

The bartender poured out another beer for a customer at a table who'd requested a refill and handed it to the waitress. Looking at Remy, he put his hands on his hips and said, "Well, Mr Davis, that's an impressive achievement. Slaying a werewolf and preparing canned spaghetti, both in the same week."

Remy beamed. "I know, isn't it?" He leaned back, basking in the warm glow of the gnome's admiration.

Por shook a finger at him. "Make sure you tell Taylor about that, too. The spaghetti. I'm sure she'll be very impressed."

So what he's saying is that I can emphasize how valuable to

the company I am even more by touting my personal achieve-
ments that aren't directly related to anything to do with the
agency. Yes, Taylor really will have no choice but to admit she's
better off with me around.

"Right, then," he stated, slapped the bar's surface, and left another business card under his palm. "Bill me, as usual. You know how good I am at paying my tab in a timely fashion. I need to get back to accomplishing things. Thanks for all your advice, Por!"

He slid from his stool to the floor, swayed, and waved as he headed to the entrance, where Stanislaw awaited him. He wasn't quite sure, though, why the gnome constantly shook his head.

EPILOGUE

Sotto Suolo, Chelsea, New York City

Remy stepped up to the front entrance of the restaurant. He felt a brief pang of unease when he recalled the dread of the place he'd had the first time he'd been there. But that was before he knew the proverbial score.

With Taylor meeting him, he had nothing to fear.

"Mr Davis!" The hostess greeted him as she opened the door. "Please step inside. Ms Steele is waiting for you."

"Good to know, thank you," he acknowledged.

The woman showed him to the extreme rear corner. He noticed that no one else was present in the dining area out of respect for their privacy.

The vampire sat, as she had on that first fateful evening, with her face hidden in shadow. Not that it was necessary anymore, but he supposed it was tradition.

"So," he said as he seated himself across from her, "I've learned to make my own spaghetti—and quite competently, I might add—but it's always better to have the professionals do it, I suppose. And I'm famished."

She waved a red-nailed hand gently. "Order whatever you want, Remington. We'll say this is my treat."

He smiled. "Much appreciated."

"Although," she added, "I'm pleased to hear that you've finally acquired a few of the basic skills that most human beings learn when they're about twelve."

"Thanks."

A waiter approached and he ordered a cup of coffee—decaf this time, given how early he'd been rising—and a platter of spaghetti with house-made meatballs and extra parmesan.

The server jotted notes on his pad. "I will have your coffee at once, sir." He trotted off toward the kitchen.

As he left, Remy sighed. "You know, I never thought I'd say this, but thanks to you, I now can't get images of five-foot naked fairies out of my head." He paused. "In certain circles, that would sound...different, wouldn't it? But, well, I wonder if it's even worse in this one. Since I've always had a strict prohibition against...other...uh, species."

He sensed rather than saw Taylor's smile. "Have you seen her again since then?" the vampire asked.

"No," he admitted. "Seeking her out was tempting, but I'd have to navigate all the preternatural politics again without getting paid for it."

She drummed her fingers on the table. "I think you will see her again and probably sooner rather than later," she explained. "The fae hate failing to get what they want after all...and that fairy wants you."

Remy swallowed and did not answer right away. Instead, he studied the menu, despite having already ordered.

"What else?" she asked. "You mentioned something about requests but did not clarify what that meant."

"Ah, yes," he responded quickly, grateful for the change of subject. "We've received no fewer than four inquiries for our services these last few days via our website."

Taylor's hand froze in place and he realized that he'd actually managed to surprise her. "We have a website?" she marveled.

He pulled his phone out and tried not to smirk too hard. "We do now. Only a small one, granted." He tapped the Internet icon on his screen and punched in the agency's URL, then flipped the phone and slid it across the table for her to examine.

She leaned forward within her column of shade. "Well...this, ah, looks like a beta-test for a fanfiction website circa 2005."

Remy shrugged. "Admittedly, web design isn't my strongest area of expertise. But I suppose it would be downright unfair if I were good at everything, anyway."

The vampire pushed the device back toward him. "No one will take us seriously based on this unless they've already heard of us and are familiar with our work." She paused. "Which is probably a good thing since I'm not interested in taking on mundane cases and other nonsense. We already have our work cut out for us managing the preternaturals in this town."

The waiter returned with his coffee. He thanked the man and immediately took a sip to keep from grinning. "So," he said into his cup, "I succeeded again. Awesome."

"That's not exactly what I meant."

"Well..." He pressed on, not allowing her to dead-end

this line of discussion. "I'm afraid I must take offense to that because I think we do need more cases. At least, I do. The more the merrier, as far as my beleaguered income situation is concerned. Even if it's mundane adultery shit or something. I know a few things about adultery."

Taylor sighed. "I don't doubt it. But you'd potentially endanger the rest of our operations—the truly important stuff—by bringing uninitiated humans into the equation."

"Not if I carefully disguise the rest of our operations from them," he protested. "Besides, I'm a human and you're a vampire. Imagine the beautiful symmetry of it. You deal with preternaturals by night, while I deal with mortals by day."

She considered this for a moment. "I might allow that but only if the mundane cases are relegated to any extra time you have after you've dealt with the things I want you to do. And please don't take that as an insult to your preeminence. View it as another learning opportunity. What we do with the agency is already quite vital. We need to ensure that our primary mission is safeguarded. Everything else can come second."

Remy fiddled with his tie.

"Oh," she went on, "and only if you can make that website at least look close to professional. You may want to hire someone else for the job."

"I'll work on it," he retorted with a wave of his hand.

The waiter came out with his food. He thanked the man politely once again, accepted a coffee refill while he was at it, and dug in. Eating in silence while Taylor watched him was rather awkward— he wasn't used to dinner dates that were entirely one-sided.

Once his mouth was clear, he spoke again. "There are a few business opportunities that I thought I'd investigate tomorrow," he told her. "A couple were rather vague and might turn out to be nothing of interest...but one might require a mind-wipe."

"Go on."

He glanced around, although he knew their privacy was sacrosanct here. "It involves none other than our police commissioner. He's a busy man lately, it seems, and has been getting all kinds of phone calls from the feds. Somehow, I don't think we want a group of federal investigators roving around New York and stumbling onto preternatural activity."

"I am inclined to agree," said Taylor. "I killed several of Gabriel's and Albert's human minions. Normally, I would avoid that, but extreme circumstances call for extreme measures. But before I decide, I will await your report. We need more information."

She seemed content to think in silence while he finished his supper. He asked the waiter to deliver his compliments to the chef on the quality of the spaghetti.

The man smiled. "I will relay the message. We are honored that our most respected guests think so highly of our offerings."

Remy watched the man leave. "Perhaps, one day," he quipped, "I too will be able to cook like that."

They finally took their leave, walked together to the door, and parted with a nod once out on the sidewalk.

No sooner had he turned his back than the vampire's soft voice called, "Remington."

He turned quickly. "Yes?"

She smiled in a warm, sincere way that he'd only rarely seen but which suited her nicely, he thought. "Good work."

His gaze grew distant, but he nodded. "Yes, it was good work, wasn't it?"

A few cars sped past, breaking up the neon lights that pierced through the blackness of the city but not obscuring the way she shook her head at him. Although she was still smiling.

He waved and turned toward his car. "Talk to you tomorrow, Taylor."

AUTHOR NOTES - ISOBELLA CROWLEY

SEPTEMBER 15, 2019

Confessions

First confessions. Then thank yous - because then the thank yous will make more sense!

Izzie here. I have something to tell you.

If you're in the loop with MA's (Michael Anderle's) publishing company, this may be old news to you. But if you picked up this book from Amazon you might not have been told.

Essentially people know me as Ell Leigh Clarke, rather than Izzie.

The reason why we used the Isobella Crowley pen name on this book is because the books that I've already published as Ell are in the science-fiction genre. However, as you probably already realize, the book that you have just read is best described as Urban Fantasy.

(Mike Edit: Technically more Paranormal Fantasy with Urban Fantasy undertones, 'cause vampires... But they have dwarves and stuff too, so yeah, Urban Paranormal Fantasy! ;-))

I don't know how much you know about search engines and Amazon algorithms, but publishing both genres under the same name makes it difficult for people to find the kinds of books that they want. People looking for science-fiction and the usual space opera shenanigans would be confused to find a random Urban Fantasy detective series on the author page of Ell Leigh Clarke. Similarly, folks looking for "comedic vampires solving crime" would be confused if they ended up only able to find series about space operas.

As such, MA and I decided to use my Urban Fantasy alter ego Isobella Crowley on the front cover, with the full intention of sharing this insight with you the first opportunity we got. If you're on our email lists you will have received messages to that effect already, and now we're bringing you behind-the-scenes after the show and laying it all out for you here.

Thank yous

As always on these collaborations, I'd like to thank MA for making this series happen. It was a ton of fun coming up with the concepts for *Moonlight Detective Agency*. I especially liked hearing that all the hard work has paid off when one of the team leaders in the JIT team let me know that it was being well received by our beta readers. It's always a risk trying something new, and appreciate the opportunity that our team, and MA, have provided in testing the waters with this concept. The detective genre needs a lot more planning and work to make sure the clues are laid into the plot, and it's something I really enjoy toying with. So, thank you!

Lots of people go into making a series like this happen.

I'd like to say a massive thank you to the team of suppliers who made this book possible: Brittany, Chiara, Nathan, Philip, Moonchild, and MA's editing team.

Thank you, guys! Your hard work, care and attention mean the world to me :)

JITers

Massive, and uber thanks also go out to our beta readers, led by Brittany, and MA's JIT team led by their high commander, Zen Steve. Thank you for all your hard work in making sure the words are published double-proofed, read and re-read. Thank you so much for all the care you put into the process.

Reviewers

Mega thanks also goes out to our Amazon reviewers. It's because of you that we get to do this full time. Without your five-star reviews and thoughtful words on Amazon we simply wouldn't have enough folks reading these space shenanigans to be able to write full time.

You are the reason these stories exist and you have no idea how frikkin' grateful I am to you.

Truly, thank you... And I'm writing this based on the reviews we've had for all our other series – and praying that you come over to this series and leave us some 5* reviews for this one too!

Readers and FB page supporters

I'd like to also thank *YOU* for reading this book. Your enthusiasm for the worlds and characters we come up with is heart-warming. Thank you for being here, for the giggles and interaction, for reading, and reviewing.

You rock, and without you, there really would be no reason to write these stories.

Confessions of a Storyteller

For those of you who don't know me already, allow me to introduce myself.

My name is Ell Leigh Clarke, more often known as Ellie.

My main collaborator on this project, MA, and I have written a number of books together and have been building up history of hilarious shenanigans and give each other shit.

(Mike Edit: I think this is something Ellie started, I responded, and now her PR is so much better that I've become the nefarious instigator of all things harassment... Like the whole sniper and aggressive-aggressive, not passive-aggressive.)

This is become a signature offering, kind of like an added bonus that you get, after reading our stories. I've even had messages from our readers telling me that they are torn between whether they read the story or the author notes at the back of the book first. As such we decided that we should continue with this tradition and just let you know that this is Ellie behind-the-scenes, but Izzie on the cover.

If you're interested I'll share with you a little bit about how I came to write urban fantasy.

8 years old, and casting spells.

This couldn't be normal.

A moment of clarity settled over me as I sat crossed-legged on my bedroom floor. Frankincense incense wafted through the shoe-box-sized room. In front of me was a sigil I'd found in an occult book. Next to me were the tarot cards I'd trekked through town looking for the previous weekend. Only the candle and a little desk lamp lit the room.

There was a strange eerie-ness that filled the room. Yet somehow I found it strangely familiar. Comforting, even.

It was late.

Everyone was either in bed, or crashed out in front of the telly downstairs.

No one needed to know what I was doing.

I'd jammed some folded-up paper under the door to stop anyone coming in.

Not that they would. But just in case.

(Mike Edit: Ok, you are EIGHT FREAKING YEARS OLD and you know how to deal with this stuff? I'm not saying you were a con artist in the making...but you totally were. I've no idea how you ended up a physicist...or an author (although the skills of a con artist are completely acceptable in writing. I like to say I'm a professional liar—I get paid to lie. This is where Ellie is allowed a LOT of response opportunity. Don't say I didn't warn you.)

<<Ellie edit: You're talking about jamming the door? I tell you about the super-frikkin-natural and your comment is about jamming the door?! Ha!>>

I glanced nervously at the candle. One stray spark on this carpet would send the whole room up in flames. I'd made extra sure it was stable. It would have to do...

I had a job to do. This spell wasn't going to work itself, but already the sigil was "activated." Just looking at it in this half-light, I could feel it doing its work, calling out into hidden dimensions, gathering power.

Looking back I couldn't tell you what the spell was even for. I can guess what type of magic it was, from the sigil...but what bothers me to this day is how an 8-year-old can even begin to get into this kind of thing as a hobby.

(Mike edit: no shit.)

Both my parents were very down-to-earth.

I doubt either of them really believed in a god...but nor did they show any signs of believing in anything else. Other than hard work and education. Those were their "gods." (They were a doctor and a teacher).

Yet somehow, one of their kids had managed to stray from the mundane.

It wasn't until a few decades later that I found out that my grandfather, who had died years before I was even born, was a Rosicrucian. (Mike edit: Ok, something for me to go look up.)

<<Ellie edit: https://www.britannica.com/topic/Rosicrucians >>

Knowing that, I started to realize there was probably something in my bloodline. Something that understood that there was more to us than the meat suits we operate through.

Something more than the tangible world.

And it was bound to come out at some point—in creative musings for stories.

After all, every time I watched something like *Vampire*

Diaries (Team DAMON!), or *Supernatural* (Dean, swoon!) there were certain things that just made sense...

So I started planning a series of stories that included British magic. The actual story structure used more of a detective or thriller structure, but magic naturally seeped in.

However, since it wasn't sci-fi, and since I used collaborators, working to my specifications, to do some of the work, it didn't seem like a good idea to publish as Ell Leigh Clarke. (As I've already mentioned, it would also confuse Amazon, because it was Urban Fantasy, rather than science fiction).

Thus was born Isobella Crowley: my magical, alter ego ;)

If you're interested in magic and mystery, and what life in Bicester, Oxfordshire was like, before I upped sticks and started wandering the globe, then this might be a series you'd be interested in reading.

Go ahead and check it out...

There are currently five books in this series. If we get enough interest from it, we may continue it...now you know that Izzie and I are closely... "related" ;)

Check it out, and if you enjoy the read, hop on the reader's email list to hear about more magical books as we publish them.

http://isobellacrowley.com/

Moonlighting

MA and I decided that we wanted to do something with the supernatural. Something with a badass female vampire and a reformed frat boy. Actually, and you've probably noticed this already, Remy has been heavily influenced by the cartoon character, Archer. I'm a huge fan. Even though Archer is a complete dick, he still manages to endear the audience to him. I was fascinated to figure out how, and how we might reconstruct this.

MA wanted Taylor to be a terrifying, "strong female" type because...well, I can only assume he's going through something. 12

(Mike edit: Too many nice vampires. I wanted something a bit darker, where she wasn't afraid of a little blood lost. Or truly she is a dark creature with the clothes of someone cultured.)

However, two characters does not series make.

As you probably know by now MA and I have hilarious conversations every time we chinwag, and the tangents and sidebars get more pronounced when we're in creative mode.

Think of it as a writers' room with 20 different personalities each trying to one-up each other and come up with the funniest concepts possible. That's kind of the vibe that happens when we do these concept calls *with just the two of us*. Yep, we both have multiple personalities that come to the fore in this mode. It's scary...and oddly hilarious.

(I hope that our level of output somehow matches what goes on in a writers' room, but I wouldn't like to make that presumption).

You can sample what our calls look like here: https://youtu.be/BGTeDnvRMrk

You can also see a bunch of snippets on Facebook: www.ellleighclarke.com

...and if you want to see the more regular updates, we

publish most of our "chinwags" on Patreon: www. Patreon.com/ellleighclarke.

Anyhoo, it was during one of these calls, right at the beginning, that MA referenced another TV show. The show that was on air before I was even born. Okay I might be exaggerating a little bit, cos I don't know exactly when it was. However it's fairly old, and because it's also American, I hadn't seen it. (I grew up in England, and the first American shows I remember watching were *Friends* and *Frasier*).

You might have heard of it though. *Moonlighting*? Anyway, he liked it as a concept having never seen it himself and only heard other people (women!) talk about it. He explained that it was popular because it has Bruce Willis in it. Suddenly I was much more interested in checking out. It also has Cybil Sheppard in it too. I vaguely remember watching her as a kid in the show named *Cybil* and she was awesome in that. So off I went to watch a few episodes and we decided to reconvene a few weeks later.

Luckily I was able to find the show almost in its entirety on You Tube. This is the link that I slipped to MA because I literally(!) could not stop laughing: https://youtu. be/eYqwLgrYFas?t=1661

You may want to check it out but if you're not at your computer the clip shows Bruce Willis's character completely hung over and hanging off the back of Cybil's office door by his jacket! She comes into the room oblivious, only to be scared out of her wits by his presence. He then proceeds to have all the answers to her "problems" and suggests that he will do her a favor and let her sleep with him!

I figured this was the kind of logic that our Remy might

use in the event that he wasn't scared to death of Taylor taking him apart.

Anyway, check out the clip if you fancy it. It's well worth the effort-to-giggle ratio!

And on that note, I should hand over to my collaborator. We have a word count limit on how much we can write at the back of the book and I want him to have the opportunity to say something entertaining.

From me, thank you again for reading. Do connect with me over on Facebook or something, and I'll look forward to writing to you again in the next set of author notes. Mwah!

Ellie x

"And I want him to have the opportunity to say something *entertaining.*" – Isabella Crowley, AKA Ell Leigh Clarke AKA Ellie.

Damn, with a comment like that, I only have up to go!

So, I'm just back from eating in the NYNY hotel (Il Fornaio for breakfast), where I dashed over to the Excalibur because it has a sugar store (no, really) called Lick. Lick has a fairly decent selection of esoteric soda pop.

No Coke or Pepsi here.

Which is fine, I can get my Coke habit solved at grocery stores, and I'm learning that doing rituals to cause the downfall of Pepsi, Inc. is frowned upon.

No, seriously. *It is.* Surprising, I know.

The only problem (I've found out) is Big Red is bottled under license by Pepsi. Darn my luck! If I succeed in one area by getting rid of Pepsi, Inc. I have to be ready to accept my precious Big Red—in a bottle—might not be so easily procured.

Dammit, *quandaries*.

So, I guess a slight introduction is relevant here. I live (often, for the most part) on the Strip in Las Vegas. I go to the Aria hotel for lunch and dinner because it's the closest place that has some of my favorite restaurants, Javier's and Five-Fifty Pizza (but I ask for the pizza well done.)

However, my closest WALKING favorite breakfast location is over in the NYNY Hotel.

It's about a half-mile walk each way, so a nice way to get a mile of walking done in the morning. Right before I chug my recently acquired Big Red which—#probably—negates all the benefits of the walk in the first place.

IT DOES NOT SURPRISE ME IN THE LEAST

I'm already on record saying that I believe Ellie is one of the smartest people I know. I typically explain the way I judge intelligence is it takes smarts to provide short, concise, quality explanations from a lot of data blathered about a subject.

(On this scale, I'm back w/the apes.)

Ellie can listen to a five-minute conversation (coming one-way from me) and then distill it down to one or two paragraphs. I call that *linguistica magicka*.

<<Ellie edit: hahhaha—that's pretty funny! I like it.>>

However, this is the first time I've heard of her effort with the tarot cards and sigils at eight years old. I think I was playing with those eight-inch-tall Spider-Man action heroes at that age.

(Look up 1973 Action Hero Spider-man eight-inch-tall —it has clothes and a squishy head, I kid you not.)

<<Ellie edit: yeah, I think that is proper child develop-

ment. To this day I don't like games or puzzles. I see them as a waste of brain resources—which they're not. I realize that now. Even poker I struggle with and half the time get myself knocked out because I'm tired of the effort a game is taking! It's a huge disadvantage. >>

Obviously, we can see which of us is going to go to theoretical physics between the two of us. Hint: It wasn't me.

When I first saw the pen name she had chosen for Urban Fantasy / Paranormal stuff I admit to just a bit of professional jealousy. It really is an EXCELLENT pen name.

<<Ellie edit: oh sweet! I remember you saying it was cool, but I didn't think a pro like yourself would be *jealous*. YAY! That's kind of worth taking a screenshot of and bringing it up at a well-timed moment in our next debate over titling something…! Tee heee…. >>

I suppose Alexander Crowley is open…

<<Ellie edit: I guess? But that would confuse Amazon too… because he's already published a ton of books which aren't something your fans would appreciate. ;-P >>

MORE ON TAYLOR

When creating Taylor, I wanted the reader to know that underneath, she really is a monster. This is why I had the one scene in the beginning where her jaw unhinges, and we can imagine her biting off the head of the werewolf.

That is not something nice vampires do.

Further, she keeps Remy on guard with how ho-hum she is about murder—his specifically, if he does something heinous.

Like being late for his appointment.

I like to think she would say: "I have ninety-nine problems but dealing with idiocy won't be one."

DONUTS

At this Lick candy store (Excalibur Hotel, upstairs next to the buffet.) I saw a shirt I thought was hilarious.

"I got 99 doughnuts 'cause a bitch ate one."

<<Ellie edit – haha that's another good one. Gosh, you're on fire today. Must be the sugar. Hey, so this Lick must be different from the Lick we have here in Texas. Lick here is an ice cream parlor... Which is pretty dope. >>

SHE HAS YOUR BACK.

Ok, so I've said that Ellie was smart. However, she has this knack for going along with stuff (sometimes to her detriment.)

I was looking at funny t-shirts (see 99 doughnuts) and I found one that would be good for her connecting her intelligence with her type of friendship.

"THAT'S A HORRIBLE IDEA!
WHAT TIME?"

<<Ellie Edit: OMG. I have no idea what you're talking about... Actually, no, you're right. But I wanna know what thing you're referring to, specifically... You mean being friends with you, right? That's where this is going... ! That is sooo my kinda t-shirt. Oh, and Jason last night at poker had another awesome one on. It was upside down text saying: "Because I was inverted", and it references that line from Top Gun where he's explaining what he was doing, improving international relations. Soooo funny! >>

AND ONE FOR ME

"I RUN ON COKE, CHAOS, AND CUSS WORDS."

Thank you for reading our stories, and I hope to see you at the end of book 02 ;-)

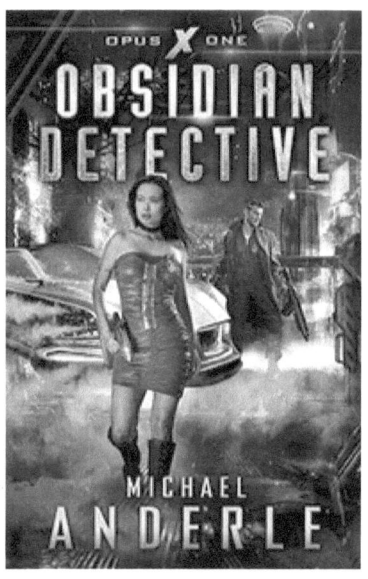

Pre-order now to have the book arrive on your Kindle November 1st.

Two Rebels whose Worlds Collide on a Planetary Level.
On the fringes of human space, a murder will light a fuse and send two different people colliding together.

She lives on Earth, where peace among the population is a given. He is on the fringe of society where authority is how much firepower you wield.

She is from the powerful, the elite. He is with the military.

Both want the truth – but is revealing the truth good for society?

Two years ago, a small moon in a far off system was set to be the location of the first intergalactic war between humans and an alien race.

It never happened. However, something was found many are willing to kill to keep a secret.

Now, they have killed the wrong people.

How many will need to die to keep the truth hidden?

As many as is needed.

He will have vengeance no matter the cost. *She will dig for the truth. No matter how risky the truth is to reveal.*

Coming November 1st from Amazon and other Digital Book Stores

with Michael Anderle

Darkest Before The Dawn (3)

Dawn Arrives (4)

Interplanetary Spy For Hire
with Michael Anderle

Expelled

Deuces Wild
with Michael Anderle

Beyond The Frontiers (1)

Rampage (2)

Labyrinth (3)

Birthright (4)

The Sword-Mage Chronicles

Awakening

Taken

Heist

Resistance

Legba

Storm

CONNECT WITH MICHAEL ANDERLE

Michael Anderle Social
  Website:
  http://www.lmbpn.com

Email List:
  http://lmbpn.com/email/

Facebook Here:
  www.facebook.com/TheKurtherianGambitBooks/